MW00875724

SALT & THE SISTERS

THE SIREN'S CURSE BOOK 3

A.L. KNORR

Edited by
NICOLA AQUINO

Edited by
THERESA HULL

INTELLECTUALLY PROMISCUOUS PRESS

PROLOGUE

White gravel crunched under Jozef's shoes as he strode up the long walkway to his family's villa. He hadn't been on these grounds in forty years, and his stomach gave a sickening twist to think of what it meant to be setting foot here now.

Claudius had found him. Rather, someone in his father's employ had found him, and delivered the only message that could have compelled Jozef to return to Gibraltar.

Your father is dying.

The sea air lifted the curls at Jozef's temples as he halted in front of the big double doors and closed his eyes. He stopped himself from using the big brass lionshead knocker, but only just. Estranged from his father he might be, but this was still Jozef's home. After Jozef stepped into the foyer, the door snicked quietly closed behind him. In spite of the gulf that had separated Jozef from Claudius all those years ago, it felt good to be home.

He half expected the smell of Gabriela's baking to greet him, to see her sweet, plump face smiling up at him. But

Gabriela had died twenty-seven years ago. They'd exchanged rare letters on the condition that she never reveal his whereabouts to Claudius or any of his cronies—until the day when he'd received a letter from Gabriela's daughter with the sad news that her mother had passed from pneumonia.

"Master Drakief?"

It was a brittle, sullen voice he did not recognize.

Jozef looked up the steps to where a man in a black blazer stood on the landing. The two men studied one another.

"You must be Mr. Heller?" Jozef guessed.

Mr. Heller was a tall, spare man with a close-cropped head of snow-white hair. He took the few steps down from the landing to the foyer and extended a hand to Jozef.

"The prodigal son has returned," he said in an accent that was pure local. He shook Jozef's hand but his gaze was pure ice. "Your neglect of your father has not done him any favors, as you'll see for yourself. Had you come home sooner, he might not be suffering as he is."

Jozef released the man's hand, unsure of whether to laugh at his assumptive insolence, or to make an attempt to defend himself. Instead, he closed his face from all expression. Suddenly, it no longer felt good to be at home. This man may have been Claudius's caregiver for the past few years, but he knew nothing about Jozef or what had driven a wedge between father and son. He doubted Heller even knew the true biological nature of the man he cared for.

Upon that thought, Jozef was once again hit with the same cold wonderment which had plagued him on the flight over—*why* was his father dying? As an Atlantean, Claudius was blessed (if you wanted to look at it as a blessing) with a much longer lifespan than any human. Jozef knew Atlanteans who were three hundred years old. His father was only a little more than half that. Jozef had been born when Claudius was in his seventies and in every memory he had of his father, Jozef remembered Claudius as an iron-hard, vital man.

"I'll show you to his room." Mr. Heller turned and led Jozef up the steps. He paused and sent his frigid judgment over his shoulder at Jozef again, like tossing a bucket of cold water over Jozef's head. He spoke with a thinly disguised contempt, his upper lip curling. "Unless of course you'd rather take some time to freshen up, have some tea, perhaps?"

"I know the way, thank you."

Jozef passed Mr. Heller, leaving him on the steps with that disgust on his face. The welcome Jozef had received thus far did not bode well for the reception he expected from his father. Claudius must not have told Heller anything good about Jozef for Heller to treat him this way.

Jozef found himself compartmentalizing as he journeyed through the large villa toward his father's personal suite. Claudius had been a wonderful father while Jozef was a boy. He'd raised Jozef with a strict but loving hand, and nurtured the young lad into his chosen path of oceanographer. Claudius had curbed his own desire for Jozef to become involved in his investing activities and his passionate desire to find the ruins of their people's native city. Instead, he allowed his son to pursue his heart's passion.

Until Jozef's heart's passion took the form of a beautiful siren named Bel.

Jozef paused outside the door to his father's bedroom, sucking in a stabilizing breath. He pushed his way inside, walking silently on the thick carpeting toward the four-poster bed.

Claudius was asleep, and it was a good thing because Jozef could sooner have stopped the tide than kept the shock from his face at the sight of him. How much his father had aged since their last face-to-face encounter!

Claudius had lost most of his hair. The pink skin of his skull seemed stretched thin over his scalp and the bones of his face. His cheeks and forehead were mottled with age spots and the hands which rested on the red coverlet were bony and beginning to twist with arthritis. His eyes were closed and his face turned slightly away from where his son stood looking down upon him.

Jozef's eyes welled with tears and a hand covered his mouth to mute the sound of his ragged breathing. His chest felt tight as a well of grief rose like a bubble in a swamp. His fingers pinched his nose shut against the sob. He made a sound like a choked cough as tears over-spilled and streaked down his cheeks.

At the sound, Claudius's lids cracked open. He turned his head slowly, like it was on a rusty pivot desperately in want of oil. His formerly vibrant eyes were watery, the whites tinged with yellow. But what Jozef saw in them brought another crippling wrack of pain.

They were overflowing with love.

"My son." His voice crackled with age. He lifted a hand to reach for Jozef.

Jozef came to his knees beside the bed and took his father's hand, a fresh sob coming at the feeling of the fragile bones. His father had always been powerful, broad-shouldered, and capable. He'd always stood straight with his chest out, shoulders back, and an ambitious glint in his eye. Jozef hardly recognized the wasted figure making a thin lump under the bedding. He put his forehead down on the back of his father's hand.

Claudius made a shushing sound and rested his other hand on Jozef's curls.

"You came home." Claudius spoke as if sighing. "I can die a happy man."

Guilt flooded Jozef's body, making him feel tremulous and weak. He raised his head to look at his father and found he couldn't speak around the tightness in his throat. He'd been wrong to stay away so long. His father had done the unforgiveable and yet, somehow at the bitter end of it all, there was nothing but forgiveness in Jozef's heart. It was easy to hate his father as long as he'd stayed away, but Jozef had a soft heart. He'd been told this since he was a boy. He could no longer be angry. The crimes were old, so old, and did not matter in this moment. His father really was dying. Jozef knew it now in a way he had been unable to know it when simply reading the words in the handwritten letter from Heller, when standing in his former office back in Gdansk.

"You would have made an excellent intelligence agent," his father said in that papery voice. "You've been near impossible to track."

Jozef sniffed and found pieces of his voice. "I knew how not to be found."

It was only when Jozef had begun to relax and had allowed his name to be mentioned in an article about the salvage of *The Sybellen* that Claudius's staff had been able to locate him—now the resident oceanographer of one of the best salvage companies in Europe.

Jozef had ignored all the attempts Claudius's lawyers had made to talk to him about his inheritance. But he couldn't ignore the hand-written letter from Mr. Heller: Claudius was dying and...

...unless you want to live the rest of your life in regret, you'll return to Gibraltar at once.

Jozef had been there the night Mira had gone into the Baltic, leaving her daughter in tears on the beach. He'd watched breathlessly from the scrubby trees where the golden sand met the thick thatch of prickly growth separating the beach from the country road. He'd felt like a criminal. Shame had burned within him for watching the private moment between sirens—between mother and daughter—but he had to know: Was the woman who seemed so physically like Bel, but so different in character, *his* Sybellen?

She'd looked like Bel, was the right shape and size, but she was so different in personality. She spoke with a different accent, she claimed to be only in her thirties and—so convincingly—seemed completely without any memory of her life before Canada.

The first step had been proving to himself that she was Mer.

She was. He'd seen it for himself, but too late.

When Jozef had come to emotional terms with the fact that Mira had really gone—probably for years—Jozef ignored the letter no longer. He resigned from Novak's salvage operation and got on the first available flight home to Gibraltar.

"If you can forgive your old father," Claudius was saying, "then he can die with a peaceful ending. Can you do that?"

Jozef nodded and brushed the tears from his cheeks. "For what it's worth, you have my forgiveness." Jozef did not say that it was Bel and her people whose forgiveness

Claudius needed to seek. The time for hurtful words had passed. "Forgive me for staying away for so long."

Claudius coughed quietly. "It is a good thing we have long lives. If we were human, I would have been without a son for half a lifetime. As it is, I am thankful for the decades of happy memories I have with you." His father's fingers grasped Jozef's with a fierceness that surprised him. "We learned too late, Jozef. You must be careful."

For a moment Jozef felt totally lost. Had Claudius also lost part of his mind as his body failed?

"Father?"

"Loukas, he..." Claudius paused to take a breath and it was obvious that the talking was tiring him. "He made the discovery so late. Too late for either of us."

Jozef frowned at the mention of the researcher and he wondered why they were talking about Loukas. "What did he discover?"

"It isn't good for us to live out all our days on land. You must promise me that you'll swim in the sea. Saltwater, it must be saltwater." Claudius half lifted his head from the pillow in his fervor to explain.

"Shh, you're getting upset." Jozef put a hand on Claudius's shoulder. "I do swim, father. I always have. I love the ocean." It felt strange to be reminding his own father of his passion for the water and all the life within. It was something that had defined Jozef for as long as he could remember.

"Loukas is dead." Claudius let his head rest on the pillow again. "And what killed him is now killing me."

"What do you mean?"

"Loukas called it a wasting disease. A human doctor would diagnose it as MS."

"Multiple sclerosis?"

Claudius nodded. "It has similar symptoms but a different cause. Loukas began to study it toward the end but he got too disabled to finish. His early research showed that not enough sunlight weakens our immune system. We felt justified in living like humans. But after..."

Claudius stopped and took a few breaths.

"Take your time," Jozef said, helping his father take a sip from the glass of water on the bedside table.

When Claudius resumed, he spoke more slowly.

"After, he learned that not enough saltwater wastes us in a different way." An airy laugh came out on a cough. "How is that for irony? We used to be so disdainful of those of us who lived entirely in the ocean. Who can be disdainful now?"

Jozef had an uncomfortable thought. If what his father was saying was true, Atlanteans could never fully live on land, nor at sea, always requiring both—the amphibians of the mammalian world. Atlanteans who spent their lives entirely underwater were known to be sickly, and Loukas had confirmed it while he was still a young man. Jozef could remember the self-congratulatory and superior tones of Claudius's friends as they lauded Loukas for his findings and settled even more firmly into their land-based lives of opulence and wealth. Jozef wondered how many of those members of his father's inner circle were now suffering themselves. Or dead.

"You must rest now." Jozef squeezed his father's hand gently. "I understand that you're trying to tell me to look after myself so that I don't suffer in the way you are, but believe me father, you don't need to worry on that account."

"I'll rest soon." Claudius closed his eyes and when they opened again it was in a slow drift. His fingers gripped Jozef with a new energy and his old eyes burned. "I have better news, my son."

"Shall we talk later? After you've had some lunch?"

"There is no later. There is only now. We *found* it, Jozef." Claudius smiled at his boy, deep wrinkles appearing at the corners of his eyes.

"What did you find, Father?"

"What I've been looking for since before you were born! What I've been looking for all of my life. *We found Atlantis.*"

Jozef gave his father a soft smile, which he hoped didn't appear too bitter. "That was Okeanos you found Father, or have you forgotten? You already took everything of value from it. There is no orichalcum left. There might not even be much artwork left from what I've been told by your lawyers."

Claudius shook his head. "I'm not talking about Okeanos. Okeanos is in the Azores, as you know full well. Atlantis is in Africa. It used to be a coastline, but the Sahara swallowed its ruins over the centuries. You can actually see it from satellite!"

Claudius husked another dry laugh, this one with genuine humor in it. He hit Jozef's hand with his own, a soft slap of camaraderie.

He continued, "It was right in front of us the whole time. Right in front of our noses!"

Jozef's doubt diminished a little, but not much. "How do you know it's Atlantis?"

Claudius gestured to a box on the old wooden desk by the window. "There, my files."

Jozef retrieved the leather-covered wooden box and sat on the edge of his father's bed. Opening the lid revealed a pile of file folders. He picked up the first one and opened it, flipping though the research. It was full of articles, including both typed and hand-written pages. Notes were scribbled in the margins of most pages, and there were photographs of sandy looking stones and broken rubble that didn't look very interesting.

"The one of Mauritania." Claudius gave a low cough but he was smiling. "The Richat Structure."

Jozef paused in his rifling through the pages to stare at his father. "The Eye of Africa?"

He knew this anomaly. Scientists had been trying to figure out its nature and genesis for decades.

"The very same," Claudius said.

Plucking the satellite image labeled 'Mauritania' and 'Richat Structure' by hand, Jozef set the box aside and held the image out for both of them to see.

"You see it?" Claudius asked after a while.

Jozef's throat tightened as he stared at the tawny wasteland of the Sahara, and the undeniable perfectly circular structure stamped into the desert.

"So far from the ocean, though," Jozef observed, his gaze wandering the wasteland between the ruin of Atlantis and the western coast of Africa.

Claudius made a sound in the back of his throat which could have been humor, could have been annoyance. "We examined thousands of kilometers of coastline but never thought to look inland, or even in a desert location. A lot can change over so many millennia. Even so, all things considered, it is not so far from the Atlantic—only five-hundred-eighty-five kilometers."

Jozef could easily see the concentric circles Atlantis was famous for. It was a shape which did not happen naturally. He could even recall Plato's description of Atlantis given how often his father had made him recite it as a young boy.

"Alternate zones of sea and land, larger and smaller, encircling one another," Jozef recited. "Two of land, three of water..."

Jozef and his father finished the quote from the *Critias* together.

"Turned as if with a lathe each having its circumference equidistant every way from the center."

"Do you see the mountain range on the north side?"

Jozef nodded. He could easily see the smooth rivulet scars from some long dried up water source. "I can see the evidence of the rivers and waterfalls, too."

Jozef found his throat closing up with emotion again. His doubt was dissolving like dew in the morning sun.

A mathematical equation scribbled on the side of the document caught his eye.

"What's this?"

"That's the conversion from stadia to kilometers. Plato's measurements work."

"And the springs?" Jozef recalled from Plato's description that two springs fed the center acropolis of Atlantis, one of hot water and the other of cold. "Did you find evidence of these in the center?"

"Yes, we found evidence of freshwater in the heart, and saltwater in the surrounding area."

Jozef took a deep breath and released it slowly. The evidence was enough and he knew his father had been meticulous with it.

"You did it."

"My second biggest regret is that I shall never see it in person," Claudius said.

Jozef's eyes cut to his father. "And the first?"

Claudius held his son's gaze. "You know the first already." His father gently patted Jozef's forearm. "You can go through this as you like. This research is yours now. You have the biggest discovery of the century on your lap there, my son. I cannot think of a better person to steward its release."

Claudius's fingers tightened on Jozef's arm. "Atlantis will have to be acknowledged officially. No longer can they call it a myth, or worse—pseudo-history." The former disdain for the way historians dismissed the existence of Atlantis surfaced in Jozef's father.

"I look forward to going through all of this." Jozef flipped the lid of the box closed and patted it. "But now I want you to rest."

Claudius's twisted fingers grasped Jozef's hand again. "There is something else, something…" he seemed to search for words.

"What is it, Father?"

"I do not wish to lose the forgiveness you have given your dying father," Claudius said, "but there is something you must see. It is better if you see for yourself than if I waste breath trying to describe…"

His body arched forward as he was wracked with a dry, hacking cough. To Jozef, it sounded like Claudius's lungs were made of kindling and filled with sawdust.

"Shh." Jozef reached for the glass of water beside the bed and put it into his father's outstretched hand.

His father lifted the glass to his lips, but gestured at the drawer in the bedside table.

Jozef pulled open the drawer and inside found a letter addressed to him, but the address was a Stalingrad apartment Jozef had not lived in for fourteen years. The envelope was heavy.

Inside was a set of three keys, but while two of them were simple brass keys and ordinary, the last was a small

cylindrical key of gray metal. One of the brass keys he actually recognized from its unusual fleur-de-lis shaped bow—it
was the key to the outer door of Loukas's labs. It was a key
to the last place Jozef would ever want to return.

Opening the letter revealed his father's own scrawl,
begging him to come home. It said that he must—

*...come home at once. There is no double of the cylin-
drical key attached, and a life hangs in the balance...*

It was manipulative, and maddeningly vague.

"Whose life hangs in the balance, Father? Yours?" Jozef
swallowed down a lump in his throat. Was there some way
his earlier presence might have staved off this awful death?

Heller's barbed words of greeting floated back to him.

*Your neglect of your father has not done him any favors,
as you'll see for yourself. Had you come home sooner, he
might not be suffering as he is.*

"You must see for yourself, my son. The rest of the keys
you will need are in my desk drawer." Claudius gave Jozef
the glass of water and his eyelids drifted closed at an uneven
rate. Even his pupils seemed to be of different sizes.

"Rest then, that's all you must do now." Jozef dropped a
kiss on his father's dry, cool forehead.

He left the room, feeling the weight of the keys he'd
dropped into his pocket.

ONE

Antoni let out a long, frustrated raspberry and leaned back in his chair, rubbing his hands vigorously over his eyes.

"Not going well?" I moved to stand behind him and massage his shoulders.

Antoni had spent the better part of two days flipping through the photographs on the tablet we'd retrieved from the Group of Winterthür men. His eyes were glassy, and pink in the corners where he'd been rubbing them. A mass of paper covered with handwritten scrawl—Antoni's attempt at translation—covered the table as if a small tornado had shredded a scrapbook.

"I don't think I can do this," he said, not for the first time this morning. "I just don't have enough of the language, and whoever took these photographs only cared about the location of the gemstones and what they could do, not the story behind them."

I looked back at my mom where she was standing in the doorway, leaning against the doorjamb with her arms crossed in front of her stomach. "You sure you don't want to give it another try?"

"I told you, sunshine. The writing is Atlantean, not Mer. We're lucky that any of us has even seen it before."

"Lucky," Antoni muttered thoughtfully.

Mom and I looked at Antoni. He'd pulled his hair up into jagged spikes and looked like a troubled hedgehog.

"You look like you're having an idea," I said.

"Lusi." Antoni looked up at me so I moved to the chair beside him to save his neck.

"Lusi?" I knew who he meant, I wasn't sure why I pretended I didn't just then.

"The woman who taught me what little I know. She's the only one who can help us."

Mira strode forward and took a seat across from Antoni. "But how do we get ahold of her? Do you still have her phone number?"

"Or maybe an email address?" My fingertips felt a little cool at the thought that Antoni might have kept his ex's contact information. I ignored the jealousy rapping quietly at the door of my heart. I wouldn't let it in. This was too important, and Antoni didn't deserve anything but trust from me.

Antoni's brow wrinkled and he shook his head. "No. I promised her I wouldn't keep it."

I cocked my head at my sweetheart. "That was an odd thing to promise her. Did you have a falling out?"

"No, we parted on good terms. She just...didn't want to stay in touch. I'm sure she had her reasons." Antoni's face lit up suddenly. "But we don't need her phone number. You can *call* her to us."

"Only if I know her full siren name. Do you know it?"

Antoni's face fell again. "I only ever knew her by Lusi; she never gave me any other name or even a last name."

"Well, there goes that idea." Mira sat back in her chair

and pulled up one knee. She laced her fingers over her knee and set her chin on her hands, face thoughtful.

Antoni chewed his cheek, a slash between his brows. He grabbed the tablet, fingers dancing across the screen. "Maybe not. She showed me all these monuments in Warsaw and told me they were about her." Antoni's hazel eyes flashed up at me and Mom as he punched terms into the search bar. "I thought she was joking, of course. Just having a laugh at my expense."

A page full of writing popped up on the tablet. The title was *The Mermaid of Warsaw*.

I skootched my chair closer to Antoni so I could read the small screen.

Two images were visible on the right-hand side. The top one displayed a coat of arms with a bright red background behind a blond mermaid with a raised sword in one hand and a shield in the other. A crown sat above the crest and the caption read, *The current coat of arms of Warsaw*.

"Whoa," I breathed. "Mom, come take a look at this."

Mom came to my other side as all three of us peered at the article.

The image below the current coat of arms was an older coat of arms. It depicted a similar image, but green with a beast that was less a mermaid and more of a hybrid creature: a woman with a tail and dragon's wings and strange, duck-like feet.

"She said this one was made before anyone in Warsaw got a good look at her," said Antoni, pointing to the green one. "Hideous, isn't it?"

"Sixteen-fifty-two?" Mom said under her breath, reading the caption. "Just how old *is* she?"

"The creature first appeared on the coat of arms in thirteen-ninety," I read aloud, pointing at where the date appeared. My skin shivered with gooseflesh and I gaped up at my mom. "Is that possible? Can a mermaid really live that long?"

Mom lifted a shoulder, but wonder was etched across her face. "Why not?"

"Look at all the monuments." Antoni scrolled down the page with his thumb. "I can still hardly believe that these are of the woman I knew."

Five more creations were shown on the page, three free-standing statues, all of which depicted a beautiful mermaid with a sword raised over her head and shield in her other hand. One was a crest affixed to a wall, also of a mermaid in the midst of attack, and the last was a more recent, more demure and modern statue which was roughly the form of a mermaid but depicted without weapons.

Many more coats of arms done at various points throughout history were also on display.

"Scroll up, let's read what it says." I patted Antoni's arm and he scrolled back to the top.

"The legend of the Warsaw mermaid," my mother read out loud as we each skimmed the text. "It says she was trapped by a merchant but rescued by fishermen, and ever since, she has been the protector of the city."

I laughed with delight at the next part. "*The Little Mermaid* statue in Copenhagen is of her sister!"

"Look," Antoni said, and his voice was strangely breathless. "It's right there in black and white."

I read aloud again, the hairs spindling straight up to standing on the back of my neck. "Polish *syrenka* is cognate with siren, but she is more properly a fresh-water mermaid called *Melusina*."

Antoni and I shared a disbelieving look.

"Lusi," he said, followed by, "Melusina. That's it, right? That has to be it?"

Mira nodded. "That's her name, all right." She put a hand on my shoulder. "I don't know about you but after reading all of that, I'm dying to meet this six-hundred-something year old mermaid warrior, and not just for her ability to read Atlantean. How about you?"

I could only nod in reply.

TO CALL LUSI, I walked down to the beach and to the stone outcrop I had used to call my mother. I went alone at sunset and settled myself on the stones, my toes dangling in the Baltic. Closing my eyes, I let myself tune in to the sound of the water. Waves lapped gently against the stones, and shushed softly against the sandy beach behind me. I let my thoughts drift down past the waterline and into the symphonic sounds of the underwater world.

Melusina.

I let the name drift from my mind the way someone might let a paper boat bob lazily from their fingertips.

Melusina, my mind whispered, sending the word out through the water like a silent shockwave.

At first there was nothing. Nothing but the sounds of clicks and snaps and burbles of the underwater universe.

Melusina.

More urgently this time. I couldn't tell how long I waited or how many times I asked for her attention, but there was no mistaking the tug of resistance when she finally did respond. The resistance took me by surprise. When I'd called Mom, she had been incapable of resisting. Perhaps Lusi was more powerful because she was just *so old.* Old and strong. I felt like she'd heard every time I'd thought her name, but was choosing to ignore me. I wondered what it was like to have someone else invade your mind and call your name. Shoving that thought aside, I refocused. Rather than just beckoning her to come to me, I tried going a little deeper into our connection.

We need you.

I felt a stubborn resistance to acknowledge my presence.

I'm not going away, I thought at her. *Sorry,* I added as an afterthought.

Communicating this way was nebulous and tricky. I wished I could explain in more detail why I was disturbing her, but knew I'd only confuse and annoy her further.

I asked her to come and didn't stop asking until she grudgingly acknowledged by letting her resistance dissolve. She wasn't happy about it. I could feel her displeasure as keenly as my own reluctance to disturb her life.

But she was coming, and that was all that mattered.

The world came rushing back in on me as I opened my eyes. Sounds invaded my ears and wind tugged at my hair. It was dark, and the indigo horizon winked with a few stars. I got up, feeling stiff, and headed for home.

On the road, halfway between the rock outcrop and the back gate leading to the corner of the yard, I saw Antoni. He stopped walking when he saw me and let me come to him.

"I was getting worried." He dropped a kiss on my lips and put an arm around my shoulders as he turned to face home.

"It took a while."

"But you did it? You reached her?" Antoni looked down at me as we walked, his face was half lit by the shafts of light from a nearby street lamp. Concern marred his features.

"I reached her."

"Do you know when she'll arrive?"

"Soon. Sorry, that's the best I can do."

"So cryptic." Antoni tried to smile but I could see the worry in his eyes.

"What are you worried about?" I asked, even though I thought I knew.

Antoni let out a breath, but his smile disappeared. "It's weird, right? Meeting an ex? I don't want it to be awkward."

"It will be." I couldn't keep myself from replying honestly. "But that's not your fault. You have an ex, she happens to be a siren, one that we need. I'm grateful that you met her. If you hadn't, we'd be stumped by this whole mystery."

He cleared his throat as we reached the gate and he lifted the latch to swing it open, letting me pass through first.

"Is there anything I can do to make it easier for you?" he asked.

Now that question was a little harder to answer. Did he want me to say that I secretly wanted him to send Lusi signals that I was the only woman—correction, the only siren—for him? I wanted her to know that whatever had been between them was long over and would never be rekindled. I wanted Antoni to shoot me loving glances in her presence, give me secret-not-so-secret touches of his fingertips. I wanted her to see nothing but a flat emotionless gaze when he looked at her.

It was all foolishness. My rational mind knew that. I didn't think I'd be feeling this way if Lusi had been a human woman. Scratch that, I *knew* I wouldn't be feeling this way. But Lusi wasn't human. She was a siren, and an extremely old and experienced one at that. She was my lover's ex and what that meant was not as clear to me as if she'd been just a girl.

"You do it all already," was what came out of my mouth after all the internal rambling and emotion, tumbling around in my mind like pebbles in the backwash. "It's a relationship you had in University, you don't need to *do* anything. It's lucky you knew her at all, even if you didn't know what she was."

Antoni still looked miserable. "I feel stupid."

"Why?" I stopped him and put my hands on his arms.

"Because she *did* tell me who she was. Plain as day. She showed me the artwork around the city, even taught me bits and pieces of what I thought was a made-up language. But it was all real! She knew I would never believe her, so she just kept adding to it, spinning what sounded like a fairy tale. That's why I feel stupid." His expression was pained. "It's embarrassing."

I reached up and gave him a hug. In that instant, all of the conflicted and irrational feelings—the jealousy, the uncertainty, the awkwardness—evaporated. Nothing mattered but making him feel better.

"You shouldn't feel stupid. You only reacted the same way any human would react when presented with such a story. The world doesn't know we exist."

"Well, someone in Warsaw does, otherwise why would all those artists depict Lusi—a real live mermaid—on their crests and in their parks?"

I released Antoni and stepped back. "We can ask her when she arrives if you want."

"I love you," he said, suddenly.

"I know."

We crossed the yard in silence and slipped into the house to tell the others to expect a very important guest.

TWO

The rumbly tones of a motorbike grew louder as a machine approached that sounded like it had been rudely awakened from a nap.

When a slim rider turned in through the Novak Manor's open gates on what looked like an antique motorbike, I got up from where I'd been sitting on the front step. Behind me, the front door of the manor opened and my mother stepped outside. She came down the steps and we made our way onto the pavement of the roundabout together as the rider brought the bike to a stop.

Lusi kicked the stand down and let the bike lean on it.

Time stood still as she just stared at Mom and me, and we stared at her.

It was impossible to see her face behind a shiny blue-green helmet with a black faceplate. She was dressed in dark brown leather—a slim-fitting cropped motorcycle jacket and leather riding trousers. Her matching boots were laced up to mid-shin. The black leather gloves covering her hands looked soft and well worn. She took those off first, her fingers long and tapered and her skin as pale as mine. The hands journeyed up to the strap of her helmet where it was fastened under the side of her jaw. Unsnapping the clasp, she put both hands flat on the sides of her helmet and removed it.

A tumble of blond hair spilled out, but didn't fall far as it was jaggedly shorn to just under her ears. Either her hair was supremely mussed from the long journey under the helmet, or she'd cut it herself with a blunt blade, leaving its edges rough and uneven. Her hair was the color of wheat, but when it caught the sun coming through the trees, it glinted more silver than gold. It fell over her face enough that I couldn't see any of her features clearly. She got off her bike, turned her back to us, and carefully set the helmet over one of the handlebars. Raking her hands through her hair, she seemed to take a breath before she turned to face us.

I got my first good look at the oldest mermaid I'd ever met, possibly the oldest one alive.

She didn't look happy.

Two straight slashes of eyebrows pulled tight to the center of her brow as she peered at us. The eyes beneath them were as green as emeralds and just as hard. She unzipped her jacket and I caught a flash of metal under one arm. I glanced at Mom, but didn't have time to ask if she'd seen what I had seen before Lusi reached us.

She was taller than either of us, slim-waisted, long-legged, broad-shouldered for a woman, and with powerful looking thighs straining at her leathers. Her face was beautiful, there was no denying that, but it had a quality that made me want to look away. I didn't, but it took effort. Lusi's skin had the look of polished marble, like her skin would be cold and hard if I had the courage to touch it. Except for a straight scar on her upper lip and another on her neck, her skin was smooth and flawless, opaque and unmarred. Yet I could see the age behind her eyes.

She stopped in front of us, looking from me to my mother and back again.

"I've had many unusual days in my time," she said.

My lips parted in surprise at the sound. What little voice she had was a rasp of dry air passing through a tight throat. Startled, my eyes dropped to her neck and it was then that I noticed a third scar. A thin line of white ran across her windpipe. A small puckered circle at the centre of her throat became visible as the sun came out and it threw a small shadow.

"But this one is a standout," she continued in that husk of a sound. Her eyes cut to Mom standing to my right. "The Sovereign." Her gaze drifted back to me. "And an elemental."

She took a step closer and looked down at me. Our eyes met and held, hers were flinty, yet curious. She bared her teeth when she spoke.

"You rang?"

I finally found my voice. "I apologize for interrupting… whatever it was you were doing when I called you, but when you learn why I asked you here, I hope you'll understand."

"Get on with it then," she said.

I nodded and gestured to the door to welcome her in. "Thank you for coming." I said, feeling like I sounded supremely lame.

She made a sound that I didn't know how to interpret. Was it a grunt? A sound of agreement? She strode past us and made her way up the steps. I heard her mutter roughly as she reached the front door.

"Didn't have much of a choice."

Just as Lusi was reaching for the doorknob, it twisted and opened from the inside.

Antoni and Lusi stood face to face. I couldn't see Lusi's expression, but Antoni's eyes looked glued open and unable to look away. They were a pair of frozen figures for a moment.

Emun's head appeared over Antoni's shoulder.

"Hello," he said cheerily to Lusi. "Glad to see you've made it. Come on in." Emun patted Antoni firmly on the shoulder as if to wake him up, and Antoni stepped aside.

I was close enough now to see the side of Lusi's face as her eyes settled on Emun. They widened in surprise.

She turned her head and looked at me, then back at my mother before facing Emun again. "The Sovereign, an elemental, an ex-boyfriend, *and* a triton. I left Warsaw early this morning in a sour mood, but just seeing the four of you together has already made it worthwhile."

Lusi stepped over the threshold and into the foyer, and Mom and I followed. When Antoni closed the door behind me, he gave me a weak smile.

"I thought your kind was extinct," Lusi said to Emun.

"I get that a lot," Emun replied.

The five of us stood in a misshapen circle facing one another.

Lusi was looking at Antoni and her expression was stony.

Antoni finally spoke. "I'm sorry, Lusi. I know I made you a promise, and I would have kept it and left you alone except for these two." He gestured to me and Mom.

"So, you figured out what I am, then. Finally." When Lusi spoke, the stony expression melted away and she appeared to relax. Her eyes, now appearing dark in the dim light of the foyer, glinted with what I thought was humor and she winked at Antoni.

The friendly gesture made me realize just how stiffly Antoni, Mom, and I were all standing—like soldiers at attention. Lusi's arms dangled, relaxed at her sides as she leaned into one hip like a horse dozing under a tree. Emun had his hands on his hips and an earnest look on his face as he looked from one face to another, waiting for something interesting to happen. I got the feeling he found the whole thing amusing.

It was Emun who broke the tableau. He cleared his throat and a dimple appeared briefly in his cheek.

"Why don't we have a seat in there." He gestured to the parlor where my mother had told us her incredible story. "Would anyone like anything to drink? Adalbert and Sera are off today, so I'm happy to fetch anything your heart desires."

"I'll help," I said, needing the relief of leaving the room even for a moment.

Emun and I shared a look as we headed to the kitchen.

"What do you think happened to her voice?" I asked, keeping my own voice at a whisper. "It's not a cold. Did you see her scar?"

Emun nodded as he grabbed a tray and pulled some glasses and mugs from the cupboard and I put on the kettle. "I wonder if her siren voice still works."

I blinked for a second. I hadn't even thought about her siren voice.

"Why don't you ask her?" I suggested.

"*You* ask her." Emun elbowed me in the shoulder as I was putting teabags into the teapot. That same dimple appeared in his cheek. "She's intimidating as hell."

"I noticed." I would have teased Emun about being intimidated, because up until I'd met Lusi, Emun had been the most intimidating Mer I'd ever met—well, until I realized he was a softie on the inside. There was no question that Lusi was not someone to make an enemy of. The fact that I'd called her here using my power already put me in an awkward position of being responsible for how this all went down.

"You know, I think there's a gun under her jacket?" I whispered as we settled the water, coffee, and tea on two trays.

He didn't even blink. "That doesn't surprise me in the least."

As Emun and I carried the trays of drinks into the parlor, I overheard Antoni commenting on Lusi's haircut. I guess she'd had long hair when they'd known one another. I looked for my mom but she wasn't in the room.

"Where's Mira?" Emun asked as we set the trays down on the coffee table in front of the sofa.

"She went to get the tablet," Antoni explained. "It was charging in Adalbert and Sera's office."

Lusi's eyes were on me as I sat next to Antoni. I held her gaze without flinching. Her earrings caught my eye—small rough-cut aquamarines, both of them. She noticed that I'd noticed.

Her gaze flicked from my own ears to my neck to my hands.

"I can't wear one," I explained, picking up the teapot and beginning to pour.

For the first time since I'd met her, Lusi looked taken off-guard. "What do you mean you can't wear one? You *have* to wear one."

I shook my head. "They're poisonous to me. It's part of why we asked you to come."

Lusi looked at me like my face had sprung an extra mouth.

Mom entered the room carrying the tablet and a folder full of the photographs we'd enlarged and printed. She sat next to Lusi, but not too close, and set the folder and tablet on the wide expanse of the table. Flipping open the folder, she pulled out six photographs and set them in a line in front of Lusi.

"Antoni tells us you know how to read Atlantean," Mom said, sitting back and picking up one of the cups of tea.

Lusi gazed at the photographs, her eyes slowly scanning the images of the ruins in front of her. She shifted forward on the couch. "Where did you get these?"

Given how raspy Lusi's voice was, it was difficult to make out tone, but there was a stunned look on her face as she picked up one of the photographs to examine it more closely.

"It's a long story, which we'd be happy to tell if you'll agree to help us," Emun answered.

"Help you to do what?" She tore her eyes away from the photos to look up at Emun.

"We want to find the source of the siren's curse." I set down my tea and put my hands on my knees. "Understanding what these fragments say should help put us on the right track, but we can't read them."

"At least, not well," Antoni added.

Lusi looked at Antoni, and a smile quirked at the corners of her lips but didn't quite break all the way through. "You remembered some of what I taught you, did you?"

"A little."

"And you thought it was all made up."

"There was a lot you told me that I thought was made up," Antoni replied. "But it was all true, wasn't it? All that artwork, all those crests and statues. They really are of you."

Lusi let out a long breath. "I shouldn't have told you. I really should give up drinking," she added. "It makes me sloppy. Maybe I thought you'd forget, maybe I thought it didn't matter because you were leaving Warsaw anyway. It was irresponsible and stupid of me."

"We're glad you did tell him, because what he knew probably saved his life," I told her.

Lusi listened quietly as Antoni, Emun, and I relayed the story about the Group of Winterthür and the retrieval of all the gems we'd found. We told her that the gems allowed humans to breathe underwater and that the men from Winterthür had planned to sell them to the highest bidder. We told her that we'd brought the gems back here and had originally thought to return them to as many sirens as we could, until Emun had posed the question about the curse.

Lusi's eyes glittered dangerously as Mira then told her a short version of what happened to Okeanos and the Mer who lived there.

"Okeanos was my home," Lusi told us, then looked at my mother. "It was a very long time before you were born. Until Warsaw became my home."

"How is it that a mermaid makes her home in a land-locked city?" I asked.

Lusi had lost a little of her intimidation factor as the day wore on and we'd given her our secrets. She hadn't called us crazy and gotten back on her motorcycle. She even seemed interested. Now that the ice had been broken, I felt comfortable enough to probe a little.

"The Vistula river flows through Warsaw and then north to the Baltic," she explained. "I have access to it through an underground passage leading from my home. It is easy to get to water whenever I wish, freshwater immediately, or salt if I take the time to go all the way to the Baltic." She made a little jab at the air with her chin. "If you want to call the Baltic salty." She looked at me. "It's how I was able to hear your call. I was swimming at the time, in the Vistula."

I found it enlightening that she'd been able to hear my voice while swimming in freshwater, but didn't bring it up.

"You never wanted to return to Okeanos?" Mom asked.

"Like I said, Warsaw is my home now. It will be my home until I die; I'll never leave it again. I made that mistake before, and I'll not repeat it." She shot me a look. "Unless, of course, I get a call I cannot ignore."

"I won't do that to you again," I replied, putting my palms up in a defensive gesture before I could stop myself. "But we would appreciate your help."

"I think you've given yourself an impossible task, but good luck to you," Lusi said, looking down at the images before her again. "I'll do what I can to help. If by some miracle you can actually change things for sirens, then I'll be grateful." She jerked her chin toward Emun in that way I was coming to know as a quirk of hers. "And if breaking the curse means there's a few more of *him* around, I'll thank you for that, too."

I shared looks of relief with Antoni and my mother, but when I glanced at Emun, he was gazing at Lusi with both dimples in full view.

THREE

"She's a piece of work, isn't she?" Emun's knees cracked as he took two steps down and sat next to me.

I'd parked myself on the steps of the front porch again. It was the best place to enjoy the spring sunshine since the house buffered the wind coming off the Baltic. With a fresh coffee and one of Sera's biscuits—pulled from the freezer and microwaved—it was a corner of paradise. The biscuits, shot through with cinnamon and raisins, often filled the house with a mouthwatering scent as they were baking and were best fresh from the oven, but warm from the microwave was a close second.

"Who?" I responded as the warm buttered biscuit melted in my mouth, rendering my mind nearly vacant with pleasure. A second later, it clicked. "Lusi?"

Emun nodded and gave a crooked smile at the crumbs at the corner of my mouth.

I wiped my mouth on my napkin and took a swig of coffee.

"Sure." I shrugged and made my tone disinterested. "You know, if you think a hundreds of years old mermaid protector is a piece of work. That's *so* dark ages if you ask me."

Emun knocked my shoulder with his and gave an indignant snort which turned into a laugh. "For a second there, I thought you were serious."

I went back to eating my biscuit.

"How long do you think its going to take her to..." he swirled his fingers in the air mystically.

"Translate?"

He blew out a breath with puffed cheeks. "If you want to call it that. It's a confusing jumble of primitive images and glyphs. If you ask me, no one could make sense of it."

"I guess we'll see."

"Antoni is helping her," Emun added with a sideways glance.

"That's nice of him," I replied airily, and took another bite.

My phone vibrated from the pocket of my hoodie. I set down my coffee and fished it out. I swallowed as I read the number on the screen.

"Three-fifty? What country is that?"

"Can't help you there." Emun snagged the rest of the biscuit from my fingers as I gaped at the screen.

"Hey!"

"Aren't you going to answer it?" Emun's cheeks bulged as he said this around what was left of my biscuit.

"You're such a...a brother!" Pushing the talk button, I brought the phone to my ear. "Hello?"

"Targa?"

The voice was masculine, accented, and not one I recognized.

"Who is this?"

"It's Jozef."

I snapped upright and my eyes widened.

"What? Who is it?" Emun asked. I practically heard Emun swallowing the big chunk of biscuit before it was ready to go down his pipe.

"I know you don't know me that well," Jozef was saying, "and we were never formally introduced, but maybe you heard your mother mention me once or twice?"

"She did," I replied. "Where are you?"

"Well, that's the thing." He sounded a little apologetic, even sheepish. "I'm here, and I'd really like to see you."

"Here as in Poland? Here as in Gdansk?" I got to my feet, feeling my limbs pulsing with adrenaline. My stomach was doing enthusiastic backflips.

"Uh..." He cleared his throat, sounding nervous. "I'm pretty nearby."

I spluttered. "We've been looking for you! You've been impossible to find. You resigned, left no reason, no forwarding address."

"Wow, I—I..."

He took in a big breath but I couldn't tell if it was relief or mounting anxiety.

"I had no idea," he said. "I'm sorry to have made it so hard for you. So, it would be all right if I popped by for a visit, then?"

"All right?" I began to laugh at the absurdity of the phone call, and how he'd just plopped himself into my lap after all the effort we'd expended looking for him. "Get here as soon as you can, for Pete's sake! Don't waste a moment."

Jozef gave a chuckle and this time I could hear the relief in it.

My eyes were drawn to movement by the front gate. Jozef appeared on foot, and stepped into the driveway. He was holding a cell phone to his ear. He saw Emun and me standing on the front steps and I could see his surprise even at a distance.

"Oh!" Jozef's face split in a grin. He lifted a hand and waved at us. "Hello, there."

I ended the call and went down the steps. Emun followed me.

"That's Jozef," I said over my shoulder, my own face splitting in a grin.

"So I see."

Jozef crossed the grounds and we met in the middle on the patch of grass in the center of the roundabout.

Jozef looked as I remembered him—ruggedly handsome, with a trim beard and curly brown hair. His eyes were shining.

He held out his hand to shake mine but I went right past it and gave him a hug. I felt him give a startled laugh, and then his arms went around me and squeezed.

"You look so much like your mother," he said. "I'm sure you hear that all the time."

He released me and I introduced Emun and Jozef to one another.

"He's my brother," I said, enjoying the way it felt to call Emun my family, even if he was more than a century older than me.

Jozef looked so startled that for a moment he looked like a figurine from a funhouse—eyes stretched wide, mouth gaping. "Brother?"

"It's a long story," Emun said as he shook Jozef's hand. "I hope you can tell how happy we are to see you."

My heart was jumping. "I can't wait to tell Mom," I said. "I'll go get her."

Jozef's hand reached out and snagged my wrist. He

pulled me back around to face him, his face now both shocked and pale.

"She's here!?"

"Yeah, of course. Where else would she be?" I blinked at Jozef's surprise. He really hadn't expected her to be home. "She lives here."

"I thought...I thought she—" Jozef seemed unable to finish what it was that he thought.

Emun and I shared a confused glance and then stared at Jozef, still waiting for him to finish. Then it clicked into place like a puzzle piece. Jozef was aware of the *Dyás*. He thought she was gone.

"You thought she was in her salt-cycle." My eyes narrowed a fraction. "But how did you know she'd left in the first place?"

Jozef's mouth closed, then opened. A thin sheen of sweat had appeared on his brow. "I hope you can forgive me, it was all done with the intention of helping Mira. I was there..." he trailed off, weakly.

"You *saw* us that night?" I felt my eyes pop with incredulity. At first, I was horrified that such an intimate moment had been viewed by a stranger. It had been the most traumatic night of my life, and I'd had an audience? My cheeks flushed with heat at the thought of how I'd let everything go on the beach the night my mother had left, how I'd bawled like a baby, like a person whose heart was broken and would never heal.

"I'm so sorry." Jozef looked stricken. "It was a personal moment and I regret the intrusion, but I was trying so hard to reach Mira, to see if she was who I thought she was. And if she was, to see if I could trigger her memories. I followed you down to the beach that night. I'm sorry."

I closed my eyes and made an effort to steady my breathing. I had to remind myself that this was not Jozef the professional colleague at the salvage company, this was Jozef, my mother's true love and soul mate. A confusion of emotions roiled together—embarrassment, outrage, the joy and incredulity that Jozef was here now, excitement for my mother to be reunited with him, indignation. I opened my eyes and he was studying my face, worry marring his dark eyes. I also realized it was only Jozef and me standing on the grass now.

"Where did Emun go?" I asked.

"Jozef?"

We both whirled to face my mom where she stood at the top of the steps, her face was a blend of joy and shock. My heart gave a high leap at the sight of her. I'd never seen an expression on Mira's face that rivaled anything like what I was seeing in this moment. It was like she was someone else. Like, right now, she was pure...

"Bel?"

Jozef realized it too, just from the sight of her.

Mom thundered down the steps and ran across the lawn to where Jozef had swung his arms wide. She barreled into him and the two of them went down to their knees on the edge of the driveway.

Watching them, my heart pounded and my eyes misted. Their faces were overflowing with emotion. They were both crying, and laughing, and talking, and hugging one another, and touching one another's faces, and kissing.

"It's you," Jozef breathed into her hair. "It's really you, Bel. How can this be?"

I took a few steps back and reluctantly turned my back on them and headed for the front porch. I didn't want to leave Mom at such a critical moment, but I also felt like an intruder.

I heard my mother murmuring, her voice thick with everything—happiness, sadness, regret, longing, joy.

"I remember you. I remember it all now. I'm so sorry."

"You didn't know me. It's okay," Jozef whispered.

Emun and Antoni were peering through the glass of the windows beside the front door. Their faces were glued on the reunited lovers on the front lawn, still on their knees, still wrapped wholly up in one another. I waved at them and they disappeared from the windows. Stepping inside, I closed the door behind me, leaving my mom and Jozef to their private moment.

Emun stood in the foyer under the chandelier, one hand thoughtfully on his chin, partially hiding a little smile. Antoni came to me and I stepped into his arms, grateful for a hug. My body was trembling.

"We know a little bit what they feel like, don't we?" he murmured into my hair.

"A little," I agreed. Antoni and I had never been separated by so many years, and neither one of us had ever suffered an amnesia as complete as the one my mother had; after all, she'd literally lived two different lives. Jozef was a lover from a previous lifetime. But love was love, and separation was separation.

Several minutes passed and we waited quietly for Mom and Jozef to come into the house. It felt like a long time before we heard their footsteps on the stairs. The door opened and Mom came in, leading Jozef by the hand. She looked flushed and overjoyed, and her shirt was damp and there was still moisture on her face. Jozef looked both downright dazed and deliriously happy, like someone had blown by him at Mach speed and a big pile of money swirled around him.

Emun was seated on the large staircase. Antoni and I

stood in front of the archway into the parlor, his arm around me.

There was a silence so pregnant with emotion that no one knew what to say.

"So, we found Jozef," I said, just to break the tension.

Mom gave a sob-laugh and fresh siren tears poured over her cheeks. The water stain at the neck of her shirt slowly spread.

I realized at that moment that I had never seen my mother so happy. Oh yes, she'd been happy with my father, Nathan, when she wasn't suffering from the *Dyás*. But she had been Mira, then. The look in her eyes now, the smile, the full and open joy in her face had not simply been a rarity in my life, but an impossibility. In this moment, with Jozef's hand in hers, somehow it completed the circularity of her journey. It was the last key in the last lock that allowed her to be who she really was, fully and completely.

She was Sybellen *and* Mira, and she was happy.

FOUR

That evening after supper was over, the house was quiet, and the fire was lit in the front sitting room. Holding a mug of hot tea in my hands, I stared unseeing at the fire and blew at the steam meditatively. Antoni held a book open on his lap, flipping the pages slowly with one hand, his other arm over the back of the sofa behind me.

"When do you think it'll be safe to go upstairs?" Emun asked. He lay stretched out on the sofa, eyes closed and fingers laced over his chest.

"You can go upstairs anytime," I said with a laugh. "In case you haven't noticed, this place is massive. You're not going to disturb them."

"His room is next to Mira's," Antoni murmured without looking up from his book. "I don't think he's worried about disturbing them, so much as the other way around."

"Right." Mom wouldn't care who might hear her 'reunion celebrations' with her long-lost love, but Jozef might, and Emun would definitely want to skip out on any of that audio.

Footsteps on the stairs lifted Antoni's head from his

book and my own gaze snapped from the fire to the doorway, where whoever was coming down was sure to appear in a moment.

Emun still hadn't opened his eyes. "Sounds like I might have the all-clear to go to bed. I don't know about you guys, but with all the emotion and excitement of the last couple of days, I'm exhausted."

A moment later Lusi appeared, carrying the tablet.

"It's Lusi," I told Emun.

His eyes flew open and he popped upright to see for himself.

Antoni set the book he'd been reading on the side table and I handed him my tea so he could put it on the coaster.

"A breakthrough?" I asked, sliding forward with an excitement I tried to temper to avoid disappointment.

"Maybe," she replied, sitting next to Emun, who'd slid over to make room. "It's a start, but I think you'll have a lot of questions still." She pulled a folded piece of legal paper with messy handwriting on it from the pocket of her hooded sweater.

Emun peered at the page as she unfolded it. I got up and took the space next to Lusi. She shifted over toward Emun, who slid down a little too, although he didn't move as far as she had, I noticed. They were touching at the hip and shoulder.

Peering at the page, I realized I couldn't make sense of anything she'd written down.

"What language is that?"

"It's shorthand." Emun saved Lusi from having to reply. "It's English, it's just a faster way of writing. Secretaries used to use it when taking notes at meetings."

"Can you read it?" Lusi asked Emun.

He shook his head. "I never learned, I just know what it

looks like. I didn't think anyone used it anymore. It's very mid-century of you."

She made a sound in her throat which I thought had to be a laugh. It was hard to tell.

"If you mean mid-*nineteenth* century, then yes," she responded with a smile. She looked at Antoni and then at me. "Did you want to call Sybellen down so she can be here for this?"

"Uh..." Antoni seemed ready to respond but then looked at me for an answer instead. This was pretty important, but I was loath to interrupt her private time with Jozef.

"Let's start without her. You can give us a primer and we'll catch her up when she comes down...or in the morning."

Lusi looked surprised. "Are you sure?"

"She and Jozef need some time alone," I replied shortly.

"Okay. Well, this won't take very long. There weren't a lot of photos to study and what was there seems like a partial story, anyway." She flattened the sheet out and referenced it from time to time as she talked.

"The mosaic starts mid-legend and tells of a triton who found a large, six-sided rock. The rock was blue, and precious, that much is clear in the imagery, but the glyphs talk about it like it was more than precious, it was mystical." She touched the gem in her ear.

"We know for sure that's true. Does it tell you how the triton knew that?" I asked.

"Sort of," Lusi went on. "It says he took this large column home—probably to Okeanos—with him and hid it in a cave. It stayed there for a long time. It doesn't say how long, but we might be talking decades here, possibly centuries. Until eventually he decided he wanted to make a gift for a siren he'd fallen in love with. He broke the column and took a small piece with him to a jeweler, where he had it made into a ring."

"Let me guess." Emun got to his feet and paced to the fireplace and halfway back. I'd learned that pacing was a favorite past-time of the thinking Emun. "After he gave it to his siren lover, they realized that it freed her from the salt curse and allowed them to be together without her having to endure any land cycles?"

"Essentially, yes."

"Do you think he knew it would help her, or was it an accidental discovery?" Antoni asked, closing the book and setting it on the table beside the couch.

"Don't know," Lusi replied, "and I don't think it really matters for your purposes, does it?"

I shook my head. "No, what I'm more interested in is where he found it, and how it ended up in a million tiny pieces under a magical dome in Okeanos."

Lusi cocked her head and looked at me. "I can answer one of those for you, but it's not going to make you happy."

"Put us out of our misery, please." Emun had stopped pacing and crossed his arms.

"He found it in Atlantis, I know that from the glyphs. It was near a white stone temple and the stone was threaded with blue. There's a symbol that looks like this." She took a chewed-up stub of a pencil and doodled a simple ring of three concentric circles on the legal paper.

Antoni threw his head back and groaned loudly.

"What?" Lusi looked up at him, startled.

"I'm so stupid. *Of course* it means Atlantis!"

"Yeah, it's simple in retrospect," Lusi said, "but maybe not to the untrained eye."

"It looks like a bulls-eye," I said.

"Or a shockwave," Emun offered.

"Or it looks exactly the way Plato described Atlantis," Antoni said with another groan.

"Don't beat yourself up, Antoni," Lusi replied in a clipped tone.

My guess was that patience wasn't Lusi's strongest point and she had more to say.

She continued, "The other thing that's important is that the columnar was a piece broken off of a much larger chunk."

"That was the blue blob at the broken end of the first tile!" Antoni nodded, his cheeks flushing with pink. "I thought it was a body of water."

"Nope, it has angular edges, just like the jagged edges of the column depicted in the mosaic."

I felt Emun's gaze snap from Lusi to me. "Then that's where we have to look."

I gave him a withering look which he read perfectly, for he voiced my exact thoughts aloud.

"In the ruins of Atlantis." His tone expressed fully just how impossible he knew this to be.

"Yeah, the city that all of archaeology has failed to find and believes to be completely bogus," Antoni added.

"Pretty much," Lusi said, putting the page on the table in front of her knees. "Sorry there was no more to it than that."

The room fell silent, broken only by the snaps and crackles of the dwindling fire and the thin buzz of electric lamps. A blanket of hopelessness enveloped Antoni, Emun, and me.

I sat back against the couch with a sigh, rubbing my eyes. I suddenly felt so tired.

"Don't give up that easily." Lusi's voice came from beside me and I felt a light, comforting pat on my knee.

"You're young, you have a whole siren-lifetime ahead of you to find Atlantis and see if you can set things straight."

"What odds would you give us?" I opened my eyes to gaze at the strange siren beside me. Her words were encouraging, but even with hardly any voice at all I could hear her doubt.

She shrugged.

Emun wandered back to the couch and sort of collapsed into it, rather than sitting down. I guessed his pacing was done for the night.

Two sets of footsteps on the stairs wasn't enough to rouse any of us from our grim silence. We didn't even turn around to greet Mira and Jozef when they walked in.

"Wow." My mom came into view on the right, standing between the fire and where Emun had just deflated. Jozef appeared a moment later just behind her. "Who died?"

No one responded. The fire gave a pop.

"Are you guys okay?" Jozef asked, stepping closer to my mom. His brows pinched together.

"Well, no one died," I replied finally. Someone had to put them out of their misery, and drop them into the misery of our dead-end.

I told them what Lusi had learned. She spoke up a few times to clarify things. As we talked, Jozef's eyes widened and he took a seat in the single chair a few feet from our couch. He seemed to sink into it slowly, dreamlike, and listen like his life depended upon him reciting back all he'd heard.

When Lusi explained where the original, larger gem had been found, he seemed to come alive. He looked up at my mom and then back at me. I could see the whites of his eyes.

Fascinated at the play of emotions and expression

shifting and cavorting on Jozef's features, I stopped telling the story and let Lusi finish.

When she'd told the rest of it, the only face in the room that had any liveliness in it at all was Jozef's.

"If you don't share whatever it is you know right now," I said to him, watching his knees begin to bounce in an agitated way, "then I'm going to put a frog under your pillow tonight."

Jozef got to his feet, his face looking near to exploding with excitement. "You're not going to believe what I have to tell you," he began.

"Try us," I said.

"I know the location of Atlantis," said Jozef with a Cheshire-cat-like grin.

Our response was almost comical, as jaws dropped. Then all of us started talking at once, questions tumbling over each other like an avalanche. Jozef held up his hands for calm.

"All of you know my heritage. The reason I left Novak Salvage was that I received a letter informing me my father was ill." Jozef summarized his activities of the past couple of months succinctly, ending with, "We have access to all of Claudius's research."

FIVE

The next morning saw us all up early to say goodbye to Lusi. She wished us luck, but it was pretty obvious that she didn't really believe we had much chance of success. It was better that way, I thought, for her to not have high hopes. I wouldn't have been keen on having the world's siren population knowing what we were up to. If we failed, no one would know except for us.

The rest of the morning was spent on the phone: to the office to free Antoni from work, to Ivan to prepare the plane, to Adam for a driver, and to Sera to inform her we would be away. But within hours our bags were packed and in a pile on the front porch.

It was strange and exciting, preparing for this adventure. We outfitted ourselves with only a few changes of clothing. Jozef assured us that he had equipment for the kind of desert outing we were in for. Thinking of the desert made me think of Petra, where she'd had her elemental transformation. I wondered what she was up to now.

I sent texts to Georjie and Saxony to let them know what we were up to. Georjie and I had talked on a weekly basis after she'd left Poland for Scotland, but Saxony had seemed so busy at Arcturus that she hardly had time to exchange texts. She promised she'd catch me up properly over her spring break.

Adam pulled the largest of the Novak SUVs up in front of the house and he, Antoni, and Emun loaded the luggage into the back. Jozef came out with Mom a few moments later and we said goodbye to Sera and Adalbert, who had managed to return before we left.

The vehicle had six seats in the back, three facing front and three facing back. Antoni and I settled in the seats with our backs to the driver's cabin. Mom and Jozef sat side by side on the front facing bench seat and entwined their fingers. Emun stepped in and took the seat beside my mom.

"Everything has happened so fast." Jozef gazed at my mother as if still hardly daring to believe that she was in fact flesh and blood and not some ghost of his imagination.

"There are still a few things I don't understand," I began, then laughed. "Okay, there're a lot of things I don't understand." I was directing these words at Jozef. "You didn't think my mom was here yesterday when you arrived."

"No, I was certain she wasn't, in fact. I thought she'd be somewhere in the middle of the Atlantic by now, or farther."

"So, what was your original plan, then? Why did you come back to Gdansk?" Given that Jozef's father had recently passed away, it would not have been a great time to leave home. Yet, here he was.

Jozef coughed into his curled fist, retrieved a bottle of water from the cup holder in the door, and took a few long swallows. I thought his eyes seemed a little red and my heart reached out to him. I knew what it was to lose a father, but I had been so young. Young people seemed to bounce back from death more quickly than adults did.

"I came to find you, Targa. I thought you might be able to help me find your mother." He leaned forward and put the bottle back in its pocket and settled back, lifting a shoulder in a shrug. "If not you, then who?"

"You know about the *Dyás*," I stated. "And you saw how much Mom was suffering before I finally made her go. Why did you think I would help you make her come back?"

"Because of what I found in Loukas's research."

Antoni and I shared a look. "More than just Atlantis? Are you talking about his...dissections?"

"No." Jozef frowned and two lines appeared beside his mouth. He looked ill at the mention of Loukas's scientific work on mermaids. "I knew that sirens needed the gems to be able to live without the *Dyás* hanging over them, torturing them. But I learned a lot more about how it became that way, at least in Loukas's mind. It's only a theory, but it made sense to me."

"You know about the curse?" My heart began to speed up a little.

But Jozef shook his head. "Not the curse, no."

"Let him explain," Mom said gently. Her expression said he'd already filled her in on what he was about to tell us. She looked calm and had been thoughtful and quiet all morning. Fair enough; it was a lot for her to process.

"When my father gave me the key to Loukas's labs and library, I found a journal he kept for his thoughts as he was working. Most of it was scribblings that made no sense to me, but part of it was a theory on why there were no tritons." Jozef braced his shoulder against the door as Adam took the on-ramp and began to speed up. "See, tritons had been gone so long that no one alive believed they existed."

"But Loukas did?" I asked.

Jozef nodded. "He thought it went against the natural order of things for a species to only have females, but he couldn't pinpoint any place in time where the tritons had gone extinct. There were no strange events, no illnesses, nothing that might be a cause for the elimination of one gender."

"Mira said she saw something in Loukas's journals that referenced crossbreeds," Emun said, one knee bouncing up and down.

"Yes, that factors into his theory," Jozef agreed. "See, at some point in time, an Atlantean or a group of them discovered the gems' value. That group made a commitment to one another that if they ever crossed paths with a siren, they'd do their level best to steal her gem. It was a way of disabling them without a violent attack. They knew that sirens without gems began to cycle, and some of them ran the risk of losing their minds."

"Why would they steal the gem as opposed to just killing the sirens outright?" Antoni asked.

"Who knows?" Jozef replied. "Loukas asked the same question. He theorized that they didn't want to out and out start a war they probably wouldn't win. He thought that if an Atlantean attacked a siren one on one, they'd lose. But the thinking went that if an Atlantean could catch a siren off guard and steal her gem, then he could get away from her. Atlanteans would collect the gems. They earned bragging rights to their friends, maybe they were even rewarded when they turned it in to someone."

"Someone like your father?" I asked, keeping my tone as neutral as possible.

Jozef winced, but agreed. "Yes, someone like my father. Only we're talking centuries ago. Over time, Loukas thought that this activity of stealing gems from sirens became a part of Atlantean culture. If there was a plan or an end game in mind, it has been lost to time, but in the meantime, Atlanteans raised their children to do this. It became hardwired."

"Like that guy in the bar." Emun's eyes were fixed on Jozef's face and his brow was wrinkled thoughtfully. "It was like he knew he was supposed to take gems away, that it would weaken sirens, but beyond that it was all up to fate. Like it was a superstition or something."

"Yes, that was one of the words Loukas used in his ramblings."

"How did the gems end up back in Okeanos, then?"

Jozef paled a little and looked out the window for a moment before resuming the story. "That was my father's idea, his and his lieutenants. Over the years, my father and Loukas groomed their Atlantean friends and friends-of-friends to bring any stolen gemstones to them. They'd amassed quite a collection, as you know. After they'd mined all the orichalcum from Okeanos and left its interiors mostly in ruins, they put the gems inside and had someone put up a magical barrier to make them inaccessible."

Antoni and I looked at one another with wide eyes. We'd seen these magically protected gems. We'd even seen the magic kill.

Emun had been there too but his mind was on something else. "So, concerning the lack of tritons...I'm not sure I understand yet."

Jozef nodded. "Loukas thought that the decline and eventual extinction"—he paused here and gestured to Emun––"obviously he was wrong about the extinction part—happened as an accidental byproduct of the sirens slowly losing their gemstones."

"Because of the crossbreeding," Antoni interjected with a nod to Mom. "The note she saw in Loukas's lab when she was rescuing Fimia."

"Yes. The sirens having to cycle meant that they bred mainly with human men, rather than Mer, because tritons didn't have to cycle, and generally stayed underwater."

"I certainly haven't," Emun replied.

"No, but tritons of old did, according to what we understand. So the sirens had no choice but to mate with men, and as a result..."

"Male offspring were human, and female offspring were sirens," I finished.

"Exactly." Jozef gave a deep nod, keeping his eyes on me. "And over time, this meant that with no new tritons to replace the ones who died, they just became less and less common, until they were rare, and then finally, nonexistent. Over time they fell into the realm of myth, with almost no sirens alive today even believing that they ever existed at all."

"Even the curse isn't seen as a curse," Mom added. "Sirens alive today don't see it that way because it's the way life has always been. It's the way it was for their mothers, and their grandmothers."

There was silence in the car for a few minutes. Adam turned the SUV onto the airport road. We were nearly there.

"So you discovered all of this," I said to Jozef as we all swayed in our seats when the SUV cornered, "after your father died and gave you the keys to Loukas's stuff. And you wanted to find my Mom..."

"I wanted your help to find her and give her a gemstone. It never occurred in my wildest dreams that you'd have done that for her already." Jozef's eyes seemed a little glassy and he looked away. I saw him swallow, fighting to keep his emotion under control.

The SUV came to a halt in the parking lot and we could see Ivan and his co-pilot waiting on the tarmac near our plane. Adam and Antoni pulled out the bags and passed them to their owners.

Mom and I shared a grim look as we heaved our bags onto our shoulders and headed for the plane.

"I'm glad I asked him all that stuff *before* we got into the air," I muttered.

"Yeah, it'll be lights out from now until Gibraltar."

"Too bad the gemstone doesn't cure the flying sickness."

"No, but maybe on the way back…" She let her sentence trail off without finishing it.

"You think the flying sickness is part of the curse?"

She shrugged. "One can always hope."

SIX

"This isn't the only reason I was so desperate for you to come to Gibraltar with me," Jozef said, his hands laying flat over the satellite imagery and documents we'd been perusing.

We'd been in Gibraltar for just over twelve hours. Mom and I had slept away half that time. Since we'd woken we had done little else but pore over the Atlantis documents while snacking on fruit and hard-boiled eggs.

I looked up from the photograph of The Richat Structure at these words. Antoni and Emun paused in what they were doing as well.

Jozef's eyes were all for my mother. "I have something else to show you, something even more... well, I don't know if exciting is the right word, but...honestly I've been wracking my brains trying to find the right words to tell you but I find myself at a loss, just like my father was. I just have to show you."

Mom stood up. Antoni, Emun, and I all shared a look. We hadn't specifically been invited by Jozef to come and see this thing he was clearly so nervous to show my mother, but there was no way I was going to sit this out...whatever it was.

Jozef wiped a hand across his brow. "We have to return to Loukas's lab. I'm sure it's the last place in the world you would ever want to go back to, considering what he did there."

My gaze darted to my mom. "Where he dissected sirens?"

A cold hand slipped around my heart and began to squeeze at the thought of it.

Jozef nodded. "That's the place." He looked a little green himself as he got up from the table.

Antoni took my hand as we followed Jozef through the manor and out into the back gardens. It was just the way my mother had described it. Topiaries, trickling fountains, and borders of flowers decorated the large courtyard and pathways. We passed through this courtyard and headed toward a free-standing building at the rear of the property. It was boarded up and to say it needed a spot of repairs was a massive understatement. There had to be a resident ghost or two.

Ivy crawled through the crevices between the bricks, and soft fuzzy mosses crept up the lowest stones from the damp ground. The door Jozef led us to—at the bottom of a long, narrow stairwell leading below ground level—looked newer than everything else. It was a metal door, painted black, and crusted with several locking mechanisms.

"Looks like Loukas stepped up security," Mom said.

Jozef nodded as he fished a set of keys from his pocket and began to unlock the door, lock by lock. When he swung the door open, a musty smell drifted from the doorway. We followed Jozef inside. The space within was pristine with stainless-steel surfaces and several computers. A door to the right drew my eye—also new, metallic, and painted with the same black finish as the entrance.

"That's where you found Fimia?" I pointed at the closed door across the room.

Mom nodded and I saw a shudder pass through her.

"Is it just me or does this place feel evil?" Emun muttered, his dark blue eyes scanning the table and bookshelves, boxes and computers. Everything was covered in dust, and several cobwebs dangled from corners and in the spaces between the bookshelves.

"With your help, perhaps we can exorcise a few of the demons," Jozef answered.

But he didn't lead us to the doorway where Fimia had been kept in an aquarium and slowly starved. He headed straight for the back wall. A plain plastic cover hid a panel of numbered buttons and a small circular keyhole. Jozef punched in a code and inserted a cylindrical key. The panel blinked to life with a muted yellow glow and there was a creaking sound. A gentle breeze came from nowhere and drifted past my face. It smelled of mildew and salt.

Antoni took a step back and pulled me with him at the sudden noise and the mysterious wind. His eyes darted about, looking for the source.

"It's a secret doorway," Jozef explained.

What had looked moments ago like a seam in the wall, had cracked open and was widening before our eyes as a door swung inward. Shadows tinged with a false green light yawned from within. I could hear a slow but steady electronic beep.

Jozef entered and reached for something near the doorway. A fluorescent light flickered above our heads, revealing a small chamber.

A long computer screen blinked dimly in front of a set

of chairs. Below it was a panel of complex boards with dials and switches. A film of dust had formed over everything. Just like the rest of the lab, no one had been in here for a very long time. In the corner of the room was a semi-circular rod holding a curtain, like privacy curtains in hospital. It was hanging in front of what I thought might be another doorway.

Jozef reached for the curtain and drew it back.

My mother gave a low cry and covered her mouth with one hand. She walked up to the glass Jozef had revealed and put her hand on it.

Jozef had revealed a circular tank with a heavy silver lid and a sturdy looking base, with several cables connecting it to the panel against the wall.

Inside the tank was a mermaid.

The room was so quiet that I could hear my own heartbeat. I left Antoni and Emun in the doorway and went to stand beside my mother. I could not have torn my eyes from the siren within the tank if I had wanted to.

"Is she dead?"

She looked dead. Her eyes were closed and her body lay relaxed against the bottom of the tank, her tail curled in front of her torso. Her fins disappeared beneath her head, like a pillow, and her hands were together in front of her nose, almost in prayer.

"She's in what Loukas called diapause," Jozef answered. "That beeping sound is her heartbeat."

"So slow?" Antoni asked, his voice quiet and awed. "It can't be more than fifteen beats a minute."

"Something like that."

The mermaid had dark skin, but long white hair that drifted in the water like a cloud above her head, and a black tail. She was so thin that muscular striations were visible on her arms, belly, and chest. A small aquamarine dangled from a thin chain fastened around her neck.

"This is what you must have looked like when you came out of diapause," I said to Mom. My stomach squirmed at how fragile the siren in the tank appeared—like her bones might snap if the water around her shifted too much.

"And Emun, too." Antoni stood close enough to my back for me to feel the comforting heat of him. I leaned against his warmth and solidity, fighting the cold filling my heart.

I finally tore my gaze away from the comatose siren when my mother moved in my peripheral vision. Mom put both hands on the glass and looked at the siren, but tears were now over-spilling her cheeks and running down her neck. Only then did I realize that she *knew* this siren.

"Who is she?"

Mom took time to find her voice and when she faced me, I realized that she was in a strange ecstasy of emotion—both elated and grieving.

"It's Nike," she said. "Annikephoros, the siren sorceress who saved my life by reversing my age." She took a breath and her eyes softened. "The sorceress who gave me you."

It felt like my eyes were going to pop out of my head and I stared at the sleeping mermaid again. "This is Nike? But..."

"I thought she had blue hair," interjected Emun, stepping to my left side and peering down at Nike's fragile form. Even the siren's face was sharp, the cheekbones jutting and her features seeming too big for the bones of the face that held them.

"She did," Jozef answered. "Loukas actually records that in his notes. After they put her in this chamber, he documented that her hair turned white some time later. You can still see a little of the blue at the very ends if you look closely."

I looked, and yes, I saw it. The very ends of her hair were a darker shade that the rest, a shade that looked more like shadow in the water and dim light of the tank—a barely-there tint of sky-blue.

"How do we wake her?" Mom looked over at Jozef and took her hands away from the tank. She wiped at the moisture running down her face.

I fished in my pocket for the small packet of travel tissues I kept for the inconvenience of siren tears. Pulling one out of the sack, I handed it to her. She took it and gave me a wobbly smile. After thinking about it for a second, I gave her the whole packet. She gave a sodden chuckle and took that, too.

Jozef looked pained. "Well, that's the tricky part. I don't know." He gestured to the computers and to the room we'd passed through. "We have all of Loukas's notes. He was good at documenting everything. But what I've read so far suggests that this is the first time he'd ever done this—forced a siren into diapause."

"This is a special chamber, obviously," Emun said, moving to get a closer look at the vintage computers and the complicated looking panels. He murmured to himself as he began to read some of the writing on the panel below the screen. "Some of this is her vitals, which must be coming from the clip over her finger."

Blinking, my gaze shot back to Nike's hands. There was a pale plastic clip fastened over the skin just below the base of her pinkie fingernail. The clip had a thin cable coming out of one side, which disappeared underneath Nike's arm and shoulder.

"I hadn't even noticed that." I felt Antoni's breath against the top of my head.

"Me either," I added. "I noticed her fingernails, but not that thing."

Nike's fingernails were so long they had begun to corkscrew.

Jozef nodded. "It's a high-pressure chamber, made to mimic the deepest of underwater sea environments exactly. When he put her in here, he writes of slowly increasing the pressure and documenting what happened to her vitals. Initially, he was trying to learn at what point sirens might...expire."

"Expire?" Antoni echoed sharply. "He might have killed her—this one-of-a-kind siren—for his experiment, and not even cared?"

"That was Loukas." Jozef looked regretful. "Science was worth every cost to him, and certainly siren lives didn't matter."

"Like a nazi," I said, feeling my lip curl with disgust.

Emun agreed and leaned over to frown at the panel. He bent to blow the dust away from one of the small screens on the dashboard.

"So, he wanted to know the limits of siren endurance in terms of depth," I summarized, more for myself to understand what had happened here than for anyone else, "and she eventually just fell asleep?"

"Exactly." Jozef scratched at his temple. "He forced her into a kind of hibernation, and then, according to the dates in his research and what my father told me before he passed—Loukas got sick and the experiments came to a halt. She's been here ever since."

"You have all the notes Loukas left as he increased the pressure." Emun straightened and looked at Jozef, his eyes intense with hope. "Our best bet is to reverse whatever it was he did exactly. To do anything else might be too risky."

Jozef was nodding. "That's what I was thinking as well, but I think the ultimate call has to be Sybellen's." He took my Mom's hand. "This is your friend's life that hangs in the balance. Loukas believed that changing the pressure too quickly one way or the other might result in organ failure. I don't know if that's likely for a siren or not, but..." His mouth opened and closed, as though he was trying to decide whether to add anything to that statement or not. "Well, he seemed to think there was a risk, so I wanted you to know. I could have tried when I first found her, but I was too afraid I'd mess it up. And I also thought that the first thing she should see when she does wake up, is a friendly face. I know I could have told you sooner, when I first saw you in Gdansk, but I didn't know how you'd react and I didn't want you to spend several hours on a plane fraught with worry and upset. I hope I didn't do badly."

"You did well," Mom replied quickly, and some of the concern on Jozef's brow eased away.

Mom's eyes found ours, one after the other before finally settling on Jozef.

"We'll do it as Emun suggested," she said. "It's the only thing that makes sense."

"You're sure?" Jozef's brow crinkled and he looked tired.

Mom nodded, and in contrast, her expression was hopeful and eager. "Let's get her out of there."

SEVEN

"Okay," Emun said, gesturing to the complicated and dusty dashboard. "This panel looks like something NASA might have used to launch the space shuttle. How do we get her out of there without hurting her?" His eyes flashed to the still, emaciated form drifting peacefully in the tank. "Or killing her."

Silence stretched out, each face looking as concerned and unsure as the next.

Finally, Antoni reached toward the shelving unit above the computer panel and pulled down a book, looked at it, set it aside, then pulled down another. "There must be something in here that can help us."

Jozef and Mom began to pull books off the shelf, too, reading titles and scanning a few pages to determine whether the content might be helpful or not.

"I think what we'd be looking for is something in Loukas's notes," said Jozef, his eyes ticking back and forth across the pages of another book before setting it aside on the growing stack. "He was meticulous about note-keeping, just as any scientist should be."

"Ha, yeah, thanks Loukas," I snarled sarcastically. "Too bad he was about as ethical as Nero."

"Here's a notebook with scribbles in it," Antoni said after fanning the pages of a black, leather-bound book no thicker than a pinky finger. He scanned it quickly and handed it to Jozef. "I don't think it's written in English, though. So, good luck."

He pulled down another notebook, this one thick and brown, also without a title.

"What's that?" I asked, peering over Antoni's shoulder as he opened it to where a skinny brown ribbon marked a page.

"More notes, but they may as well be in Urdu for all the sense they make."

"May I see it?" Mom held out her hand and Antoni gave it to her. She flipped through a few pages, eyes scanning, brows pinching. It looked like she didn't disagree with Antoni's sentiments.

"Here, look at this," Emun said suddenly and shifted to stand beside Jozef. "It's a graph with a timetable running across the top."

The five of us crowded around the small book as Emun pressed it flat on the table, open for all of us to see. He flipped through it slowly, the end of his index finger tracing horizontally across the page.

"Look. These numbers look random, but if you flip back to the front of the notebook, a column down the left-hand side denotes everything on this line as PSI."

"Pounds per square inch." Even I knew that one.

Emun nodded. "Yep, and this one," his finger traced down to the next line, "is marked as TDS, which is Total Dissolved Solids."

"What does that mean?" I asked.

"It's how you measure salinity," Emun answered, his eyes flashing up at me and back down to the page. He pointed out the initialism below TDS. "But I'm not sure what this one means."

"EC," Mom read aloud.

"Electrical Conductivity," replied Jozef. In his voice was a tone like a key had unlocked something in his brain. "I think you've found something here, Emun. May I see it?"

Emun let Jozef study the other marks on the front left page. "Oxygen, G over KG, that's the ratio of salt to seawater. PSU, THC…"

"THC?" I couldn't keep the look of shock from my face. "What's that need to be measured for?"

"It's not what you think," Jozef explained, the dimple in his left cheek making an appearance, though he didn't fully smile. "THC means Thermohaline Circulation."

"Oh."

"What's PSU?" Mom asked.

"Practical Salinity Unit," Jozef said, his eyes back on the page. "It's an extraneous measurement, actually, because it's a combination of two other measurements he's already taking."

Jozef flipped through a few of the pages, then he turned around and faced the panel, looking from the notebook to the panel and back again. Emun peered over one shoulder and Mom peered over the other. Antoni and I squeezed in at the sides.

Jozef jabbed a finger at each marking on the left side of the first page and found a corresponding marking on the paneling in front of us.

"It's all here," Mom said, her voice low but thrumming with energy. "If we just do everything that Loukas did to put her in this state, but in reverse…"

"And at exactly the same time intervals," Emun added.

Jozef was nodding. He looked at my Mom. "She should wake up."

"How long?" I asked, reaching across Emun and pawing at Jozef's shoulder. "How long will it take, can you tell that?"

He turned to me and then his eyes flashed back down to the notes and he noticed the time and date of the first entry, then flipped through the book and found the last entry.

"Eight hours, thirty-seven minutes, forty seconds," he replied, looking back up at me and then to my Mom. "But we'd better be precise. We don't know what it will do to her if we mess it up."

"What if the system's broken?" Mom turned to look at Nike, curled up in the seawater. She put a hand on the glass. "She's been down here for years. What if in that time something in the computer, or the parts making the pressure don't work anymore?"

"We can't worry about that." Jozef put a hand on her shoulder. "We'll have to do the best we can with the information we have. No one has disturbed this room in a very long time. There's no reason to think this setup has stopped working. If it had, Nike would probably be dead by now, but she's not."

"I think we should write out the instructions and make them really clear," Antoni suggested, ever the organized project manager. "We have to know exactly what to do and at what time to do it. I can hardly make out some of those handwritten notations."

Jozef nodded. "I'll reverse engineer it and put it into a form everyone can read and follow."

Mom's eyes were wide and glassy, worried and hopeful. I crossed to her and took her hand.

"She'll be okay, Mom. Sirens are bloody tough."

She smiled and squeezed my hand, then nodded.

ONE MIGHT THINK that tweaking a bunch of buttons and knobs for a little over eight hours would be an easy job. In actuality, it took all of us rotating on ninety-minute shifts and it was still mentally exhausting. There were eight adjustments to make during the course of Nike's waking. The adjustments were made frequently and not all at the same time for each metric. Each bit of data had its own reversed timeline and we were collectively terrified of what it might do to Nike if we so much as stepped a half degree or two seconds out of the timeline.

"How did Loukas know what he was doing?" Antoni asked when the two of us were on shift together and nearing the end of the process.

"Maybe Loukas didn't do it? Maybe he had someone else do it for him, someone who knew more," I suggested, not really focusing on the answer as I watched the clock. My fingers hovered over the knob marked 'PSU.'

Antoni went quiet as we counted down the seconds. "Okay. Do it."

I made the adjustment and we both looked at the timeline, checked off the change, and mentally marked what was next.

"He must have taken actual measurements as he lowered some sensitive device down to the ocean floor where a siren would fall into diapause, and then just mimicked it." Antoni's chair creaked as he shifted closer to the panels. He seemed to find the whole thing fascinating.

"He'd have to go at a speed a mermaid would naturally

swim down to the bottom, synthesizing the environment and pressure and salt and all that exactly." I brought my fingers to my temples, where a dull headache had begun to take root just behind my eyes. That was no surprise. I'd been staring at the screens and the timeline taped over the panel for over an hour.

The door creaked on its hinges but neither Antoni nor I turned around.

"Almost time for a shift change."

I felt Jozef's presence behind us, but not Mom's.

"Where's Mom?" I'd assumed she'd be joining Jozef for his shift as she had previously.

"She's having a late-night snack." It was Emun's voice. "I'll be Jozef's co-pilot for this shift."

I heard Antoni's stomach growl, and my own grumbled to match it.

"What's she having?" I asked.

"Cheese and crackers and fruit," Jozef answered, sounding apologetic. "It was all I could put together on short notice."

"That sounds amazing." My stomach gurgled in agreement.

All went quiet as Antoni held up a hand with his five fingers out stiff then lowered them one by one in a count-down. At zero, he adjusted the oxygen. There was a respon-sive burble from the tank. A few minutes later the shift change bell went off, which was just my cell phone set to alarm. Antoni and I passed the seats to Jozef and Emun for the last shift.

My eyes were itchy and my head throbbed. I wanted nothing more than to eat dinner and go to bed. It was closing in on ten in the evening. Still early by my regular routine, but it felt much later to my tired brain.

"Last shift," I murmured.

There was no way any of us would miss the ending of the last shift, no matter how tired or drained we were.

I glanced at the still form of Nike in the glass tube. The machine had begun to make noises at the third hour, which I'd found unsettling. Bubbling and whooshing noises filled the room as it did whatever it needed to do to adjust the environment inside the tank. I'd gotten used to them, but I'd be happy when I didn't have to listen to them anymore. Sometimes there were creaks and high-pitched whines, almost whistles, which made me freeze and cringe, thinking that at any moment the whole thing would crack open and Nike would slither out, dead.

Antoni took my hand as we made our way back to the house. The night air smelled sweet and fresh, like rain. We found Mom in the kitchen, perched on top of the counter and guzzling a glass of water.

When Jozef had said cheese and crackers and fruit, I had assumed those cheap orange crackers and some chunks of cheddar, maybe some apple slices. But what had been laid out on two large cutting boards was five different cheeses, sourdough and almond crackers with bits of nuts embedded in them, dried pears, fresh figs and grapes, and quince jelly.

Antoni and I fell on the spread like starving sharks.

"Did Jozef and Emun eat?" I asked through a mouthful of Roquefort and grape. "I forgot to ask them."

Mom nodded. "After Nike's awake and we've settled her in bed, we can go get more groceries."

"These dried pears are amazing." Antoni rolled his eyes with pleasure.

We filled our growling bellies and I went to lie down on the couch in the library until the last shift was over. The headache began to ease and I must have dozed a bit because it seemed in the next moment that Antoni was kissing my cheek and telling me time was up.

We joined Emun and Jozef as the last adjustment was made and we watched the clock count down to zero, all of us on our feet and tense. Eyes on Nike, we held our collective breath and waited. Mom stood the closest, giving Nike a familiar face to see when she woke up.

Nothing happened.

Time passed in agonizing slowness. Mom crouched and brought her face close to Nike's face. She put her hand on the glass and stared at her friend expectantly. A moment later she tapped her fingernails lightly on the glass.

"Come on, Nike."

A lump rose in my throat as time went by and there was still no change. Nike's heartbeat was steady and slow. In fact, now that I was noticing it, it hadn't changed its pace much during the entire transition.

"Shouldn't her heart be going faster?" Emun gave voice to my thought.

"Annikephoros," Mom whispered to the glass.

There was no visible response, but the small echo of her heartbeat did speed up, just a little.

Mom turned her head sharply and looked up at me. "Call her."

Antoni and Emun's expressions brightened with hope and they both nodded.

"Call her?" Jozef looked perplexed. "Like...telepathically?"

"I don't know if I can," I said to my Mom, surprised at her suggestion. "I think she has to be in the ocean"

"Just try?" Her eyes pleaded. "What have you got to lose?"

I nodded and closed my eyes, working to block out the electronic sounds of the room, the smell of mildew and dust, the creaks and whooshing noises of the tank.

Annikephoros.

The smell of the room seemed to intensify, a deep earth dampness, like a grave.

Annikephoros.

The bubbling of the tank and the breathing of the people around me sounded like they were coming through a microphone placed right beside my head. The beep of Nike's heartbeat battered against my skull like a cricket bat. My own heartbeat sped up and my eyes screwed shut as I fought to keep the noises and smells out of my line of communication.

It was no good.

I opened my eyes and was not surprised to see that there was no change. I shook my head. "I can't. But let me go down to the beach. It might not work but it's worth a shot."

"I'll come with you," Antoni said, making to follow me as I turned away.

I gave him a smile, tremulous at the corners, but still a smile. "Thanks, love, but I'd rather go alone."

He nodded. "Of course, sorry."

I kissed him and climbed out of the dank basement, immediately feeling completely different as I took fresh sea air into my lungs. Crossing the yard full of tangled overgrowth, I picked my way across large black boulders. Soon I was standing on a pebbly shore. The sky was as black as velvet. The clouds obscured most of the stars but the moon was a dusty orb, like a giant thumb had smudged ink across a bone-white blob of paint.

Kicking off my sneakers, I stood with my feet in the saltwater. Every deep breath worked to clear my mind like a wind carries away smoke. The throbbing of my temples disappeared. I closed my eyes and let myself reach out to Nike.

Annikephoros.

Almost immediately, an explosion of teal fireworks made of a fine spray of water went off behind my eyes. I couldn't halt the laugh of delight at the sudden display of beauty.

I'm here.

My heart began to gallop. Never before had I actually 'heard' a siren I had called. But her response was unmistakeable. I could only assume our connection was so strong because she was a sorceress. Along with those words were more fireworks, and a warm pulsing presence unlike any other I had sensed. She felt like the first ray of sunlight warming the upper layers of a cool ocean. She felt weightless and sleepy, dreamy and patient. Most surprising of all, it felt like a hug from someone who had been waiting for me for a long time. My pulse fluttered at the feel of her, the energy that didn't come from physical health, but magic.

You're awake?

I waited for a response but there was none, not in words anyway. Instead, her whole presence swelled and washed over me.

"She's awake!"

My eyes flew open and I spun around, my feet grinding into the sand. Antoni's form was visible in the distance, one arm up and waving. Even in the dim moonlight, his face was open and bright.

I bolted from the beach, leaving my sneakers and leaping over the boulders barefoot. I flew into Antoni's open arms and he lifted me off the ground and twirled me.

"You did it! She's awake! It happened such a short time after you left, too."

He released me and followed me down the stairs and into the room where excited voices talked over one another.

Halting in the doorway, eyes stretched wide, I saw that the tank had been drained, the water released through some pipe or other, and the front panel was open like a door. Emun's back was to Antoni and me, and a very thin pair of bare legs were draped over his right arm. A long swath of wet hair draped to the floor over his left arm. Mom was bent over and picking the hair up, looping it over itself so it wouldn't trip Emun. She had tears running down her face but she was smiling. Emun turned to the side, pausing while Jozef put a blanket over the small frame of Nike, before he turned all the way around and faced Antoni and me.

Nike lay in Emun's arms, as tiny and fragile as a sick child, but her eyes were open and full of a fierce energy. She looked at me and I felt frozen to the spot.

I knew you would come, she thought at me.

My mind skipped like a rock over choppy water. Nike sleeping and behind glass was one thing. I had felt nothing from her. But Nike awake and looking at me, even in a weakened state, was throbbing with power like a banked fire. I could feel it radiating off her and it was as beautiful to me as a summer sunrise.

Emun carried her forward and Antoni pulled me aside since I seemed to have trouble moving on my own. Only when they passed by and our eye contact broke was I able to stumble after them in a state of amazed bewilderment.

EIGHT

Knocking softly on the bedroom door where Nike had been sequestered and cared for by Mom for the last several days, I realized the door was open a crack.

"Come in," my mom said.

I poked my head inside and saw Mom sitting in a chair beside the bed where Nike lounged against fluffy pillows. The room was large and had its own fireplace. It reminded me of an art gallery with numerous large portraits decorating the striped wallpaper. Thick blue curtains had been pulled aside and the windows opened to allow the fresh sea air to comfort Nike.

Nike looked at me and smiled. "Targa. Come here and let me look at you."

She patted the coverlet beside her hip with long fingers. I noted that her nails had been trimmed to normal length, which made me look at her hair—it was now somewhat shorter, too.

"Mom wanted to give you a chance to rest and gain a little weight before I harassed you with questions," I joked. "You do look better."

Nike's body had absorbed all the calories she could put into it without making her system revolt. The muscular striations on her arms and chest were no longer visible. She was still painfully thin, but her skin had softened and her cheeks were less hollow.

"You would never be capable of harassment," Nike replied.

I crossed the carpet and sat where her palm had touched. She reached out and took my right hand in both of her cool ones.

"Now I can see you better," she said as she reached up to move a stray lock of hair away from my eye. "Coming out of hibernation like that doesn't do one's sight any favors. You are so beautiful, the near spitting image of your mother."

"Thank you," I replied. "You are beautiful, too."

And she was. In spite of her thinness, Nike had an exotic, almost unnatural, beauty. Her skin appeared dark most of the time, in a Mediterranean way, but when light from the window passed over her as the sun broke through, she somehow appeared much paler. Her gray eyes changed the way fast-moving clouds did on a stormy day, sometimes there was a flash of blue, other times a flash of green. She had small pointed ears, one of which stood out starkly against her white hair as she'd tucked her long locks behind it. And her cheekbones were high enough to make her appear elven. Her hair seemed like a being all on its own. Now that I was closer, I could see that it was lighter and puffier than any hair I'd ever seen, each strand so fine that the lightest breeze could lift it and make it sway. It reminded me of spider's silk without the stickiness. It now floated over her shoulders like a thick cloud, spilling across the pillow and bedsheets on either side of her hips.

She gazed at me for a time.

"Are you feeling better?" I asked when I'd grown uncomfortable under her scrutiny. Nike did not appear to have a malevolent bone in her body, but I still wasn't accustomed to such a penetrating gaze. It felt like she could see right through me. Maybe she could. She was a sorceress, after all.

"Much better, thank you." She closed her eyes and took a deep breath as a light breeze blew in through the window. "The smell of the ocean is healing me faster than any food or drink ever could." She opened those slate-colored eyes and smiled, a small dimple appearing in her left cheek. "You watch. I'll be back to normal within a week."

"A week!" I couldn't hide my surprise and glanced at my mother, who was watching the two of us with a satisfied smile, like she'd recently eaten a luxuriant dessert.

Mom nodded. "Sirens coming out of diapause don't take too long to recover because they've been in a resting state. While they're asleep, their bodies work slowly to heal injuries, or diseased and damaged tissue, allowing them to wake up feeling younger and healthier than before. Provided they get proper nourishment and ease back into exercise, of course."

I blinked at her. "That was quite a scientific assessment," I said. "Didn't sound like you at all."

"That's because it was from Loukas's notes," she said, her smile disappearing at the taste of the diabolical researcher's name in her mouth.

"Diapause," Nike murmured. "What a strange word."

"What do you call it?" I asked the sorceress.

"We called it *anapáfsi*," she said, the word sharp and accented. "It means the long rest in our tongue." She turned her head and looked at Mom. "Did you not teach Targa any Mer?"

Mira laughed, her eyes crinkling with genuine mirth and affection. She leaned forward. "My friend, you erased my memory of not only my language but all of the life I'd lived. How could I teach my daughter something I had forgotten?"

"Oh." Nike closed her eyes and shook her head, putting her fingertips to her temple. "I'm sorry, of course I did." She opened her eyes and looked at me, taking my hand with both of hers again. "Our memories return like our strength does. It takes a few days."

"Well, a few days to be back to normal after decades in *anapáfsi,*" I said, trying out the strange word and liking the way it felt, "is pretty incredible."

"Mer sounds good on you," Mom said, leaning back in her chair again. "Nike is doing well. We should be able to leave in a week or so."

I glanced at Nike. "I guess Mom has filled you in on our plan to go to Atlantis?"

Nike nodded. "She has." She hesitated, and an expression I couldn't name crossed her features. Doubt? Concern?

"What is it?" I asked.

"Breaking a curse is not a simple matter," she said. "A curse takes on the nature of the being who created it, and curses are rarely made by those with kind hearts. If you want to do this, you should prepare yourself."

"For what, exactly?" I hadn't figured curse-breaking was going to be like hot-wiring a car. Not that I could do that, but there was a right way and a wrong way. This was magic, and I didn't know the rules.

"I won't be able to tell you exactly, but Sybellen told me

what your friend Lusi said when she translated the glyphs on the ruins."

It was strange to hear my mother referred to as Sybellen, at least by someone in the present day. I really only thought of her as Sybellen when I thought of her past. To me, she was Mira MacAuley, and she always would be. That, and Mom.

"It's important that there are no details missed," Nike said, "tell me everything you remember."

"Even though Mom already explained?"

She nodded. "Yes, because you might remember a tiny, seemingly irrelevant detail that her mind thought was unimportant and so discarded it."

"I see." I shifted on the bed and pulled my sock feet up, crossing my legs and clearing my throat. "Well, it came in disjointed bits of information, because whoever took the photographs wasn't concerned about the story of the curse so much as the nature of the gemstones." I told her what I could remember, speaking slowly and trying not to forget any details. "We did bring the tablet if you want to see it," I finished.

"Your mom showed it to me already," said Nike. "I don't read Atlantean either and you are extremely lucky to have found someone who did."

"She was willing once we explained what we needed it for."

"Yes, any siren would be," Nike agreed. Her eyes skimmed my collarbones, my earlobes, my wrists. "I notice that your gemstone is not visible."

I looked at my Mom, surprised that Nike would bring it up.

Mom straightened in her chair. "I hadn't gotten to that part yet."

"What part?"

"Targa is kind of...allergic to the stones."

Nike's eyes clouded as they darted from Mom to me and she became very still. "Is this true?"

I nodded. "If they touch my skin, they burn me and sap all my energy." It was an understatement. The gemstones had felt like they were killing me when I'd been under a pile of them deep in those caves.

"Sybellen, I hope you don't mind, but I need to speak to Targa alone." Nike looked at Mom, her expression serious as death.

Mom's eyes widened. "Why?"

"Because I need to say something that is for her ears only."

Mom's brows drew together in irritation. "That much is obvious. I don't understand what you could possibly want to say to my daughter that you can't say to me? We're all sirens. We all want the curse undone. We're in this together, and of all the people in the world, I am the one who loves her the most. I should be here."

"I am a sorceress," Nike reminded her gently. "You asked for my help. I am giving it."

"But..."

"We're dealing with magic. It won't always make sense to you."

"But it will make sense to Targa?"

"Targa is the only one who will truly understand."

Mom stared at Nike with a challenge in her eyes, but Nike did not look away, did not even wither under the glare of her Sovereign.

Mom finally let out a breath and got to her feet. "Fine, but I don't like it."

"You don't have to like it," Nike said, following my mother with her eyes as she left the room.

The door snicked shut behind my mom.

I turned and faced Nike. My heart had ratcheted up a notch and I let out a low laugh to cover up the anxiety growing in my chest like a weed.

"At least she didn't slam the door," I said.

"There's going to be a lot of things she doesn't like about what is to come if you pursue this." Nike's eyes, now a soft gray like the sky before a spring rain, came to my face. They were full of sorrow.

"You need to understand what it is you are committing yourself to," she said. "You above anyone else, for this quest will cost you the most."

"Why me?"

"Because the gemstones are poison to you."

"I figured that probably had something to do with it." I still wasn't sure why Nike looked so grim, her mouth set in a straight thin line.

"Whoever made the curse was someone like you."

"An elemental?"

"That isn't the only thing that makes you who you are, but it is a characteristic that makes you rare. It could be that, it could be something else."

"But you don't know?"

She shook her head. "No, all I can tell you is that you are the secret key to breaking the curse. There is not another siren alive, at least to my knowledge, who ever reacted to the gemstones the way you do. There is something about *you*, Targa."

I absorbed this quietly. "Okay, but you could have said all of that with Mom still in the room. So why did you send her away? What is it that she cannot hear?"

She took my hand again and squeezed it. "You need to decide if you're willing to give your life to break this curse, because that could be what it takes."

My mouth and throat suddenly felt as dry as the desert. "What do you mean?"

"I mean that you and the curse-maker have something that binds you, something that makes you alike. But you'll only be able to break the curse if you are stronger than them."

"Stronger in what way?" My heart had begun to pound hard and heavy. "Physically? Emotionally? Mentally?"

"All of it."

"Who is the judge?"

"The curse is."

This was a confusing answer, but it was magic we were dealing with so it wasn't like there was a rulebook to reference. It reminded me of how the Salt made new Sovereigns. It didn't provide specific rules or look you in the face and deliver a report card on your performance. The ascension to the crown was either given to you or it wasn't, and no one was able to refute the judgement.

"And if I'm not?"

"Targa." She leaned forward away from her pillow and gazed into my eyes. "If you're not, you'll die."

NINE

"Are you okay?" Antoni whispered in my ear before planting a kiss on my neck. "You barely ate and you've hardly said a thing since you went to visit Nike."

We lay spooning in the big bed in the room Jozef had given us while we waited for Nike's strength to return. It was down the hall and around the corner from Jozef's own room, where he and Mom were sleeping.

"I'm okay," I said softly and squeezed his arm where it rested in front of my chest.

Peering in the gloom at the small round clock on the bedside table, I saw that it was close to midnight. Rain spattered against the window panes and ran down in long streams. I'd been following the patterns they made between the panes for quite a while now, blinking in the dark. We had retired to bed shortly after ten-thirty and since then, I'd been meditating. I hadn't shared what Nike had told me with anyone.

"I thought you'd be asleep by now," I whispered to Antoni.

"I've been listening to you think." Antoni said. I could hear the smile in his voice. "It's quite loud, you know."

I found a laugh for him. What could I say to Antoni? He was just as likely to be resistant to allowing the plan to go forward as my mother would be, but I kept thinking how it would be if the situation was reversed and it was Antoni whose life was in danger. How would I feel? Obviously I didn't want to lose the love of my life, but I would never forbid him to do anything. Everyone had their own path, their own reasons, their own convictions for the choices they made. It wasn't right or fair to forbid someone from doing something because you were afraid of them getting hurt, or of losing them.

And then there was the fact that I had died once before, and it had been the beginning of a whole new wonderful life. Sometimes death was death, and sometimes death was a beginning. Who was to say which was which?

"I'm here if you want to talk," Antoni said, and relaxed down into his pillow. He snuggled his chest up to my back and sighed deeply.

This was one of the many things I loved about Antoni. He'd never force me to tell him anything I didn't wish to. He'd never cajole me or pry secrets from me. He let me be, trusting that if it was something he needed to know, that I would tell him.

Tears sprang to my eyes and my mouth wobbled at the thought of my own death. Not for myself, though I didn't want to die, but for how much Antoni, my mom, and my friends would suffer. I was loved, and I was shown that love regularly. My death would hurt them.

And what if I could break the curse with my death? Wouldn't it be worth it to stop all the suffering that sirens and husbands and sons of sirens had to endure the world over? I had seen firsthand what the curse had done to my mother, both while my father had been alive, and during the time before she went into the Baltic. I had held on to her so tightly and it had taken so much from her. She had given so much to me, sacrificed so much to raise me, and stay with me even after I'd become an adult. She had shown me how powerful love was. All of those painful lessons, those agonizing memories of my mother's weariness as the curse weighed on her, they still brought tears to my eyes if I thought about them too much.

It all had to have been for a reason.

I could have been born a boy, abandoned as a baby or a toddler the way Emun and Michal had been. I could have never known my own mother. If I'd been born male, my father would have raised me until he died, and then I'd have gone to my grandparents on my father's side. Never knowing where I'd come from and who my mother was, just that she'd abandoned me.

How many male children had had just this kind of life? Over the centuries that had passed, they were innumerable. There was a tragic example in the Novak family itself— where Michal had been raised by elderly relatives after Mattis followed Sybellen into the storm.

And I had one chance to stop it all for good. How could I look myself in the mirror every day and know that I'd turned my back on them? I may as well tattoo the word 'self-ish' across my forehead and be done with it, because that would be what I saw.

I had a chance. Nike said that I had to be stronger than whoever set the curse and there was no way of knowing anything about that person. They'd had a vindictive streak, that much was obvious. I had to be better than *that*, didn't I? I could never dream of cursing an entire species. I couldn't even fathom what would make an individual want to do such a thing.

"Hey." Antoni's hand found my shoulder and he gently nudged my back flat so he could see me. His fingertips found my cheeks and rubbed away the tears I hadn't even known were falling. "Shh."

I turned. My arms snaked around his neck and he held me as the tears flowed. He kissed my face, my lips, my cheeks, my jaw, anywhere he could reach, trying to comfort me. I could feel the confusion pouring off him, but still he did not force me to talk.

Finally, when the moisture began to ebb, I released him and pulled myself up to sitting. He slid up beside me and rested against the headboard. Plucking a tissue from the box on his side of the bed, he handed it to me.

"Sorry," I sniffled, blowing my nose and dabbing at my face. "It's very inconvenient when I cry." I gestured to his pajama top and our pillows, which were now soaked.

"If you think I'm concerned about that," he murmured, "you don't know me very well."

He stripped off his top and tossed it on the floor beside the bed, then he flipped both of our pillows over so the dry side was up.

I found my voice. "I've been wrestling with myself about whether or not I should tell you what's going through my mind."

Antoni nodded in the gloom, his eyes catching and reflecting a little of the moonlight coming in through the windows. "Okay. You know you don't have to, but I sure would like to make you feel better if I can." He paused, uncertain if he should continue. "I'm guessing it has some-thing to do with Nike."

I nodded, then shook my head. "Not with Nike personally, no. But she told me that the reason the gems hurt me is because I'm the only one who can break the curse."

I could feel his surprise, even though he didn't move. His forehead wrinkled in the dim light. "I don't understand."

I explained to him what Nike had said, as precisely as I could remember, only leaving out the part that I could die. Antoni listened attentively, and when I got to the end of it, I said, "So, she said that breaking the curse could be dangerous for me."

"I can't say I understand what form that danger could take," he finally said after a long silence. He put a hand on my face. "While the thought of my sweetheart in danger isn't a happy one, we're in the business of curse-breaking. What I know about magic wouldn't even fill a postage stamp, but this curse..." He paused and shook his head. "It's stood for thousands of years. I never for a moment imagined that breaking it would be like dumping water on a campfire."

"So, you're not surprised?"

"Surprised, no. And we should have guessed it would have something to do with you personally, because you are the only siren who can't touch the gemstones without great pain. It's a pretty big hint, now that I think about it."

"What would you do?"

He let out a long breath. "I honestly don't know, Targa. Even if I did know, I'm not sure I would say."

"There's a chance I could get hurt," I continued, unsurprised at his careful neutrality. "But there's a chance I could break the curse and prevent all the future generations of sirens and their families from having to suffer the same awful things my mother had to suffer. Wouldn't that be worth it?"

"It's your call to make," Antoni replied, ever the diplomat. "You already know that I would walk through fire to prevent you from being hurt, so of course I don't want anything to happen to you. But some decisions are bigger than us." He took another long breath and there was a shudder in it this time. He took my hand as we sat there leaning against the headboard, hip to hip. "Whatever decision you make, I'll back you."

"Just like that, huh?"

His fingers twined through mine and he lifted my hand and kissed my knuckles. "It's not easy, but people have been watching their loved ones walk into known danger for all of recorded history. How many families said goodbye to their sons, husbands, uncles, during the big wars of the world? They were sad, of course they were. They were terrified, as I would be and as I am now. They were also proud, and sometimes, it was the right thing to do. Sometimes, most times," he corrected, "those boys didn't make it home. But some of those boys became heroes, and without them wars would have been lost and many countries would look very different today than they do now. It was freedom they were fighting for, and that was worth everything. So, who would I be to tell you to stay home and be safe, when your people are not free?"

So, he understood. It was my life in danger, not just my health. He was even able to relate my reasonings to something that made sense to him.

My heart flooded with the warmth of love for him and I pulled him into another hug. I didn't think I knew anyone else who would have said what he'd said, who could have shown me that they understood and would also stand beside me without judgement no matter what I decided.

"I love you, Antoni." I couldn't have stopped the words

if I had wanted to. They spilled from my lips, the way the tears had begun to spill from my eyes again.

He squeezed me so tightly that the muscles of his arms and chest quivered.

When he released me, I took his face in my hands and showered kisses on his lips, his cheeks, his jaw, his neck—kisses of adoration and gratitude. I felt the moisture of his tears against my lips, mingling with my own.

I knew what I had to do. All of my deliberating and agonizing was done. My decision was made. I had to give myself over to my mission, no matter the outcome. If I didn't try, I wouldn't be Targa, and if he didn't allow me to try, he wouldn't be Antoni.

When you love someone, you let them go, and that was what he was doing for me.

My kisses turned urgent, hungry, and he rose under my hands, his heart pounding strong and loud. He wrapped an arm around my waist and in one motion slid me down in the bed. He slid down beside me and his lips crushed mine. His weight pressed against me, comforting me. Words were no longer needed.

Our choices define who we are. I just had to be me, and he just had to be him. It was that simple.

TEN

Once my decision was made, I was at peace with it. Peace didn't mean that I wasn't nervous, or that I wasn't sending out requests to the universe to be on my side. A curse was an evil thing. Surely nature was not pleased with it. Sirens certainly were not, but this curse was so old that most didn't even know it was a curse anymore.

Nike continued to regain strength, so after breakfast a few days after making my decision, we agreed that we should start packing and formulating a more specific plan.

Returning from the boathouse after a swim, my hair and clothes still damp, I made my way along the path leading around the side of the villa.

Across one of the many broad lawns and through a scraggly line of trees was a large outbuilding which looked something like another villa, only plainer. I knew it was the garage. I could hear the sound of men's voices and heavy things being moved across a gritty floor.

Two of the four garage doors were up and an array of boxes and bins were spread out on the gravel in front. A pile of sleeping bags and tents in canvas sacks lay in a heap in front of the grill of an ancient vehicle whose logo I didn't recognize.

"Can I help?" I approached Jozef where he was lifting down more boxes, shoving off the lids and rifling through the insides.

He looked up and smiled, the corners of his eyes wrinkling, his dark eyes sparkling.

"That would be great," he replied. "Most of this stuff is so old that it's likely useless, but some of it is still in good condition. We're just trying to separate the wheat from the chaff before we take an inventory and make a list of what we still need."

"Easy enough." I pulled down a box from the wooden shelves and carried it into the sunlight. Opening it up revealed a jumble of equipment from antique flashlights to small propane stoves.

Antoni dangled a rag in front of my face. I grinned up at him and grabbed it. I pulled out the items one at a time, cleaned each one, and tested to see whether it worked. What was broken went into a box Antoni had scrawled 'busted' on, and what worked was sorted by category so Jozef could select the best of what he had.

"Went camping a lot when you were younger, did you?" Antoni said just before he sneezed three times. He held an old tarp out by one corner. There was a sound of sand and grit tumbling down it and spattering on the ground.

"Some," Jozef replied, his voice nearly lost behind the old vehicle. There was the sound of metal clanking, and rusty hinges squeaking. "My dad also had an affinity for bush craft for a while."

"Does bush craft include desert craft?" I asked, clicking the power button of a huge square metal flashlight, not expecting it to work. It didn't, but I put it in the "needs parts" box as it might only need a new battery.

"I've never been to a desert," Jozef said, carrying a metal toolbox out from behind the truck and setting it on the work bench. Next, he pulled out a greasy pair of antique jumper cables. Those went into the 'busted' box.

"Understandable given your choice of career," I replied, "but not understandable given how old you are. You were never curious?"

"Oh, sure." Jozef plucked a wooden mallet out of the toolbox and set it on the bench. He frowned and pulled out a bit of broken spring next, holding it up and watching it dangle like he was trying to figure out what it was for.

"That's a slinky," Antoni said with a laugh. "A toy."

"A broken toy." Jozef tossed it in with the junk. "All joking aside, I don't think we fully understand the job we've carved out for ourselves."

"Why don't you outline it for us, then?" Antoni straightened and his back gave a little crackle.

"We'll have to drive from the nearest city with an airport across kilometers of vacant desert wasteland with more supplies than I care to think about," Jozef began, continuing to dig through the toolbox as he talked. "What we *should* be doing is reporting the discovery to an archaeological society and letting them organize a professional excavation."

I looked up at him and frowned. "That would take way too long and would involve way too many people."

Jozef put up a defensive hand, his fingers black with grease. "I'm not saying we are doing the wrong thing, I'm just saying that we're going to get into trouble for digging there without sanction."

"We're trying to break a curse, not just unearth Atlantis."

He nodded. "I know, that's why I'm stifling the professional in me. I might be an oceanographer, but the way you treat an underwater archaeological discovery isn't any different to how you treat one on land in terms of due process. A professional team could excavate the site quickly. We're a team of five people."

I saw his point but he was neglecting to factor in a few important details.

"We're a team of five supernaturals and one buff guy." I winked at Antoni.

Antoni made a little bow and said, "Thank you."

Jozef gave me a look from under his brows. "Yeah, we're a team of water-dwelling supernaturals. Our powers are greatly diminished when we're on land."

"Not our strength," I reminded him.

"No, but even with four physically strong supernaturals, one sorceress, and one strong human," he nodded at Antoni, "how long do you think it'll take to excavate forty to fifty circular kilometers of compressed sand and rubble? How deep do you think Atlantis is buried?"

These were rhetorical questions, and I saw his point.

Jozef saw the doubt on my face and it emboldened him to continue listing the challenges we'd be facing. "We'll have to drive across the desert in a caravan with at least three vehicles, possibly four. We'll have to set up a long-term camp. Water will be the biggest issue, as there are no water sources within four hundred kilometers or more. We'll have to bring all of our food, prepare for sandstorms and extreme heat, blazing hot sun..."

I stood up, not liking where Jozef was going with this.

Maybe he was being realistic, but just maybe he didn't realize who he was dealing with, either.

"First of all, why drive when we can fly directly to the site?" I proposed, picking up the crumpled tarp I'd found shoved in the bottom of the box. I began to shake it out and fold it.

"There's nowhere for a plane to land," Jozef pointed out. "It's very rough terrain."

"Not a plane, no. But a helicopter can land in any wide, open space."

Jozef looked thoughtful. "I don't have a copter. I don't even know anyone who can fly one, and I don't think we're going to trust just anyone with this mission. Are we?"

"We don't have a chopper either, but we do have a pilot who works only for Novak. He can fly anything with wings or blades." I was exaggerating for effect, because I didn't actually know that Ivan could fly *anything*, but I did know for sure he could fly a chopper.

"You trust him?" Jozef asked.

"With my life."

"Does he know what you are?"

"No, but he doesn't have to. He'll do as he's asked and he'll keep everything confidential. He's a pro. And there's no reason he needs to know about our supernatural abilities."

"It's highly unlikely you'll be able to keep it a secret from him," Jozef said with a doubtful shrug.

Antoni was listening thoughtfully, his gaze bouncing back and forth between Jozef and me as Jozef threw up objections and I broke them down.

"If he has to get let in on it, it's not the worst thing in the world, is it?" Antoni ventured. "I mean, *I* know. Martinius knew."

I'd have to think that through, but I knew Jozef was right. If we were going to involve Ivan in this mission, it would be easier if he knew why we were doing it. I couldn't discount that ever-present stop-gap—making Ivan forget anything that needed to be forgotten by using my siren voice on him.

"Okay, so the traveling part could be made easier," Jozef admitted. "We fly to the nearest city and charter a chopper. I suppose Ivan could fly back and forth to the nearest city for supplies as they were needed."

I nodded, feeling a little better now that Jozef seemed to be coming around to the idea.

"But that doesn't solve the problem of the digging." Jozef cocked his head in my direction and sent an inquisitive smile my way. "Or do you have a solution for that, too, Supergirl?"

All at once it hit me like a blast of wind off a stormy sea. I almost laughed out loud but settled for a huge grin.

"I just might," I replied.

Antoni and Jozef shared a confused glance.

Reaching into my back pocket for my cell phone, I turned it on and began to pound out a text to Georjie and Saxony. I wandered away from the garage, keeping my back to the men so they couldn't see the hopeful and excited look on my face. No use getting them all hopped up if she said no.

Halfway through writing the text I just got impatient. I deleted the text, switched my phone over to contacts, found Georjie, and dialed her.

A few rings later, my beautiful bestie's lovely liquid voice poured into my ear.

"Well, look who's on the line. Your ears must have been

burning," she said, a smile in her voice. "I dreamt about you last night. We were back in grade three, and do you remember the day Gavin Campbell farted into a ziploc bag and then hid it in his desk? Said he was saving it for the last day of school—"

"Georjie..." My voice was tense with hope. It got her attention.

"Yeah?"

"Sorry to interrupt. You can tell me how the dream turned out later. Please tell me you have a way of contacting Petra?"

"Ha! What are you up to? Don't do anything fun without me!"

"You're in Scotland," I reminded her.

"Yeah, I know. I'm only kidding. But what do you want Petra for?"

I gave her the bare bones of the mission and told her about Atlantis. I didn't dare look back over my shoulder at Jozef's face as I told her. He'd wanted to swear us all to secrecy, but my promise not to keep secrets from my two best friends trumped any promise made afterward. Georjie knew what and who I was, we'd been through life and death situations together. I didn't feel a single twinge of shame at spilling our secret, though I did ask Georjie to keep it to herself.

When I got to the part where we'd be excavating in Atlantis, Georjie gave a low whistle.

"Petra would kill to be part of that."

"Yeah, and I'd kill to have her on the team. Georjie, we really need her if we're going to pull this off sometime before the end of the century. Do you have a way of getting a hold of her?"

"Up until last week, I didn't, but she happened to call

the other day, asking if she could send me a sample of some dirt to analyze."

I knew Georjie didn't mean a scientific analysis. Part of Georjie's powers as a Wise—an earth elemental—was that she had the ability to 'see' the past happenings on a particular patch of land when holding earth from that land in her hands.

"I thought you had to be standing on the same ground as you are holding it in your hand?"

"Turns out, no," she said. "I do have to be standing barefoot, but I can see the history of a particular lump of earth from anywhere. It was a neat discovery."

"You'll have to tell me more about that when all this is over," I replied, swallowing the lump in my throat down. I sure hoped I was still around when all this was over.

"Of course, just as I expect the nitty gritty details of whatever madness you're up to while you're out in the desert. Anyway, give me a second."

There was silence while Georjie went into her phone contacts. Then, "I found it. I'll share it with you, okay?"

"Great. Thanks, Georjie."

A moment later my phone buzzed and Petra's contact number popped into my feed. I didn't recognize the country code, but that was no surprise.

Georjie and I said goodbye and I dialed Petra's number, not knowing or really caring if she was asleep or not. It rang twice before she picked up.

"I know who you are," Petra's voice blazed on hard and loud. "If you don't stop calling me I swear I'll personally..."

"Petra?" I interrupted.

She stopped talking for a second. "You're not a revenue agency scammer."

I laughed. "Definitely not."

"Targa?" Her voice lit up like she was thrilled to hear from me, and it warmed me from the inside out. Georjie, Saxony and I never had a chance to get to know Petra very well. First we'd been colleagues, and then she'd gone on some crazy solo vigilante mission and completely destroyed Field Station Eleven where evil people had plotted evil things. She was the most badass person I'd ever met, and I didn't like to think I intimidated easily.

"Yeah," I said, "it's me."

"What an awesome surprise!" And she really sounded like she thought so, which warmed me even more. "Where are you?"

"Gibraltar, where are you?"

"Gibraltar, wow. You do get around."

I noticed she dodged answering my question, but that didn't surprise me. Petra had turned full on enemy-of-the-state, the state being any corporation owned by or linked to The Nakesh Corporation.

"You must have got my number from Georjie," she said. "I don't give my info out."

"Yeah, I hope that was okay."

"Sure, sure," she replied, but I felt her interest cooling. She was wondering why I had called and what I wanted.

"I'll get straight to the point," I said.

"Okay," she replied in the same all-business tone.

"We found Atlantis."

Nothing. Dead air.

"Petra?"

"I'm here," she replied. Her tone was now closed; I couldn't tell if she believed me or not.

"We found it and we need to excavate it, and quickly." I launched into a rapid explanation about the siren's curse,

how we knew the location of Atlantis, and why we needed
to go there.

She listened quietly. I found myself hoping she hadn't
hung up, but I never heard a click so I didn't stop talking
until the story was out. When I was finished, I shut up and
didn't say anything again until she did.

"You're not messing with me?" she asked.

"I wouldn't do that to you, Petra. I would never."

"I believe you."

Relief lifted a weight from my shoulders like a yoke
carrying huge buckets of cement had fallen to the ground.

"Thank you. The reason I'm telling you is not just
because you're an archaeologist, but because we're going to
need your help."

"I'm not an archaeologist yet."

"Close enough, plus you have a way of moving sand like
no one I've ever seen. Will you help us?"

I knew Petra had things going on. She had a brilliant
hacker boyfriend, and goodness knew where she was in the
world and what vigilante mission she was on right now. But
I was hoping that the temptation of Atlantis would be too
much for her to turn down.

I was right.

"I'm kind of busy," she said haltingly, but I could hear
the smile in her voice. "But when a fellow elemental calls
and says they found Atlantis, well." She took a deep breath.
"That's not something I can say no to."

"Great." I couldn't keep the grin from splitting my face
in two. "When do you think you can be here?"

"In Gibraltar?"

"Yeah, we're hoping to leave in less than a week. You
could fly with us."

"I can't leave that soon," she said, and my heart fell. It

buoyed again when she followed it up with, "But I can meet you in Mauritania if you tell me where you'll be."

I let out a long breath but the thrilled pounding of my heart did not ease up. "We'll be landing in the nearest city to the ruins. I'll text you the info when it's nailed down. I can't tell you what this means to me."

"Yeah, well, it's Atlantis, I can't tell you what it means to me either. It's a once-in-a-century kind of find." She paused and then said, hurriedly, "I have to go. Text me the details?"

I said I would and then I hung up. I couldn't help but clench my fist around my phone and do a victory punch into the sky in excitement. I whooped with joy and turned to face Antoni and Jozef, who were both staring at me like I'd lost my mind.

"Petra's going to meet us in Mauritania," I said, directing this statement at Antoni, who had never met her but knew who she was and what she could do.

"Who?" Jozef looked bemused.

Antoni straightened up and his eyes widened. "The *Euroklydon*?"

I nodded and hurried over to Antoni where I threw myself at him. He caught me in a bear hug.

"That's unbelievable, Targa. How did you get her to say yes?"

"It wasn't hard," I replied, pulling back, my feet touching the ground again. "I said Atlantis and she was all over it."

Jozef's expression was on the verge of thunderous. "You just told a total stranger that we have the location of Atlantis?"

"She's not a total stranger, she's a passionate archaeologist, and she's The Euroklydon."

Jozef blinked in further confusion. "She's a storm from the Bible? Forgive me, I'm really not following."

I turned to clamp a hand on Jozef's shoulder. "I don't mean to over-promise, but she's a helluva lot more than a storm, dude."

ELEVEN

"There! Will you look at that!"

Ivan's awe-filled cry through the headset had every head swiveling quickly to find the best view as the aircraft crested another gentle red and rocky dune.

From my place next to the window, I had a clear view of the massive circular shape visible in the rubbly, barren terrain of the desert below. Beside me, Antoni reached for my hand where it rested on my thigh. I looked up at him and squeezed his hand back before my gaze went back to the Eye of Africa growing ever larger.

"The Richat Structure." Emun was in the co-pilot's seat beside Ivan, his face so close to the window that his flight helmet bumped into the glass. "Atlantis has been visible from above this whole time."

"It looks like a meteor strike," Mom's voice came crackling through the headsets. "Only it's a little too symmetrical. It looks like a perfect bulls-eye."

"That's what they thought it was up until the sixties," answered Jozef from where he and my mother were seated behind Antoni and me. Then Jozef laughed. "I mean, they thought it was an impact site, not a bulls-eye."

Ivan had flown us from Gibraltar to Nouakchott, the capital of Mauritania and the largest city of the Sahara. There, the sirens had rested before we met up with Petra and gathered water, food, and supplies while Ivan familiarized himself with the Bell 430 helicopter he'd chartered. Our ride was an ugly eight-seater bird that could land and take off easily from the uneven, hard-packed rubble of the Sahara.

So far, all was going according to plan. Ivan had flown as low as he dared to avoid the sirens feeling ill or passing out. It was a refreshing change to be airborne without feeling like some monstrous kraken had its tentacles wrapped around me, pulling me back to earth. I wondered if we could always fly a chopper from now on. Scrap the bloody private jets.

"It's huge," Ivan said, his helmeted head scanning the horizon through the windscreen.

"Over forty kilometers across," Petra said. It had been a while since she had said anything.

"I thought you'd fallen asleep as soon as we left Nouakchott," Mira said with a smile in her voice.

"I did," Petra replied, laughing. "Something about the sound of the blades knocked me right out."

"Where would you like me to put us down?" Ivan directed the question to the group.

"Er, perhaps best not to land right on top of it," Antoni replied, gesturing to a flatter area to the side of the outermost ring. "There, the south side, away from all those rough gunnels."

"The geological society will already have my head for this," Jozef added as he braced a hand against the side of the helicopter while Ivan directed us in a loop toward the south.

"If we're going to dig up Atlantis anyway," Mom said, "I can't see why it matters if we land in the middle."

"We're not sure what it will do to anything beneath the rubble if we land on it," Petra replied patiently. "A true archaeologist wouldn't dream of landing on top of a dig site—"

"Amen," Jozef interjected.

Petra continued, "A true archaeologist wouldn't allow anyone to do what we're about to do. The Richat Structure is a mystery that has baffled researchers from almost every discipline since it was first discovered. There'll be a lot of academic types up in arms when they learn what we've done."

"What, unearthed Atlantis?" Antoni called over the sound of the blades as Ivan shifted gears for landing. "They should be toasting the find of the century!"

I looked back over my shoulder at Petra's face. Her mouth twitched. "Archaeologists are rarely that gracious."

"I thought you were an archeologist," Jozef said, also looking at Petra.

She bared her teeth in a feral smile. "Not yet. I've delayed my studies in favor of a couple of other projects."

"What other projects?" Jozef probed, keen interest in his tone. "Also in the field of archaeology?"

Petra shook her head and looked back out the window as the ground beneath us surged closer. "More in the field of corporate demolition."

Antoni and I shared a look of startled amusement at that comment.

"Nice and easy," Ivan's voice came through the headset as the landing skids of the chopper touched down. The blades had raised a red cloud of dust that obscured the horizon. He shut down the Bell's engine and the whine began to slow. "Best give it a few minutes to calm down out there before stepping out."

Metallic snapping sounds echoed through the craft as seatbelts and shoulder braces were released. As I twisted to stow my harness, my eye caught Nike's face as she lifted the headset off her ears. She looked pale and tired.

"You okay, Nike?"

Her gray eyes found mine and she gave me a weak smile. "Not built for helicopters, I'm afraid," she replied in that strange accent and gentle voice I had grown to love.

Mom gave a chuckle and touched Nike's cheek, brushing a stray strand of white locks away from her friend's face. "Nike's not built for any kind of life above sea-level."

I felt a twist of concern and guilt as I watched Nike slowly unsnap her safety harness and fumble for the hat we'd found for her. I wondered, not for the first time, if we should have left her behind. I had put the question to my mother and she'd said Nike would never stand to be left behind. Besides, it was a curse we were dealing with. The odds that we'd need someone with some magical know-how were high. Mom had assured me that we'd take good care of Nike, and get her back to the ocean as soon as possible—whether we succeeded or failed at our mission.

Emun was the first to step out onto the baked earth. A wash of hot, dry air swept through the helicopter as Ivan opened the door on his side.

"Smells like..." Antoni paused, searching for words, "dry?"

"A mermaid's worst nightmare." I put the light white fabric of my headcovering over my hair and draped it loosely in front of my face before following Antoni out from under the chopper's door. "Of course, Atlantis had to be in the desert. If it was in the ocean, it would be too easy."

In with the supplies we'd picked up in Nouakchott were thin white tunics, robes, and headscarves. It took only moments to understand why Bedouins wore full-body light coverings in the dry heat and intense sun of the desert. Already, my lips felt dry. After I'd wrapped myself in fabric, I guzzled some water.

Mom, Petra, and Nike followed us out and we stepped away from the chopper, blinking in the morning sun of the desert. We looked like ghostly nomads in our white tunics and head coverings. Only Petra had eschewed a tunic, and I wondered if it was her prior time in the desert, or the fact that she was practically made of sand herself that gave her some kind of immunity to the stifling heat.

"Nothing about this is going to be easy," Nike said as she sheltered her eyes and scanned the horizon.

I looked at her uncertainly, recalling the conversation we'd had about my possible role in this. I felt like the bulls-eye stamped into the desert wasn't the only target around. I wasn't sure if she'd been referring to the dig part of the operation, or the breaking of the curse. I didn't ask her to clarify.

"You can't even tell what you're looking at from ground-level," Emun commented, peering to the north over what looked like softly undulating ranges of broken wasteland. "No wonder it wasn't discovered until we started sending satellites into space. It doesn't look like anything at all."

Antoni grabbed his backpack from under the seat, unzipped it, and rummaged inside. Pulling out the Kirlian photography device we planned to use as a compass, he offered it to me. "Would you like to do the honors?"

"Uh, she'd better not," Mom said, grabbing the device as I was reaching for it.

"I wasn't going to touch the gemstone, Mom, believe me," I said with humor. "A little overprotectivey, much?"

"I'd rather not take any chances," she muttered, turning away from me. "How does this thing work?"

"There's a gem already inside," Antoni explained. "All you have to do is turn it on and then hold down the capture button."

I heard a click as Mum flicked the on switch. We all crowded around her, waiting as her thumb pressed down the capture button and held it.

The machine made several quiet ticking sounds and a bright teal light shot from the eye like a laser.

"Geez murphy," Petra jumped back as the laser penetrated the ground at her feet. The beam followed an angled path from where Mom held the device toward the north and disappeared beneath the dusty soil.

The ticking sound increased in speed and took on a grinding scream between the ticks.

Mom looked up at Emun and then to Antoni. "Is that normal?"

Antoni frowned. "Most definitely *not* normal."

He reached for the machine as the sound became so grating that Nike and I covered our ears.

There was a loud sharp crack and a whining hiss, and the teal laser went out.

We stood there in startled silence for a half-minute.

"It wasn't me," Mom said, handing the device back to Antoni. "I did exactly as you said."

Antoni took the device back. A thin wisp of smoke issued from the eye. He gave me a puzzled frown.

"What do you suppose that means?" Petra voiced what all of us were thinking.

"It means we don't have a compass anymore," Jozef said.

"But we don't need it," I suggested. "Before it fuzzed out, the laser beam was pointing straight into the Richat Structure. Am I right?"

There were a few mumbled agreements.

"So, we figured we had to dig already. The device just confirmed that the rest of the aquamarine, whatever is left of it, is buried in there somewhere." I looked over at Petra. "You're on deck."

My stomach did a little flip of apprehension. I'd seen what Petra could do, but at times I questioned my own memory of what had happened on Saltford's beach. Was she really as powerful as I remembered her to be? I hoped so, because she was my idea and if she couldn't help us, not only would I be embarrassed, we'd be up a certain creek without a paddle.

Petra stared across the expanse before us, then smiled and rubbed her hands together. "You might want to stand back."

IT BEGAN AS A DUST DEVIL. A small, almost elegant, swirl of sand lifted and rose into the air, just a stone's throw from where we stood. If Petra hadn't been staring intently at that very spot, I would have thought the tiny whirlwind was naturally occurring. When she began to move her fingers in an elegant dance, making spiral shapes with her long slender arms, I knew it had begun. I couldn't help but smile.

"You're going to love this," I told Antoni under my breath. "What I can do with water, Petra can do with...well, anything else, pretty much."

The dust devil became a double-helix of sand particles. The spectacle was way too organized to be anything but magic. Our necks craned as we watched the helix spiral high into the sky. Bits of sand were caught by the wind, scattered and blown off course, but the bulk of it arched high and began to descend far to the east of us.

"There will be dunes where there weren't any before," Petra said calmly as her hands danced in the air in front of her—pushing and pulling the sands of the Sahara, a snakecharmer drawing a cobra from its basket. "Would you like one big one or a bunch of smaller ones?"

"Jozef?" My mom said after a few moments of no one answering. I saw her elbow him in my periphery. "It's your call."

I tore my eyes from the continuous stream of sand spiraling upward from the ground in front of us to look at my mother's long-lost love.

His face was pale but his expression was amazed, his mouth open and eyes wide.

"Uh, several smaller ones would be preferable. Please."

"You got it." Petra began to walk as the column of sand thickened. A second spiral joined the first and quickly, like a sheet of rain moving across the land, pouring up from the earth instead of down, the two columns became one large one. The sound of sand moving was like a fine rain, a neverending grainy swoosh.

Petra's arms moved for a while, adding helixes and columns of sand to the first large one, connecting them and adding more. Eventually, she put her hands down and the sandstorm continued.

Suddenly, her chin jerked up. A loud hiss erupted from the Richat Structure as a huge, dark mass of earth and sandy rubble lifted and threw itself in a scattering rain of sand far beyond the edge of the outer circle.

"As long as I live," I heard Antoni say beside me over

the continual hiss and sizzle, "I'll never see anything like this again."

"Oh, you don't know that," I replied with a smile, my own gaze glued to the massive arch now blocking out part of the sunlight. "I know people who can do things."

"That's an understatement."

"Look!"

We gazed at where Nike was pointing, down into the earth before us. It wasn't much to look at yet, still just a lot of sand and stone. But here and there were ragged corners of rock that were not moving. They grew more and more visible as Petra removed the sand from over and around them.

I realized Petra was now quite a long way from us, a much smaller figure following the edge of the structure's out ring.

"She means to walk the perimeter?" Jozef asked Mom.

"I don't know." Mom bent and opened the backpack she'd dropped on the sand near her feet. "But if she is, we'd better follow her with water, and later—food. It'll take her days to walk it. It's almost forty clicks across."

"I don't think you'll have to worry about that," I said.

My mom stood up. "What's happening to her?"

Petra's arms and legs had lightened in tone, they'd turned a sandy brown color.

"She's..."

The Euroklydon's body burst into an explosion of sand, a powder puff of fine-grains which shifted for a moment before sweeping up into the air and joining the sandstorm above us all. Her clothing fell into a heap on the desert floor.

"...becoming the storm," I finished.

Jozef, alarmed, glanced back at me, the whites of his eyes visible. "What happened to her?"

"She's fine. Don't worry, Jozef." I put a hand on his shoulder. "She'll be back when she's done."

"Who *are* you people?" I heard Nike say under her breath.

I couldn't help but chuckle. Nike had reversed my mother's age all the way back to infancy, but she was surprised when an elemental could change herself into dirt? Each to their own.

I glanced at Ivan, but he was standing back and wearing mirrored sunglasses. His expression was impossible to read, but he didn't seem much different than I'd seen him look while reading a newspaper. Ever the professional. When we'd told him we were digging up Atlantis, he just nodded as though saying yes to an offered coffee.

The hiss and churn of the flying sand increased in power as Petra's storm swept the perimeter of the Richat Structure in one fast, terrifying sheet.

Nike covered her ears and Antoni hurried back to the chopper. He returned with the headgear looped over one arm and handed them out. When the last of us had our headgear in place, it was like Petra had seen and approved.

A sound like a soft never-ending thunderclap ripped across the desert, and a blast of hot air hit us in the face. Not a single particle of sand hit us, but the sky grew dark as the sandstorm grew so dense hardly any light could penetrate. The Richat Structure looked as though it was caving in as it lost the covering which had kept it hidden for millennia. A jumble of jutting stones in unnatural shapes began to emerge. But it was happening slowly, even with the tons of sand Petra was removing. Atlantis was buried deep.

An hour passed. Then another.

Nike grew tired of watching and retreated to the helicopter to sit. Ivan joined her, and soon afterward, my mom.

Antoni, Emun, Jozef and I got comfortable on the sand. No one spoke; it was impossible to hear one another anyway.

Antoni poked me in the shoulder and pointed to a section of rubble with what looked like massive toppled over pillars. A curve had become visible. Broken cylinders of stone, some with carvings, could be seen in one area, while not far away, a different color of rock had become visible. Jozef had said Atlantis had been made mainly of red, white and black stones. The site was still mainly brown, everything caked in sand and dirt. But as Petra continued her work, dumping sand across the desert, making undulating dunes and cone-shaped piles, the colors began to reveal themselves. The outermost concentric circle was visible, too, but if the inner circles were uncovered, they were too far away and behind too much flying sand to see.

The darkness Petra's storm had caused, coupled with the sun lowering itself toward the horizon, made my eyelids feel heavy.

Another couple of hours later, during which we'd only moved to fetch water, Antoni and I made our way back to the aircraft where Ivan, Nike, and Mom had closed themselves inside.

Mom opened the door when she saw Antoni and me coming. We crawled inside and she shut it again, blocking out much of the noise of the storm. I clambered into my seat and took off the headgear, rubbing my ears and wincing at their soreness from being flattened against my skull.

"Hungry?" Nike asked, and reached behind her seat to retrieve one of the coolers.

"Starving."

"I'll get the guys." Mom gave us a second to cover our ears again before cracking the door open and stepping outside. She returned a moment later with Jozef and Emun, and we shared a meal of chicken kebabs, roasted vegetables, hummus, and cans of tonic.

We agreed it made sense to set up the campsite while Petra continued her work, and divvied up the tasks before we left the helicopter, since we wouldn't be able to talk to one another. Ivan handed out little packets of soft earplugs to those of us who preferred them to the big unwieldy headgear, which would be likely to fall off when bending over. That taken care of, we stepped out of the aircraft to complete our chores.

I had thought Petra might be finished by the time the tents and gear were set up, but the sandstorm had not abated. To the south of us, where we could still see the sky, the light had dimmed and a few stars poked out of a velvety blue sky.

We played cards for a while in the chopper with all the doors open to let any breeze that happened by to sweep through it—all except for Jozef, who couldn't pull himself away from the supernatural spectacle happening just outside the Bell. When we got tired of that, I pulled out a book and crawled into the tent Antoni and I would be sharing. He crawled in after me, blue earplugs visible in his ears. He pulled out his own book, one written in Polish. It wasn't long before we were asleep.

I woke with a grimace at the ache deep inside both of my eardrums. Wincing, I slowly pulled the plugs from my ears and listened.

Nothing.

Antoni lay chest down on the roll-out foam mattress beside me, cheek smooshed into the pillow. His dark eyelashes fluttered and his eyebrows tightened. I leaned over and rained kisses on the side of his face. Slowly, he sat up, blinking and wincing.

He pulled the earplugs out of his own ears and glared at them like they were scorpions. "Ow."

"I agree." I rubbed the skin just in front of my ears. "Sounds like she finished."

Antoni pulled a t-shirt over his head, his hair sticking up in all directions. Yawning, he jammed his feet into his sneakers. I raked my own messy mop up into a ponytail, fished in my bag for my toothbrush and toothpaste, and followed Antoni out of the tent.

Mom and Jozef's blue two-man tent was still zipped up tight. Nike's little white dome shook a little so I figured she was at least awake. Ivan had opted to make a narrow bed for himself in the helicopter, and the Bell's door was open a crack. Emun's tent was barely visible beyond Nike's, but I could see the zipper and it was done up tight. Petra's canvas pup-tent was nowhere to be seen.

"Do I smell coffee?" Antoni asked as we staggered sleepily toward where Petra was bent over a small fire.

She looked up at us as we approached. "Morning, sleepyheads."

"What time did you get to sleep?" I asked, yawning.

"I caught a few winks under the stars," she replied, checking the espresso maker by lifting its lid and peering into it. "Almost ready."

Her long dark hair was back in a low ponytail and she wore a baseball cap and a loose t-shirt over a pair of jogging pants. Her feet were bare. Her light silver eyes were full of good humor and her dark skin looked freshly washed.

"It's not fair that you look that beautiful after working all night," I croaked as I made my way over to one of the water jugs sitting underneath the aircraft. Grabbing a cup from the little stash, I filled it and dipped my toothbrush. I squeezed out some toothpaste onto the brush and stuck it into my mouth as I headed over to the fire.

I froze in place, staring at where the Richat Structure used to be. Antoni saw where I was looking just as he lifted a steaming cup to his lips. He stopped and turned.

He said something in Polish which I knew was not polite.

Antoni and I walked toward the edge of the abyss before us and stood at the edge.

Before us lay the unmistakable remains of an ancient city. It was massive, sprawling to the north as far as the eye could see, and ending with a low line of distant mountains. To the west and east it curved away gently. The concentric circles were not visible from ground-level, but I had no doubt that they were there, for the dark shadow of a long cavern was visible from where we stood.

Footsteps behind us could not tear my eyes from the find Petra had unearthed. I felt Mom come to stand beside me, and Jozef on her other side. A moment later, Emun, Nike, and Ivan appeared on the other side of Antoni.

The broken remains lay before us, the shapes of building stones, pillars, statues, and unidentified rubble which was clearly made by human hands were visible as far as the eye could see. The reason for the bulls-eye shape of the Richat Structure was now so plain and real in front of us that my vision misted as tears sprang to my eyes.

Last to join us was Petra, as her dark slender shape appeared in my periphery on the other side of Jozef.

Her voice was soft but the wind carried it to us where we stood speechless and amazed. "I give you, Atlantis."

TWELVE

I leveled the beam of a flashlight into the open Kirilian compass as Antoni operated on its interior with tiny tools from Ivan's glasses repair kit. He used the end of the small screwdriver to flip open the casing protecting the gem where it sat between three small, shining discs.

"There's the problem," Antoni said. "It's not the compass that broke, it's the gem. Look." Plucking the aquamarine from the casing, he laid it in the palm of his hand and frowned at it.

"Why would it break? That's weird." A crack down the center of the gem divided it perfectly in half.

"Good thing we brought spares." He reached into his jeans pocket and pulled out a small velvet sack pinched shut with a ribbon. Opening the sack, he upended it and a gemstone fell into his palm. He put the broken one inside the bag, tied it up again, and tucked it away. After popping the fresh gem into the reservoir, he snapped the casing closed and then the outer lid.

Petra had stopped nearby, watching curiously, her hat tilted back from her face.

He turned on the power and directed the beam toward the ruins. He held down the capture button.

The teal beam appeared, shooting toward the Richat Structure on a shallow angle and disappearing into a jumble of nearby stones.

I stared at the thin line of light, wondering what it might do to me if it made contact with my body.

The compass made a new noise, a grinding sound between the capture clicks.

"Uh oh," Petra said. "That doesn't sound good."

Just as Antoni reached for the power button, there was a cracking sound and the beam disappeared. He let out a long groan.

"I just don't get it. It never did that before."

"We're too close to the source," said Nike as she stood, folding a blanket. She stuffed it into a carry sack. She tightened the drawstring and turned away, returning to where she was breaking down her camp and packing up. "The energy coming from the original pieces is breaking the... whatever that thing is."

"So much for a compass, then." Antoni said. He and I shared an unhappy look. "Things just got exponentially more difficult."

"Try not to sound so glum," I replied. "We found Atlantis and we never thought that would happen, let alone to have dug it up in a matter of hours."

Antoni nodded, but still looked concerned. We busied ourselves with breaking down the tents. Ivan had elected to stay with the helicopter when we gave him the choice. He looked regretful, like a trek through an ancient city might be something he'd enjoy, but said that he didn't feel right leaving the rental sitting out in the desert by itself. I told him that there were no people around for hundreds of kilometers. That still didn't disabuse him of the notion that someone needed to stay with the bird. It didn't really matter, so I didn't push him, and went to help prepare for what was ahead.

"It's like the world's weirdest, coolest camping trip." I stuffed another bottle of water into my backpack and pulled the drawstring tight. Standing up, I heaved the loaded rucksack onto my shoulders.

Antoni chuckled. He'd cheered up some at the proposition of visiting Atlantis. He had his backpack on his shoulders, with our tent and rolled-up mattress strapped on. I had our food, water, sunscreen for Antoni, and other odds and ends.

Antoni said, "How many people can say they've camped out in the ruins of Atlantis?"

"No one." I squashed the urge to point out that no one else that I was aware of had battled a storm demon, fought a wraith, unseated a demon, been nearly burnt to death from the inside and survived, or manufactured a biodome using magic. The remarkable was quickly becoming my new normal. "Life is never boring. At least, not anymore."

"Was it ever?" Mom slung an arm over my shoulders and cocked an eyebrow as she looked down at me.

I thought of all the times she'd taken me swimming when I was little more than a toddler, all the times I'd seen her in her siren form when everyone else in our world was asleep. I thought about my oldest friends, Saxony and Georjayna, and what they'd been through, what they'd become. I thought of Akiko and what she'd sacrificed, my heart giving a pang as her sweet face filled my mind's eye.

"No." I smiled up at her. "I can't say it has been."

Mom kissed my forehead and released me. "It's just another adventure."

But it wasn't just another adventure, I thought as I followed Mom to the edge of the Richat Structure where the ruins of Atlantis awaited us. The fate of every siren in the world's oceans, and out of them, rested on the task we'd set for ourselves. Through my mind flashed images of crying babies, heartbroken husbands, and motherless boys. I shook my head to dislodge the unpleasant thought. Those abandoned children and heartbroken lovers were the ones we were doing this for. The heartsick sirens forced to leave their loved ones, the tearing apart of families—they were the reason for this quest.

"How big did you say it is, Jozef?" It was Nike speaking as the seven of us stood with our boots on the edge of Atlantis.

"About forty kilometers across." Jozef shifted his shoulders beneath his backpack, getting comfortable. "Give or take a few meters."

"And all we know is that we have to head in *that* direction." Petra pointed in the direction the teal laser had gone before it broke again. She let out a laugh of disbelief. "I hope I'm not the only one who realizes that this search could take years. Someone will soon notice the massive displacement of sand and the rather large mountain ranges to the east of us that weren't there yesterday. If they haven't already noticed. We are visible from space, you know. There'll be archaeologists swarming over this site in a few weeks, and a tent-city constructed before then." She peered over at me from the other side of Antoni, her silver eyes now serious. "I'm honored that you called me for help. Honored that I had an opportunity to be part of this, but now that Atlantis is bare, I'd give us less than seventy-two hours before the first visitors arrive, and when they do, it's game over. You'll never have another crack at it."

"So, you're saying this is impossible?" Antoni looked down at her.

She nodded. "That's what I'm saying."

"It won't take us seventy-two hours to find it." It was Nike, saying the words in the soft- spoken way of hers. She was quiet, but her tone was full of gravitas. It made you want to listen to hear what she would say next.

"What makes you say that?" Mira leaned forward to peer at her white-haired friend. Every set of eyes among us was now on Nike.

"Curses are insurgent by nature. The being that set the curse did so out of spite and the nature of the magic is also spiteful, rebellious, and ungovernable. It won't take us three days; it may not even take us two."

"I don't follow," I said, and saw Antoni and Petra both nodding in agreement in my periphery.

Nike's pale eyes shifted to my face. "It *wants* to be found. It knows you are here."

Cold fingers trailed up my arms and the back of my neck, and in spite of the increasing heat of the day, I shivered.

"It *wants* her to destroy it?" Antoni said, his brow wrinkling. "That doesn't make sense."

Nike shook her head.

For a moment we just stood there staring at the strange siren sorceress. She wouldn't answer Antoni's question but her eyes on my face, their solemnity and earnestness, meant she didn't have to. She would never say the words while my mother was present, but I heard them in my mind as clearly as if she'd said them out loud.

It wants to destroy you.

In that moment of realization, my jaw clenched and my heart hardened. Determination flowed through my muscles and blood like adrenaline pulsed before a sprint. I thought of how the aquamarines burned my skin like fire and took away all my strength while giving freedom to every other of my kind. Nike knew, I knew, that this was personal. Why it was personal to me, I didn't know, but either this curse was going down, or I was.

I took a deep breath and spoke before my mother had a chance to process what Nike had not said aloud. If Mom knew what was really at stake, she'd stop this whole mission in its tracks.

"Let's do this."

Navigating the ruins of the Atlantis Petra had revealed was like making our way through a labyrinth. At times, the rubble was just that—rubble, a big jumble of stones and boulders of various unusual shapes and sizes. At other times the way was so clear it was like walking a narrow road lined with collapsed buildings. At these times, we could often make out carvings and markings in the wreck of the city, large broken sculptures and decorative structures. Everything was constructed of black, white, and red stone, just as Jozef had said it would be. In other places, we had to trip, slip, and climb with both hands and feet over disjointed, angular collapsed walls and roofs. These areas were the most dangerous. There were cracks and crevices one could easily fall or slide into if one's footing was unsure.

"Look." Antoni paused at the top of a long slope of black rock riddled with cracks. Its side was so flat, it must have been a wall. Two narrow rectangular windows made black holes halfway down, and beyond that, dark earth could be seen. A few small mud puddles sat glistening among the rubble.

"Water." I climbed over the edge of the wall and stood beside Antoni. "Petra dug so deep that we've hit ground water. Well, at least that means we don't need to worry about drinking water."

The sun was now at its peak and the temperatures had climbed an astonishing amount since daybreak. I'd stripped off my button-up shirt and stuffed it into my pack, leaving just a tank top and sports bra underneath the white tunic. I'd rolled up my shorts as high as I could without chafing my inner thighs, but my feet were baking inside my hiking boots.

"So thirsty." Antoni dropped his back pack and pulled the back of his tunic away from his skin, airing himself out. He dug in his bag and withdrew a canteen. "I'm not sweaty at all but I feel like I can't get enough water," he said between gulps.

I knew exactly how he felt, and very likely it was even more keen for the Mer of our little group. It felt like I was spinning the top off my canteen every five minutes or refilling it.

Looking back over my shoulder, I watched as Mom, Jozef, and Nike picked their way along behind us. Petra had gone ahead, navigating the rough terrain like she'd been doing it since she was a little kid. Antoni followed my gaze and let out a tired laugh as we watched Petra climb a fractured slab of red stone and hop over the side, light as a gazelle.

"Is archaeology something that's in her blood, or is she tireless because she's the Euroklydon?" Emun asked as he walked past us, either determined to catch up with her or just showing off. He looked as cool as a cucumber under his white headscarf.

"I don't know." I watched Petra sail on ahead of us, almost skimming over the tops and through the valleys of this strange world we found ourselves in. "She's light as air, though."

She still hadn't cracked and donned the cumbersome long tunic the rest of us wore to ward off the heat, as I had suspected she would eventually. She wore just a baseball cap, tank top, and shorts. Her skin was nutbrown already. I guessed she'd come from somewhere sunny.

I scrunched up my toes inside my boots and grimaced at how sweaty my socks felt. I longed to take them off and let air flow through my toes. We'd agreed to stop for lunch at noon. There'd be shade then, and I'd have an opportunity to free my boiling soles from their prison.

"Come on. We're the youngest ones here." I chuckled as I thought about just how true that was. "We can't fall too far behind."

Antoni took a swig from his water bottle then leaned down and planted a kiss on my cheek. "Lead on, fearless one."

THIRTEEN

We came to a long straightaway of flat sand. The gigantic ruins of a set of stone trusses cast thick, cool shadows, so we stopped for lunch.

I headed directly for the shade, as did Mom, Nike, and Emun. Jozef and Antoni poked around the base of the ruin as Emun and I laid out a spread of cheese, meats, flatbread, apples, figs, and water. We hadn't bothered bringing utensils or plates so we took turns rinsing the dust off our hands before making our own sandwiches and finding a spot in the shade to eat and rest.

"It looks like it was once a church," Antoni said before biting into his bulging flatbread. "Is that possible?"

"A temple would be more likely." Nike had seated herself on the ground next to my mother with her back against a dark red stone.

"That's what we're looking for." Mom took a bite and grimaced at the chewiness of the bread.

"Only we're looking for white stones, right?" I began unlacing my boots, relishing in the thought of springing free my overbaked toes.

Nike nodded. "White, threaded with blue veins. That's what Lusi told you, isn't it?"

Mom nodded and took another bite, chasing this one with a gulp of water.

Peeling my sweaty socks off, I sighed with pleasure as I wriggled my toes in the open air.

"That's a great idea." Antoni began to unlace his boots with one hand while feeding himself with the other.

I luxuriated in the experience of filling my belly while my feet cooled. When I was finished eating, I lay back on the square rock I had claimed and looked up at the sky. It was peaceful here. There was only the sound of an occasional breeze and the spatter of sand against the ruins. No birds. No insects. I had never been in the desert before but I had expected...well, I didn't know what. But I hadn't expected this acute stillness. I rolled my head to the side to look at where Petra was sitting in her own contemplative silence against a stone not far from me.

"I thought the desert might have more life in it," I said to her. "Maybe not a lot of life, but some at least."

She glanced at me with those pale, otherworldly eyes. "The desert is full of life."

"So the stillness here is unusual?"

"Well, it's been buried for thousands of years. Give it a few days and it'll be teeming with activity."

A small insect with hard buzzing wings flew past, as if to illustrate her point. She looked up and watched it pass by. Smiling at me she said, "See?"

I smiled back at her. "Thank you for being here."

She gave me the smallest of nods. "You're welcome."

I found it difficult not to stare at her even as we took twenty minutes to rest and I came close to dozing there in the shade. I didn't know if we called each other friends, but

I hoped so. We were bound together by what we were and what we'd seen and done.

As if he could read my mind, Antoni said quietly so only I could hear. "She came when you called."

I rolled my head the other way to look at him. He was lying on his side, his elbow crooked and his head resting in his hand. His turban was pushed back a little and the face covering dangled beside his cheek. His hazel eyes were on Petra and then cut to me. "But she wasn't there when you made the vow with your friends. With Georjie and Saxony."

"No, she wasn't there."

"There's no one like her on Earth, you said."

I nodded, wondering what he was getting at. "She is the only one of her kind."

"The only Euroklydon. The most powerful elemental of all."

"Yes."

"And she came when you called." A dimple appeared in his cheek. "And you can summon fire and earth, if you want to."

I blinked at him. "Yes. As they could summon me."

He shook his head. "I always knew you were special, Targa. But this takes special to a whole new level."

I didn't know what to say to that.

He leaned forward and kissed me tenderly. "I want you to know that I fell in love with you before I knew you were anyone but Targa, a sassy Canadian teenager."

So, that's what he was driving at. I wondered if he was intimidated by my status. It was a thought that had never occurred to me before. Had I been worried that he loved me because I was powerful? I examined my feelings as he moved back and looked down at me through hooded eyes.

No, I decided. I wasn't worried about that. One time, I had worried that his affection for me was more thanks to my siren allure than any real attraction, but that worry had dropped off a while ago. Almost without me realizing it.

I put a hand behind his neck and pulled him back down for another kiss. When he withdrew this time, I said, "I love you too." I grinned. "Even if you're just a mundane human with no superpowers."

He flicked my nose and laughed. "Brat."

I stood up and stretched, feeling rested and ready for the afternoon. Antoni got to his feet beside me. No one else made any move to get up. Jozef was still chewing slowly and reading from a small book he held open with one hand.

I walked past the ruins of the temple and wandered farther down the broad way that stretched out in front of us. It was lined by destroyed city. Black, red, and white stones were scattered amidst dunes of sand. The shadow of a bird passed overhead and I looked up to watch it land on one of the highest mountains of rubble. It looked about, its little head snapping this way and that. Petra was right, before long the desert life would move in. With all the sand gone, the ruins would begin to decay at a much faster rate.

Antoni walked alongside not far away, bare feet in the sand and now coated with dust. He knelt to examine a small broken statue—maybe something that once graced a front door, or the top of a building.

Heat baked the desert floor, sending up waves of oven-hot air and giving the horizon the look of a mirage. Antoni and I stayed to the shadows—the only place we could handle standing barefoot.

I wandered farther down the road, drawn by a ruin with what looked like mosaics. Hoping for some artwork, I went to it and knelt to examine what was indeed a mosaic.

Brushing the dust and sand away revealed small black tiles arranged in the design of a snarling, two-headed dog. Atlantean words, which I now recognized from spending so much time looking at the images on the tablet, sat beneath the dog. The tile was perfectly level and compressed into the sand like a welcome mat. The vicious mouths of the dog's heads told me all I needed to know about what the glyphs below the image meant.

"Beware of dog," I said with a chuckle. "Even thousands of years ago they had this warning."

Antoni came up behind me and looked over my shoulder. "And now you can buy the same thing in plastic for your house."

"Must be one of the oldest warnings in the world." I got to my feet and brushed the sand off my hands.

My eye fell on another mosaic barely visible in the rubble off the main path. Climbing over the rocks, I went for a closer look. This one was purely a decorative border running the edge of a building block. I traced the design with my finger, rubbing away the dust and revealing a dark blue tile.

Pain blossomed on my fingers and I snatched my hand back with a gasp. I looked at my hand where I expected to see blistering, but there was no sign of damage.

Antoni appeared at my side a moment after he'd heard me gasp. "What's wrong?"

I wiped my hand off quickly on my shorts. The pain seared enough to bring tears to my eyes. It was like some fine filament deep in my flesh had lit up like a candle.

"I don't know. Something burnt me." I looked at the dark blue stone and gestured to it. "It happened when I touched that tile scrollwork."

Antoni frowned and bent down for a closer look. He rubbed his thumb over the tile and peered at it.

"But that's not aquamarine. It's way too dark." He looked at me, a question in his eyes.

Still rubbing my hand on my shorts, I stood up. The pain had been intense but it was starting to pass. "You're right. But it hurt me all the same. It's okay now, doesn't hurt as much as it did."

Turning away from the offending mosaic, I picked my way back to the throughway I had begun to think of as a road.

"Ow!"

The skin on the bottom of my feet lit with heat like someone was holding a torch to my soles. With a groan of agony, I leapt from the ruins and landed on a square of shade on the sand.

"Targa!" Antoni followed me down and knelt beside me where I'd sat down, brushing vigorously at the soles of my feet.

Antoni took to brushing my right foot while I worked at the left, the burning sensation so strong I was astounded that the skin was not melting away. Tears tracked down my cheeks. Antoni glanced at my face. His brow wrinkled and his eyes filled with worry. Getting an idea, he ran back to where we'd had lunch and grabbed one of the bottles of water. Sprinting back to where I sat, he was followed by Nike and Petra.

Antoni slid like a baseball player into the dust beside me, spinning the top off the bottle at the same time. He dumped the water over my feet, rubbing as he did so.

I took a shuddering breath as the pain eased. "Thank you."

"What happened?" Petra asked as she and Nike came

to a stop and knelt beside me. Petra put her hand on my shoulder. "Are you okay?"

I nodded, wiping at the moisture on my face and feeling a little silly at the tears that had come. "Something burned me. My hand and both my feet."

Nike looked sharply at Antoni's bare feet, dusty in the sand. Her gaze cut sharply to his face. "But not you? You're not hurt?"

He shook his head. "She touched a dark blue tile." He jerked his head. "Over there. And it burned her. On her way back to the road, her feet were burned as well."

Nike made a beeline for the mosaic Antoni directed her to and took a closer look while Petra helped me to my feet.

"Best put your boots back on," Petra said quietly. She eyed the terrain around us dubiously.

Nike and Antoni returned, Nike's expression was serious and her eyes were on me. "Those weren't aquamarines," she told me.

I nodded. "I know, but they burned me all the same."

"No, they didn't."

My head recoiled and I prepared a sharp retort. But before it could spring to my lips, she held out her hand. It was covered in dust, and in the sunlight it glimmered faintly.

"It's aquamarine dust. It wasn't the tiles, it was residue."

The four of us stood in silent shock for a moment, staring at the faint blue dust in Nike's palm.

"So, what does that mean?" Petra looked from one of us to the other, confused. "I must be missing something."

I explained about the conundrum of the aquamarine gemstones, how they were a gift for every siren except for me.

She listened quietly, nodding at intervals. "I wish I

could add something helpful," she said when I'd finished explaining. "All I can say is that I understand the power that stones can have. Stones are the catalyst that brought out my abilities."

Antoni looked back toward our lunch site.

"What is it?" I asked, getting to my feet.

"I was just wondering why Mira wasn't here like a shot from a gun." He jerked a thumb and gave a crooked if worried smile. "I get it now. She and Jozef are napping."

I nodded, relieved that Mom had missed this little drama.

"So, at the risk of repeating myself," Petra said, looking at Nike, who was rubbing the dust off her hand. "What does it mean?"

"It means we're close," Nike replied. "We'd better get moving. Antoni, you'd better carry her back to her boots so it doesn't happen again."

Antoni reached to pick me up.

"No, no it's okay. I can walk back."

Nike gave me a look of warning.

"I insist." I began the walk back to where Jozef and my Mom lay reclined in the shade. "I made it here without being burnt, I can make it back. And no one is to tell my Mom what happened. She'll only worry."

Nike and Petra agreed, but Antoni frowned.

"I don't like that," Antoni said. "She deserves to know. You shouldn't hide something like that from her."

I stopped Antoni and let Petra and Nike move on without us. Putting a hand on his chest I looked up into his eyes, almost pleading.

"Don't say anything to her. I need you to promise."

"Targa. No." It was a reproach.

"You must. If she knew, she could call the whole thing off."

Antoni frowned and the muscles in his jaw clenched as he ground his teeth. "Maybe we should."

I shook my head vehemently. "We've come this far, and there's too much at stake. Nothing can jeopardize what we're doing here. Please. Promise me?"

For a moment our gazes clashed and the unspoken passed between us. I had the power to make Antoni forget what he'd seen here. I had the power to force a promise from him. I had made myself a promise that I would never again use my voice on Antoni, but I'd never told him that.

"I won't tell her," he said, finally.

"Thank you." I turned for camp again.

"But, I don't like it."

"Noted."

FOURTEEN

It wasn't long after we started moving again that I felt it.

I was walking ahead of the group with Emun at my side. We'd been making our way down the broad old road in companionable silence. I put a hand on his forearm.

He stopped walking and looked at me. "What is it?"

Closing my eyes, I tuned in to a sensation that was not dissimilar to feeling your skin warm up on a hot day. It was like a heat lamp set on low was shining on only one side of my face. I opened my eyes and looked up, scanning the sky.

Emun followed my gaze. "You're freaking me out a little, baby sister," he said through the pale covering over his mouth, but not without humor.

The sun was to our left, and yes, it was warm. But the warm sensation was on my right and it was different—a little sharper. It was the presence of gems, it had to be. Only the gems could inspire that strange kind of heat. I began to climb over the rubble toward the crooked white pillars in the distance—the direction of the heat.

Mom, Jozef, and Antoni caught up to Emun and I heard Antoni ask where I was going.

"I'm not sure, but she's got an idea. We should follow." I heard Emun's shoes scuff over the stones as he climbed to follow me.

Soon the entire party was climbing and crawling among the rubble after me. As I gained ground, a better view of Atlantis spread out before us. From here it looked like it went on forever rather than being contained to a small circular depression in a vast wasteland. To the north was a darker line on the horizon, a rough and fuzzy skyline. These were the mountains Plato had written about in his description. For centuries, all treasure-hunters and archaeologists had had to go by was the account Plato gave in his dialogues called *Critias* and *Timaeus*. The Richat Structure fit his portrayal of the ancient city exactly, but the account had long ago been relegated to the world of fiction. And yet, here the city was, under my feet.

Following the feeling of heat on my skin—which I neglected to mention in case it alarmed my mom—we arrowed slowly through Atlantis toward the white ruin.

Antoni had replaced Emun at my side, as Emun had slowed and joined Nike and Petra. I could hear the low murmur of conversation from them. Mom and Jozef traveled even more slowly as Jozef stopped to take photos and make notes in a small notebook he kept in his chest pocket.

"You seem like you know where you're going," Antoni commented as he crested the same boulder I had stopped on, now looking down into a slight dip in the cityscape before us.

The sun passed behind a thick blanket of clouds, and my eye was drawn to a very faint glow emanating from between a cluster of fallen pillars. They were fat and white and leaning at dangerous angles, but even from a distance I could make out the faded markings on the pillars' tops. The clouds passed by and the sun came out again. The faint glow disappeared in the bright light. I was sure I had seen it though, however weak.

"I do." I grabbed Antoni's hand and squeezed it. I pointed toward the rubble of the temple. "We're going there."

We hopped down from the boulder and picked our way through a narrow gully between broken red bricks. Antoni and I made it to the temple ruin first and waited for the rest to catch up. The sun was too bright to see the glow. But if I stood in the gap underneath the tripod of fallen pillars and let my eyes adjust, it was there. It was like someone had lit a candle with a blue flame deep in the interior.

"Don't tell me we have to go in there," Jozef said as he and my mom approached. "That's why you're sniffing in that hole, isn't it? You think the gem is inside this temple?"

"It does fit the description Lusi gave us." Antoni threw me an anxious glance, but he didn't say anything about me making a beeline for it. "It even has a few blue threads, you just can't see them unless you wipe away the dust."

"Well, what are we waiting for?" Nike said. "It's not that big, let's see what's inside."

Nobody voiced what I was certain was on everyone's mind—what if the whole thing collapsed on us? Could Petra keep us from being crushed? I looked at the Euroklydon's face, the only face among us that was completely uncovered. She seemed unconcerned about entering the ancient hazard. That made me feel a little better.

"I'll go first," she said, nodding at me as she passed. And just like that, she ducked her head and crawled into the low triangular hole.

I followed, then Antoni and the rest of the party.

"Oh!" Petra exclaimed ahead of me as my eyes were still

adjusting to the dark. "There's light coming from somewhere."

"Cracks in the ceiling...uh...roof?" ventured Jozef from behind.

"No, it's coming from down, not up."

"It's the gem," I replied.

Silence met this statement, until Mom found her voice first. "Are you sure, Targa?"

"It is a blue glow, if that helps," Petra volunteered as she'd begun moving again. She was a dark shape ahead of me, faintly outlined with a dim teal light.

"That sounds about right." Nike's voice echoed through the narrow space. Footsteps scuffed along stone and gritted on the sandy layer that covered everything.

"Our aquamarines don't glow," Mom protested.

Someone bumped into someone else and I heard Jozef apologize and Emun tell him not to worry.

"Maybe because they're not big enough," I guessed, thinking of the large column the gemstones had been cut from and its considerable size. In the drawings there had been a ring of blue around the column, but I had thought that was artistic interpretation, not true-to-life.

Petra picked her way through an increasingly narrow passageway, which dropped away beneath us.

"Anybody claustrophobic?" I heard Emun ask.

A chorus of 'no's' followed from most of the party.

Then Nike asked, "Why, are *you* claustrophobic?"

Jozef replied with a falsetto, "No."

Everyone laughed at his high-pitch denial, and some of the tension broke.

Antoni sang the opening line to the *Ghostbusters* theme song, low and thickly accented, which made us laugh even more. Emun picked it up and the two of them serenaded us as we made our way deeper into the temple. Petra joined in with not a bad beat-box.

When they came to the end, Nike piped up. "I've obviously missed out on a lot while I was asleep. I've never heard music like that in my life."

"You have no idea," laughed Mom. "Jozef will force you to watch *The Godfather*, mark my words."

"Hey, that's a classic film. It's a must!"

The crawling in the darkness had lulled my brain into a kind of relaxed thoughtlessness where I felt the heat growing against my face and listened to the chatter around me. So when Petra stopped suddenly, I bumped into her.

"Sorry," I said.

"No worries. I'm just not sure which way to go. Any suggestions?"

We'd come to an intersection. Ahead of us lay a solid rock slab, a huge single monolith. To the right was a dark passageway full of jutting stones, crooked slabs of rock. To the left were what looked in the darkness like a set of well-worn steps. They descended and turned yet again.

Petra flicked off her flashlight and we waited for our eyes to adjust.

I could feel the heat before my eyes could see the glow.

"Left," I said. "We have to go left."

"You're right. I see the glow now," Petra added, and continued on.

The steps wound down in a large, squared-off spiral. After ten minutes of making our way down slowly in the dark Emun, was clearing his throat with nervousness.

Petra disappeared around the corner ahead of me, and a very impressed, "Wow!" floated back to the rest of us.

Taking the last corner, I saw what had impressed her. We'd entered a long room lined with pillars. Most of them were cracked, tilted, or even lying on their sides. The ceiling above us was compressed rock and earth. Ahead of us lay a flat-floored room covered in dirt, sand, rocks and rubble. Beyond the long room, which was more like a corridor between the pillars, was another pile of rubble, from behind which a strong blue glow was emanating.

Everyone spilled out of the stairway and stood in the huge corridor, staring.

"We found it," Nike said, and there was a hitch in her voice. She came to stand shoulder to shoulder with me. I felt her hand on my lower back, warm and comforting.

Petra and I were the first to walk toward the glow, whose source we had not yet laid eyes on. It was then I noticed the gullies on either side of the walkway. Dark water reflected the light from Petra's flashlight. Curious, I went to the edge and knelt for a better look. Putting my hand in the water made me laugh in surprise.

"It's fresh groundwater!"

Mom came to join me to feel for herself, and Nike followed suit.

"It's actually drinkable, how can that be?" Nike wondered aloud.

"It's been filtered by the sediment. It's moving a little bit," I said. "Can you feel it?"

Both sirens nodded and then the three of us got to our feet.

The air was not exactly fresh, but it wasn't as stale as you'd expect it to be being so far underground. I wondered if the air had circulated down here while Petra was blowing all that sand around.

We left many footprints in the dusty floor and as we drew close to the rubble at the end of the room, which I'd begun to think of it as a throne room, for reasons I couldn't quite explain, the blue glow cast itself out to us.

I knelt in front of the rubble, near one of the gullies full of water. With a gentle sweep of my hand, I pulled the water from the gully up onto the floor. With a swirling motion, the water swept away a patch of the dirt, and when it drained back into the gully, I could see faded mosaics. I shone my flashlight beam on them and saw that the tile was arranged in a swirling wave pattern in many shades of blue tile. Here and there, aquamarine tiles glittered among the rest.

I stood again, and my stomach clenched as a wave of nausea and dizziness passed through me. Reaching for my water bottle, I took large swallows.

A low growling sound reverberated from the ruin around us, coming from nowhere and everywhere.

Everyone froze.

"Did you hear that?" Jozef reached a hand out for Mom and pulled her closer to him, as if she was the one who might need protecting.

We either nodded or murmured our agreement before the group fell silent again, listening.

"Must have been rocks shifting overhead or something," Antoni suggested uneasily. The sound hadn't made me think of rocks rubbing against one another, but he could be right.

"That doesn't really make me feel any better," Emun replied, eyes lifting to the ceiling and moving along quickly, perhaps looking for a crack or falling dirt. But all overhead seemed solid and at peace.

Another, much louder growl, which clearly came from the direction of the blue glow, had us staggering backward and clustering together.

"Behind me," Petra snapped. She had both palms out, fingers open, arms extended in front of her like they were weapons...which was exactly what they were.

The growl became a juicy, ripping roar. It almost sounded like someone trying to start a chainsaw. I couldn't stop the involuntary yelp that tore from my throat, but I wasn't the only one who cried out in horror.

From behind the rubble, snarling and snapping, jumped an honest-to-goodness, absolutely massive, actual flesh-and-blood two-headed dog.

FIFTEEN

Several screams and a couple of yells filled the cavern as the slavering beast landed on paws the size of dinner plates in front of us. Its heads lowered, it glared at us out of four red-brown eyes, lips peeled back from yellowish fangs.

"I'm seeing double!" yelled Emun. "Is anyone else seeing two heads?"

My hands and fingers were tense, preparing to use the water in the gullies to at least slow down the beast if it decided to leap on us. Petra's hip bumped against mine as I stepped up beside her. No one spared a look anywhere but the dog.

"Definitely two heads," Nike confirmed, sounding awfully calm for the circumstances.

"Just like the mosaic doormat," I said, sounding far less relaxed. I mourned silently that my voice didn't work on animals.

"What should we do now?" Mom stood just behind me, in front of Antoni and Jozef. The sirens, the Euroklydon and the triton made a barrier between the mad-looking animal and those without supernatural powers.

"We have to get past him." My eyes never left the dog, who for the time being was not moving forward. He was frozen in an aggressive crouch, like he was prepared to spring. "He's on guard."

"Him?" Antoni called from behind me. Then a few moments later there was a confirmation. "Yep, that's definitely a him."

The four eyes of the dog's heads darted from me to my mom, from Nike to Emun. My own eyes narrowed, noticing this. The beast never sent a gaze in anyone else's direction. I didn't know if it was because we were in front, or if it was for another reason.

"Jozef." I fought to keep my voice low and calm.

"Yes, Targa," he replied in the same strained tone, somewhere off to my left and behind me.

"You, Antoni, and Petra, move to the right. Everyone else, move left."

"Why?"

"Please, just do it." My eyes were glued to the massive animal.

There was a shuffling sound as we began to move, always facing front. The dog gave a fresh growl and one head lowered and the other raised, but both heads kept their eyes on those of us who moved left.

"He doesn't like Mer," Mom said in wonder. "Smart girl, Targa. How did you know that?"

"It was just a guess. Mer move back."

Mom, Nike, Emun, and I took several paces back. My heart was sprinting in my chest. I reminded myself that Petra had the most effective power in this situation. If the beast decided to attack, at least she was in front of Antoni and Jozef.

The eyes remained on us, even as Petra, Jozef, and Antoni moved forward a step.

The growling ceased the farther back we went. Then, remarkably, the dog sat on its haunches and closed its mouths. In such a posture, it looked harmless and relaxed.

"Will you look at that," Jozef wondered. He looked back at Mom and gave a grin. "Boy, he really doesn't like you guys."

"We noticed," Mom replied, tightly.

Petra knelt and put her hand out in a supplicating gesture. She made a low whistle and spoke in soothing tones. "Hey boy, it's okay. We don't mean you any harm."

The dog finally tore his gaze away from us and looked over at where Petra knelt, Antoni and Jozef huddled behind her. He stared at Petra but made no move to approach. One of the heads began to pant, and a long red tongue lolled out of one mouth in a grin.

Jozef moved forward slowly, his hands down and open as well.

The dog gave a low whine in its throat, like a whistle of wanting. His thick black tail made a thump against the stones.

"You're just a big softie aren't you," Jozef said as he moved in front of Petra.

"Be careful, Jozef," Mom warned.

"I think he likes me," Jozef replied, a smile in his voice. "I always liked dogs, though my father never let us get one because we traveled too much."

I didn't bother to point out that this was no normal dog. Not only was it equipped with two heads and two sets of powerful jaws, the only way it could be alive down here was by magic.

The dog gave another whine and went down on his

elbows, his big brown eyes now on Jozef as he moved forward. One head rested its chin on the stone while the other remained perked, ears up.

Jozef was close enough to touch the dog now.

"I don't think that's a good idea, Jozef," I said.

"It's fine," he replied. And without hesitation, he crouched before the dog and lay a hand on one of the heads. The massive head actually twisted to the side to sniff Jozef's hands and the tongue snaked out and licked him.

"He's a completely different animal, now. Look a that," Nike said from where the three of us sirens now stood with Emun, our arms at our sides.

The dog suddenly flopped over on his side and made a playful kick at Jozef, an apparent request for a belly rub. Jozef laughed and obliged. The dog began to groan with pleasure deep in his throat. The groaning became a sad whine as the dog groveled for more love, putting one head in Jozef's lap while the other reached up to lick Jozef's face. It was a pitiful display from an incredibly lonely animal and it moved my heart.

"How long have you been down here all by yourself?" Jozef asked the animal, his voice suffused with sympathy.

"He's immortal," suggested Nike. "There's no easy way out of here for a dog."

"The dog on those old mosaics was two-headed," Petra reminded us. "He must be a remaining beast of Atlantis. He stayed when the city was destroyed, somehow surviving on his own."

"If you're right, then he's been down here all alone for thousands of years," said Emun. "With nothing but ground-water to sustain him."

"Definitely a magical creature," murmured Jozef in a

goofy tone, talking more to the dog than anyone else. "Aren't you?"

The dog gave another groan of pleasure as Jozef scratched his furry tummy.

"You know you can't bring him home with you, right?" Mom said with a laugh in her voice.

Jozef looked up at her and made a pouty face.

"Great, so we've made friends with an immortal two-headed dog." I clearly had to bring us all back to reality in this strange situation. "But I have to get to the gem. What's he going to do if I..."

I moved forward a few steps.

Immediately the two heads found me and began to growl. The dog rolled back to his feet and he rose to a low crouch. Lips were drawn back, fangs exposed.

I took a few steps back and he stopped growling.

"This is a problem," I said.

"It doesn't have to be." Petra had moved closer to the dog and was now patting him alongside Jozef. "I can contain him. He might lose his mind, but he can do it inside of a force-field he can't get out of."

"That's awful." Jozef looked over at Petra, alarmed.

"It's better than killing him," I said. "We wouldn't want that."

Jozef dipped his head in agreement.

"Go ahead, then." I looked at Petra. "Do the Euroklydon."

Petra made Jozef move back. Standing up, she put her hands out wide, palms facing one another. A low hum filled the cavern. Petra nodded at me.

"You can go ahead now, Targa," she said, but her voice was muffled, barely audible.

"Whoa," Antoni looked from Petra to me. "Did she just speak? I didn't hear a thing but her lips were moving."

"I heard her," said Jozef. "She's inside the forcefield with the dog."

"What if it turns and attacks her?" Nike voiced the same fear I was having.

Petra shook her head and mouthed, "He won't."

I took a few steps toward the blue glowing ruin and the dog leapt to his feet snarling and snapping. I could hear him, but just barely.

I kept walking and the dog took a run toward me, crouched and sprang. I couldn't help but stagger back, not knowing where the edge of the force-field was. The dog hit the invisible barrier, fur and tongue plastering as if against glass. A slobber mark remained visible on the field as the dog slid down the side of its curved surface. The dog shook itself, confused and startled but unhurt. He rallied quickly and made another leap, but by then I was well beyond him. Nike, Mom, and Emun followed me. Antoni joined us when he realized it had worked.

"Shall I stay here then, with Petra and the pup?" Jozef called.

"Sure." Mom answered as we navigated our way around the pile of rubble. "The pup. He's completely enamored," she muttered. "That's not going to end well."

"Poor Petra," Antoni said, picking his way across the rough terrain.

"She'll be all right," Emun said.

Heat blasted against my face as I cleared the rubble and entered a chamber filled with the teal glow. The source of the blue glow came into view. It stole the words from my mouth and the breath from my lungs.

A colossal aquamarine crystal sat in the middle of the

space. The center of the crystal was dim and shadowed, and the glow was brightest where the crystals were thinnest. Fingers of the bright blue gem—varying in widths from as narrow as a pinky to as thick as a pillar—extended out in all directions like a starburst. Though it threw a blue glow, the entire crystal was coated with dust.

My nausea was back in full force. I clenched my teeth and did my best to ignore the nausea, as well as the heat baking my face and eyes.

Nike stood beside me. In a low voice, she asked, "Are you all right?"

I nodded and looked at her. She looked as pale and sickly as I felt. Everyone washed out in the light of the giant gemstone. With her dark skin, Nike looked gray. Mom and Emun appeared green. If my complexion was suffering from the nausea or the anxiety riding low in my guts, the illumination concealed it.

"We found your source," Emun called from where he was inspecting the other side of the gem.

"Ugh," Antoni said as he swiped at the crystal and his hand came away filthy. "I guess that's what several millennia underground will get you."

"There's a dark shape in the middle," Emun commented, swiping at the gem and peering into the clean space it left behind. "Wish we could see better."

I cleared my throat. "I think I can help with that." Moving to stand in front of the gem and allowing its heat to bake my face, I spread my hands out to either side where the gullies of groundwater ran. Emun jumped back with surprise as water over-spilled the lips of the gullies and poured across the floor toward the crystal. His feet splashed through the puddle as he retreated to higher ground.

Beckoning to the soft flows on either side, I bade the

water to crawl up and over the shape of the crystal, bathing the stone as it went. The water swirled and trickled, ran and burbled in every direction. It grew blacker and dirtier by the moment. With little flicks of my fingers and wrists, I sent the dirty water back into the gullies and called up fresh water from its direction of flow. Making an endless wash-cycle, I sent the water into every seam and nook, rinsing away years of dust, grime, and sand. The glow began to brighten as the outermost shards came clean. The heart of the stone had the largest surface area and took the longest to clean, but soon that too was gleaming.

I let the water spill back into the gullies, pouring through the cracks and crevices of the stone like little water-falls. The cavern echoed with the sound of spilling water. The cascades thinned until they became narrow streams. The streams became drips and the drips slowed until they became only the occasional droplet.

"Oh my word," my mother muttered under her breath.

The rest of us were silent, but the reason for her shock was obvious.

For the shadow at the heart of the giant gemstone had become clear enough to make out. And trapped, deep inside, lying on her side and as still as a statue, was a woman.

SIXTEEN

I felt Nike as she came to stand by my side, both of us staring at the figure deep inside the crystal.

"Is she alive?" I couldn't tear my eyes from the body.

"She has to be," Nike replied softly. "She must be the source of the curse."

"But how can she be alive after all this time? She must be thousands of years old." I moved a little closer to the stone for a better look, ignoring the heat radiating off it as best I could. The nausea was making my mouth water in an unpleasant way.

"Targa, stay back please," my mother said from somewhere behind me. She sounded unsettled, worried.

"It's magic, Targa," Nike replied, and—in my periphery—I saw her glance at my mother warily.

"So, what now?" Antoni appeared on my other side, his voice as tight as my mother's.

"She has to touch it." Nike kept her tone even, but she had to have known the reaction it was going to incite.

"*Excuse me?*"

I felt Mom's hands on my shoulders pulling me backward, trying to put distance between me and the crystal.

"It's okay, Mom." I tore my eyes from the form inside the crystal and turned to look into my mother's face. I put my hands on her arms and squeezed.

"It's most certainly not okay." Her eyes had grown wide, her face even paler, now tinged with blue in the glow of the huge gem. "Targa, touching that thing could kill you. I'm surprised you're even on your feet standing so close to it."

"So? What? You want us to turn around and go back? After everything you've been through? After all we've learned? We want to break the curse. Now is our chance, probably our only chance. I *have* to do this, Mom."

She shook her head. "No, you don't, Targa. You really, really do not have to do this. Sirens have lived with the curse for millennia. I didn't even *know* I was cursed growing up in Saltford."

"And what if I can break it? What if there's a chance that no siren ever has to suffer again? No siren will ever have to abandon her baby boy, or her beloved husband. No siren will ever have to struggle and suffer the way you were suffering in Poland."

My mother's eyes misted up and she shook her head vehemently. Her face crumpled and it was a knife in my heart, but I could not let it sway me. I knew what I had to do, what I had been born to do. I could no more escape my destiny than Petra had been able to escape hers in a different desert.

"No," Mom whispered, a tear slipping down her cheek. "Please, don't. Don't do this. I can't bear to lose you." She released one of my shoulders to wipe at her tear with an angry motion. She cast about, her gaze landing on Antoni.

He stepped to my side and I felt his arm slip about my waist. I was grateful for his solid warmth.

Mom asked him, "Please, help me convince her she cannot do this."

"I can't," Antoni told her, his arm tightening about my waist. "I don't want to lose her either, but it's her choice."

Mom shook her head like a lost little girl, brushing away a tear again. "No." Her eyes implored me. "Targa…"

"What would you do if you were me?" I asked her.

I felt the heavy stares of Nike and Emun on us. I felt their concern, their loss for words. No one knew what to do.

But I did. It was clear to me. It seemed nothing had ever been clearer.

Mom didn't answer. We both knew what she would do if our roles were reversed.

"Don't forget that I grew up watching the curse eat you alive," I said. "I grew up not knowing if you'd be in your bed in the morning. I sat at your door at night, counting the lumps in your bed to make sure that I still had both a mother and a father. I know what the curse has cost you. And this isn't just your curse, it's mine too. It's every siren's burden, but it's mine to break."

Mom pulled me in for a hug and I heard a quiet sob in my ear as she swallowed her emotions. When she released me, I was swept into Antoni's arms as he crushed me against him. I never loved him more than I did in this moment. I felt like he really knew me. He'd had a week to come to terms with my choice, but I knew how much this was costing him.

"Thank you for trusting me," I whispered in his ear and I felt him nod against me.

"What are her chances?" I heard my mom ask Nike.

Antoni released me and we both listened. My heart had

begun to pound hard in my chest and I had to quell the urge to run against the crystal and just get it over with.

"I don't know, Sybellen. No one can know that."

"Why her?"

"I don't know that either. All I know is that whoever made the curse has something in common with Targa, something that makes them alike. As long as Targa is stronger than the one who made the curse, she'll be okay."

I tuned out at this point. I'd heard it already, and the heat from the gem seemed to be intensifying. I suddenly realized that my energy was being drained. If I waited any longer, I might get too weak to do whatever it was I had to do.

Letting go of Antoni's hand, I stepped toward the stone.

"Not yet," I heard my mother say, her tone sharp and alarmed.

"It's now or never," I murmured, and put my hand flat on the crystal.

WHEN THE AGONY STRUCK, I thought for certain I'd failed. Every muscle in my body tensed, and my back arched in pain. All I could see was the blue of the crystal stretching up before me, and the dark stones of the rocks high overhead. There was no way I could break a curse if I was in this state—I was dying.

There was a panicked blur of voices but I couldn't understand any of them. My bones felt like glowing rods of metal. I no longer had power over my own limbs. I couldn't have removed my hand from the crystal if I had wanted to. My breathing became shallow, for even the rise and fall of my chest felt like it was warping my ribcage where it attached to my spine.

Strange tugging sensations at my clothes, shoulders and hips came through in a dull, distant way. I tried to direct my gaze down but I couldn't move my head, all I could do was move my eyeballs. They found my hand where it touched the crystal, only it wasn't just touching the crystal anymore.

It was becoming the crystal.

No, it was *inside* the crystal, sinking farther in by the moment. I watched in horror, wheezing through the agony lancing up my arm and through my body as my hand sank farther and farther into the stone. My body shifted forward like it was being sucked into the crystal by an invisible vacuum.

Distantly, someone was screaming my name. I thought vaguely that the voices sounded like they were singing, as the sound slowed and blurred in my ears. My world was a blur of blue. Strangely, my right hand was no longer burning, and neither was my elbow. I wriggled my fingers, afraid for a moment that I'd lost all feeling and was dying from the outside in. But my fingers did move. I felt space around them. All at once, everything in me told me to press forward. That if I could survive this and make it through to the inside, I'd be okay.

I strained forward, though whether anything happened in response, I couldn't tell. I was not in control. The crystal was in front of my face, touching my chin. It held my shoulder fast now and crawled along my ribs as I sank into the massive gem. My chin sank into the stone, the skin baking hot where it touched, and that heat spread across my face as I was sucked inside. But inside the gem it was cool; I could feel it now with my whole right arm and part of my left.

The tip of my nose touched the stone, then sank through it. My eyes filled with the crystal as it swallowed my face. As my head passed through the stone, the world became blue.

Then black.

Cool air swallowed me, and in my eyes, a white light flashed.

There was a sensation of falling.

Then there was nothing.

SEVENTEEN

There was no longer any pain. That was my first thought as consciousness returned slowly to my mind, and feeling to my body. My second thought was to wonder how I ended up on the floor. Then, I wondered why it was so quiet.

My eyelids stirred and opened a crack. Aqua light flooded my retinas and I squeezed my eyes shut again. Pushing myself to sitting, I kept my eyes closed and felt around. Beneath me the surface was as smooth as glass, but covered with a gritty residue. The air was warm and humid, but smelled fresh and clean. Cracking my eyes open again, I winced at the flood of light but bore it as my eyes adjusted.

The world inside was green-blue, the color of a tropical shoreline. A large room with a strange cavernous ceiling of stalactites made of aquamarine arched over my head, as high as a cathedral. I got to my feet, my eyes now fully open. Behind me were many hollow fingers of clear gemstone, pale and illuminated.

I was inside the crystal. So, I hadn't died. But was I trapped here too? Like the woman we'd seen.

The woman. I saw her some distance away.

"Hello?" I called. My voice echoed eerily around me, bouncing off the cavern walls.

She did not stir. She lay curled up with her back to me. She wore a cream-colored robe with a brown belt at the waist. Long dark hair—thick spirals of it—spilled across the floor. Even from a distance I could easily tell that the thick shining locks belonged to a person with life and vitality. And yet she did not move or respond to my call in any way. Questions tumbled in my mind like shells caught in a riptide as I walked slowly toward the still form.

Who was she? How long had she been here? How could she still be alive? There was no way in or out of this crystal, save the way I'd come. I paused in my walking and lifted a hand to my head, trying to remember...

How *had* I gotten in here? I could remember pain, white-hot searing heat. I could remember a high-pitched singing sound. Or had it been screaming? I remembered feeling stuck, and nothing visible but a blue glaze in front of my face. Then I'd fallen. I'd woken up on the floor. Now I felt fine, physically anyway.

Was this a dream?

I looked back the way I'd come, eyes scanning the strange interior of the crystal for a doorway or a crack. But there was nothing. Only an alien landscape of hollow crystal tunnels with offshoots to more tunnels. Blue stalactites and stalagmites reached into the space from floor and ceiling.

I continued my slow walk toward the woman, calling out a greeting again.

My footsteps halted as a memory surfaced. I'd left people that I loved to be here. I was alone in this. Nike wasn't here to provide answers. My mother wasn't here to add her strength or wisdom. And Antoni wasn't here to offer support. How I'd gotten inside finally clicked back into my mind.

Looking back the way I'd come again, I peered at the crystal, trying to see through it. There were too many thousands of shades of blue and shadows cast by the crystalline structure. There was nothing to see but columns upon columns, crystals upon crystals. I had been able to see in, but I was unable to see out.

My foot crunched on something and I looked down.

Beneath the soles of my hiking boots were shards of aquamarines. Thousands of them, spread out around the woman like she'd made a bed of broken gemstones to lie in. It looked as though she'd tried to break through the crystal cathedral ceiling over her head and succeeded only in raining shards down upon herself. Many of the shards were sharp, as jaggedly pointed and nasty looking as weapons.

Crunching closer to her, I circled her and looked down upon her.

Her eyes were closed. She lay with her left arm straight out on the floor and her head resting on her bicep. Her right arm was crooked and her hand underneath her cheek. Her robes fell across her legs and small bare feet were visible from beneath them. A golden chain encircled one ankle. Her thick hair was looped back in braids at her temples and then tumbled free from a thong fastened at the back of her head. Her face was peaceful, eyes closed, her dark lashes long and soft against her cheek. Her ribs rose and fell very slowly. So she was alive.

I knelt at her side, unsure of what to do next.

My gaze went to a long aquamarine shard not far from her hand. It was shaped like a knife, with a smooth round handle and a sharp edge to the wicked blue blade.

My stomach turned inside out.

Nike's words rang in my ears—*if you are stronger than the one who set the curse, then you'll prevail. If you are weaker, then you'll die.*

Reaching for the blade, my fingers wrapped around the cool crystal. No pain. No heat. But picking it up, my hand trembled.

A thought came: *Kill her.*

Frowning, I focused on her sleeping face. Was I supposed to kill this woman to break the curse? It made some kind of sense. Kill the one who set the curse, kill the curse.

My thoughts tripped over one another. Why hadn't Nike warned me that I might have to shed someone's blood? Or was I silly not to have assumed it would be this way?

I didn't know this woman, but she was defenseless. In another life, at another time, she might have been a friend of mine, or a friend of my mother's. Given the nature of the curse, she had to be either Mer or Atlantean. She didn't have the look of a siren. Her skin had the blemishes and veins of a human. And she was here, deep in the heart of Atlantis, so wouldn't that make her most likely an Atlantean?

Wait a minute. I pulled back a little and took a breath.

Why would this woman curse herself to be locked inside a huge stone for all of eternity? Didn't it make more sense that she was not the *cause* of the curse herself, but maybe involved somehow? So if it wasn't her who made the curse, then who was it? Or was she the source of the curse and had willingly given herself to this great blue cage to...to what? Fuel the curse? Keep it alive?

I shifted from one foot to the other, frustrated.

I couldn't kill this woman without knowing for certain

that it would end the curse. What if it was a mistake? What if it made things worse?

The knife slipped from my grip and fell on the floor in front of me, and in front of the sleeping woman. It shattered into a thousand pieces. The shards sprayed outward, hitting my boots. They landed in the woman's hair, peppered her face and hand, and landed in her clothing.

Her eyes opened. Eyes so dark they looked black. She bared her teeth and her face transformed into something from a nightmare.

Startled, I screamed and made to straighten up, my heart doing cartwheels in my chest.

As fast as lightning, her hand reached for me, her fingers closing around my wrist as a hiss issued from her throat. It was a sound I'd never heard a living being make before. Another startled scream ripped from my throat before I could help it.

I yanked at my hand, trying to pull away and get to my feet. All I wanted was to get away from her.

The woman held fast, her grip like a vise. I pulled her to her feet and she staggered after me as I tried to get away from her. My boots crunched on the broken shards.

"Free me," she gasped into my face, as the horrible contorted expression began to ease. Where I'd seen evil a moment before, I now saw desperation and fear. "You must free me. It's why you've come."

"Let me go," I replied, my multi-layered siren's voice trembling with fright and adrenaline coursing through my veins.

"You must," she repeated as though she hadn't heard me —of course, Atlanteans were immune to siren voices. Her hand tightened and her lower lip quivered. "You must, it's why you've come."

I curled my fingers around hers and pried them from my wrist, relieved to see that I had the strength to do so. I didn't know what this woman's abilities were, or her intentions. All I knew was that my heart was jumping around like a jackrabbit that didn't know which way to go and I was trapped inside a massive aquamarine crystal without a way out.

Her dark eyes widened as she looked down at where I had pried her fingers loose and freed my wrist. Perhaps she thought she was stronger than me as well. I took a steadying breath, telling myself silently to at least pretend that I was the one who was in control here. We were surrounded by razor-sharp shards of aquamarine. Both of us had access to deadly weapons if we wanted them.

"Who are you?" I asked, stepping back.

Her hand slowly drifted down to her side. "Do you not know?"

I shook my head. "Do you know who I am?"

"You're the one who has come to free me. After all this time." She reached for me again and I took another step back.

"My name is Shaloris," she replied. "What is your name?"

"I'm Targa."

"You're Mer." Her dark gaze seemed to take me in as an individual for the first time since her eyes had opened. "You have the look of the Mer."

"And you're Atlantean?"

Her gaze went fuzzy again and her focus went inward. She took a few shallow breaths and her eyes misted. Her glare snapped to my face again, sharp and focused. "How long have I been in here?"

"I don't know." My voice was softer now. Now that she

didn't have a face out of a horror movie, I felt sorry for her. "A very long time."

"Thousands," she said on a tremulous whisper. "Thousands of years?"

"I think so."

I expected her expression to break, for tears to fall, for horror to contort her features once again. But instead, a panicked joy suffused her face, and the tears that came appeared to be those of happiness. She reached for me again and this time I didn't step back.

Her hands found my elbows, her dark eyes smiled into mine. "She said it would be thousands. It is time. I was right!"

Her hands swept up my arms and to my shoulders, her palms found my cheeks and touched my face with a tenderness that both frightened and disarmed me.

"You must release me," she said. "I revoked the curse years ago."

My skin prickled at the mention of the curse. A yawning dread opened wide in the deepest part of me. "But the curse continues, unless a siren wears a piece of the aquamarine that surrounds you. So it was you? You made the curse?"

"I did. I tried to revoke it. But it seems that as long as I live the curse shall go on. End my misery, end the misery of your people." Her tone went soft and breathy and another tear slipped down her cheek. Her eyelashes were wet and stuck together, her eyes shining and glassy. "You must kill me."

My insides shriveled in on themselves. How could I kill this piteous creature? How could I kill, period?

"I don't know if I can," I whispered. She still held my face and her touch was as tender as a mother.

"You are sweet and kind," she said, her hands dropping to take mine. "This task has been set before you and no other."

"Why?" I almost wailed. "Why me?"

"Ah." The sound slipped softly from her throat. A sound of quiet understanding, a moment of revelation. Her eyes shuttered closed and she released my hands to wipe her face. "Without understanding, we cannot find the courage to do what we must. You do not understand." Her eyes opened again and she looked me full in the face. "You do not know my story."

I shook my head.

She put her hands together and began to rub them back and forth. The sound of the dry skin of her palms gave me the shivers. She looked as though she was preparing to do something, warming up.

"I have strength enough to give one last gift," she said, now lifting her hands and blowing into her palms. "When you see, you shall have the strength to do what must be done."

Without another word, she reached for my face again. With the touch of her palms on my cheeks, the world around us blurred and all I could see were those large, dark, shining eyes. Eyes that were deeper than forever.

EIGHTEEN

Shaloris was seated on a wide flat rock a few meters above the teal water. Tender waves curling with foam kissed the edges of the red beach. A hot hard sun sent its heat and light down, undiluted by clouds. She pried the kernels from a head of grain snagged from a nearby field, popping them into her mouth and chewing them into a gum. The olive skin of her hands was tanned by hours in the sun.

A red-headed girl lay on her back nearby, her skirts lifted up to her thighs. Her eyes were closed as she basked in the sun, arms and shoulders bare. The sleeves of her tunic gown had been taken down and tucked under her arms. She'd made an effort to bind her thicket of wild red locks into a rope down her back, but short, tight curls sprang out in the humid air, framing her head and ears like a halo. The sun turned her hair to a bright copper fire. She had the porcelain skin of the Mer.

"Will you not swim, Mel?" asked Shaloris

Mel cracked an eye open and a green eye leveled on her friend. "Why do you refuse to call me by my true name?"

"I have known you as Mel since the day we were born. I cannot think of you any other way."

"You must," Mel replied, coming up to sitting. She got to her feet and began to untie the blue-green sash at her waist, the color of their father's house. "Mother says it is a sign of respect for a siren to be called by her full name."

"She said your *Sovereign* has to be called by her full name." Shaloris tossed her head, feeling her dark locks swaying against her back. "You are not Sisinyxa, you are just Mel."

"Eumelia," replied the other, dropping the sash and loosening the ties at her ribcage. "I am the king's daughter; I should be addressed with more respect than other sirens."

"And how should *I* be addressed in that case? I am also the king's daughter, should I invent a longer name to show I deserve reverence?" There was a teasing disdain in Shaloris' voice. It was not a new topic between the girls, and the teasing tone was not new either.

Eumelia shoved playfully at her sister's shoulder with her foot, shucking the last of her dress. She stood shamelessly naked in the sunlight.

"We do not randomly make up our siren names," Eumelia replied, eyes rolling and hands on slim hips. "The sea gives them to us."

A snort came from Shaloris in response to this. "Yes, the ocean gods hosted a ceremony and christened you thus." She lifted her arms and put on a serious, haughty expression. "No longer are you Mel, of your mother Hypatia and your father King Bozen the first, Defender of Atlantis and Protector of the Weak and Defenseless. You shall now be called Eumelia, thirteen-thousandth of your name, Minnow among the Many Mer."

Eumelia watched her sister's theatrics, a crooked smile

on her mouth. She even laughed, a little. "That's not how it happens and you know it."

"Right, you just *hear* it," Shaloris replied, the booming voice now gone but the disbelief still present.

"You're just jealous. You wish you were a siren, too."

Shaloris shrugged. "I like that you have a tail, you can escape this—" she gestured loosely at whatever lay behind and beyond them, "—whenever you want. But mother says I have magic." The darker girl's eyes glinted. "Magic more powerful than any Mer could hope to possess."

Eumelia burst out laughing. "You are Atlantean, what magic could you possibly have? You have these." The redhead pointed to her neck where a line of gills appeared and opened, waving as if saying hello. "So, you have less than half the magic that I have."

"She didn't mean that kind of magic," Shaloris replied, though she looked doubtful as to what kind of magic exactly her mother had been referring to.

Eumelia grew serious and thoughtful. "She does have something though, your mother," she said softly. "She is the only woman my own mother is afraid of, I think."

"Hypatia afraid of Valgana?" Shaloris scoffed. "What a joke."

Eumelia looked out to sea and was thoughtful for a time. The wind lifted their hair and raised gooseflesh on Eumelia's skin.

"They will try to separate us soon," said Shaloris quietly. She got to her feet and stood in front of her half-sister. "I heard them talking."

Eumelia's dark eyes widened with alarm. "Our mothers?"

"No, my mother and our father. He still comes to visit her sometimes." Shaloris cast a sidelong glance at her half-sister. It was not entirely devoid of impishness. "Does he ever visit Hypatia?"

Eumelia shook her head. "Sometimes she cries. I hear her at night. It's confusing because Father really loved her, and loves her still. I can tell." She gazed at the horizon, looking faraway and sad, but only for a moment. Her gaze snapped to her sister's face. "What did you overhear?"

"My mother wishes they had never let us play together. She says they should have raised us apart."

Eumelia cocked her head. "We both grew up at the palace, we shared nannies and tutors. It would have been impossible."

"When we were little," Shaloris lowered her voice, "my mother asked that you and Hypatia be sent away, to Okeanos perhaps. So you could be raised with your own people, instead of among Atlanteans and humans."

"I like living here," Eumelia insisted, taking her sister's hands. "I like Atlantean life. Besides, plenty of Mer choose to make their home here, not just us."

"You don't like the humans," Shaloris pulled her hands gently from her sister's grasp and averted her eyes from the siren's nakedness. Sometimes Eumelia's lack of modesty embarrassed her, though she tried to hide it. She wished she could be so free with her own body.

Eumelia shuddered. "No, they are vile and simple creatures."

"That's your mother talking."

Eumelia shrugged. "Maybe. But they are easy enough to avoid. Just don't go to the markets or the festival days. Stay at the palace or go to the temples."

"The markets and festivals are the most fun! I do wish you would come, just once."

"Mother would never allow it, and I would not care to

be among the human stink anyway." The girl's eyes sharpened and her look grew intense. "But we must not let them separate us. Let's make a blood pact!"

Shaloris frowned. "I'm not going to cut myself."

"It is better if we do. It will be more serious that way," Eumelia insisted.

Shaloris would not be convinced. "Let's just make a promise."

Eumelia rolled her eyes. "Fine, but the gods will not hear it."

"We'll hear it and that's all that matters."

The two girls crossed arms at the wrists and took opposite hands, giggling a little.

"You first," Shaloris said as the wind picked up their hair. Quite a sight the two girls would have looked to an observer. One girl tall and finely dressed in white and emerald green, her long hair blowing and swaying in the wind. Another girl with hair like a prairie fire, naked as the day she was born, her shape still lacking the curves of womanhood.

"I promise that no matter what my mother desires, she will never keep me from my sister, Shaloris."

"What about father?" whispered Shaloris, sounding serious and doubtful.

"Well," Eumelia hesitated, "he is the King, we must do what he says." She tossed her head and her face relaxed. "He would never do that anyway. It is our mothers who are at odds." She squeezed her sister's hands. "Your turn."

Giggling, Shaloris took some time to say her own version of the same words.

"Now kiss my cheeks, as I kiss yours. For a promise must be sealed with a kiss."

"Like a wedding?" Shaloris wrinkled her nose.

"Kind of like that." Eumelia puckered and leaned toward her sister. They exchanged a kiss for each cheek.

"Now tilt your head back to the sun, eyes closed," Eumelia instructed.

Shaloris obliged.

"Now spit into the wind." Eumelia made a rude horking sound in the back of her throat.

Shaloris burst out laughing. "Disgusting! You're just making things up."

Eumelia turned her head and spit in the direction of the wind, a fine round gob any farmer would have been proud of. "Well, you wouldn't do a blood pact." She shrugged. "There has to be some kind of body fluid involved."

Shaloris released her sister's hands. "I'll give you fluid," she cried, and shoved her sister hard toward the edge of the low overhang and the deep waiting water below.

Eumelia squealed with delight and turned her fall into a graceful dive.

Shaloris's eyes widened and her eyes hungrily took in the transformation that passed over her sister's frame in the space of time it took for her to hit the water's surface.

Eumelia's legs melted as if made of wax and quickly fused, transforming into a lime-green tail. It flashed wickedly in the sun. The splash was small as she slipped beneath the waves, leaving Shaloris to watch in amazement from above. Mel's lithe frame curved deep underwater and shot toward the surface, breeching in front of her sister and spinning for effect. Her long red braid had come undone and her hair was a rust-colored fan spraying droplets in every direction.

Shaloris gasped in amazement. She took off her own dress and jumped into the waves, making her own more subtle transformation. The girls played in the vast underwater world beyond their great city home and all talk of fathers and mothers, stinking humans, festivals and temples ceased. They were part of the ocean and its peace.

The sun had passed overhead and shadows were reaching their fingers across the land when Eumelia and Shaloris finally returned to the beach, two innocent children giggling together.

Eumelia spotted Hypatia and lost her smile. Her gaze and silence soon drew Shaloris's eyes as well. In a moment the girls were young princesses of Atlantis, and carefree no longer.

Hypatia did not approach; she stood on the steps and waited. Her unsmiling presence looking down like a stone gargoyle was enough to get the girls moving.

Eumelia dressed herself, and then helped Shaloris with her ties and her wet hair, looping it up and ribboning it on top of her head.

Shaloris climbed from the beach, acknowledging Hypatia from a distance with a wave. Hypatia did not acknowledge her in return. Shaloris walked the shoreline in the opposite direction, to where her caregivers waited with horses to return her to the heart of the city. She had her own mother waiting for her.

NINETEEN

Shaloris walked barefoot across the cool marble of the temple floor. In her upturned palms she held a woven basket full of fruit. The smell of summer's bounty filled her nose and she inhaled deeply before setting it on the floor beside a sparkling pool surrounded by other gifts.

Her chaperone and two Atlantean guards waited near a market stall not far away, probably drinking. The guards prevented any other visitors from entering the temple while the young princess was inside, unless of course those visitors were other royalty.

When Shaloris heard feminine voices and shoes being removed on the other side of the thick pillars separating the inner sanctum from the outer courtyard, she was consumed by a desperate desire to hide. Irrational as it was for an Atlantean princess to hide in a temple built by her own people, not even caring who it was she was hiding from, still she bolted. Driven by an impulse too complex to understand, she scampered from the inner sanctum and hid behind one of the many pillars on the opposite side of the courtyard.

The temple was open to the front, but backed by a solid wall of pink Ethiopian marble. No one would pass by her. She would wait until the other royal visitors left, and then she'd have the sanctum to herself again. Shaloris set her back against the marble and slid down until her bottom rested on the cold marble floor. Tilting her head back, she closed her eyes and waited.

There were sounds of baskets being set down and the water being touched, the ripples being watched while a question was held in the mind of the one who did the rippling. It was a ritual as old as Atlantis itself.

"You must make him a gift."

Shaloris' eyes popped open at the sudden sound of Hypatia's powerful voice. The siren made no effort to soften her tone for respect's sake.

"Mother, shhhh." It was Mel, of course. *Eumelia*, Shaloris corrected herself in her mind. It was still difficult to think of her sister as anyone but Mel. "You'll be heard."

"I want the gods to hear," Hypatia replied, not lowering her voice.

"I wasn't worried about the gods, so much as the people waiting outside."

"They are inconsequential. Why should we be ashamed of taking what is rightfully ours? I want the gods to know that I have seen the signs in the water. The throne will be yours, but you must make King Bozen a gift. An impressive one. One that no one else can make. One that he will love. One that will guarantee he will name you as his heir."

"Is there such a gift?" Eumelia asked, her voice thick with doubt.

Shaloris pressed her lips on one another in an effort to keep laughter from leaking out. It was silly of them to think that the next heir to the throne would be chosen based on a gift.

There was the sound of a small slap, and that was enough to choke off any humor Shaloris saw in the situation. Her dark brows drew down.

"Stupid girl," Hypatia muttered. "Must I do all of the thinking for you? Do you not want the throne?"

"What if I don't?" Eumelia responded, though her voice was haughtier than ever. Shaloris knew that Eumelia wanted it, she was just being difficult for her mother.

"Then you are an idiot who doesn't deserve it," Hypatia snapped back. "But you'll get it. You'll get it and I'll counsel you. You think I'll sit by and watch while Sisinyxa is given a place on the council?" The sound of a hiss followed this rhetorical question. "I'll be the first and only siren in Atlantean government."

There was a heavy silence and Shaloris was aching to peek around the column to see their faces. Did Hypatia realize her error?

"You mean...*I* will be the first and only siren in Atlantean government," Eumelia said. Her voice was soft but it was edged with steel.

"Yes, of course you. That's what I meant." Hypatia spoke quickly, skimming over her slip. "Even now Sisinyxa is weaseling her way in through Nestor, the idiot."

"She is Sovereign," replied Eumelia, with some shock in her tone. "Do you feel no love for her? No tie to the power the Salt gave her?"

"The Mer were meant for far more than those miserable, dank caves," Hypatia replied. There was the sound of flint on tinder and Shaloris knew they'd moved to the lighting of the three torches. Her voice softened a little.

"You'll see. We have given you a great gift, your father and I. He understands what it means. I've explained it to him."

"Explained..." Eumelia sounded as though she wanted to ask the question but was afraid of getting bit.

"What it means when an Atlantean and a siren really love one another. What it means for their child."

"You mean my gifts." Eumelia's voice moved to the far side of the temple.

Atlanteans who truly believed in the Atlantean pantheon would never talk so much in the temple, and certainly not about such political things in such a vulgar way. The Mer in the city did not really believe. Shaloris could see that, and it was obvious here in the way Eumelia and Hypatia went through the rituals of the temple so carelessly.

But then, would an Atlantean—one who truly believed the gods could see all—be hiding and eavesdropping within the temple, either? Shaloris felt shame heat her cheeks and wished she hadn't hidden herself. Why had she given in to such a childish impulse? An impulse borne of her desire to be invisible, unjudged. She had expected them to move through the rituals in silence and leave her in peace. Now she was in a bind. She wished she could run away, sneak out the back and hear no more. She didn't really care about the gift Hypatia was referring to, and she didn't want to hear any more of the siren's schemes. But she was stuck, and so she kept still.

"When the king chooses his heir, that heir will be accepted by the government. You'll be given a place on council, the place that Sisinyxa is trying so hard to claim." Hypatia's tone had grown thoughtful and searching, attempting to paint a clear picture of the future for her daughter. A path to power.

"You won't be given any say at first," she went on. "You'll have to wait until you are eighteen. But then you'll have a voice. Your words will carry more and more weight as time goes on. When he sees fit to step down, you'll be ready. I'll make sure of that."

"What of Shaloris?" her daughter responded.

Shaloris tensed, pushing her back up against the marble and making fists at her hips.

"What of her?" Hypatia's voice was dismissive. It sent a barb of anger through Shaloris's heart. "She is not suited to rule. She hardly speaks to anyone in public. She doesn't attend the parties hosted by the councilors or make the right friends, the way we've been doing since you were old enough to cut your food with your own knife."

"Father loves her," Eumelia responded, her voice earnest.

Shaloris squeezed her eyes shut and her heart swelled. She missed her half-sister. Eumelia was fiery and haughty, but they had grown up together. Every year that passed took them closer to womanhood and further from one another. They were on opposite sides of a war between only four people. A war most of Atlantis was unaware of, except for maybe its most astute politicians, the ones who could look ahead and predict things.

Shaloris wanted to leap out from behind the pillar and tell Hypatia that she was being awful. Tell her that she—Shaloris—did not want the throne anyway. There was no need for the scheming or the politicking. Couldn't she just leave them both alone?

"Of course he loves her, but that will not be what he bases his decision on. It will be based on strength, your willingness to step up and take power, wield it with confidence.

King Bozen admires courage and tenacity, boldness and craftiness."

"And what, if I should be chosen, would you want me to change? Atlantis is already the most powerful nation in the world. Is there so much work to be done?"

Hypatia cackled dryly and its sound was like ice-chips hitting Shaloris in the eardrums.

"There is always work to be done. Ousting all the wretched humans, for one thing."

Shaloris stifled a gasp of horror. Atlanteans and humans had built this city side by side. They had toiled together for hundreds of years to turn Atlantis from a small seaside village into a powerful nation where peoples of all kind were welcome. It was the Mer who had come along later, after the city had become what it was today. And now Hypatia was talking about getting rid of them? They were more than half the population and they were *needed*. They made up the bulk of Atlantis's inventors, creators, doctors, builders, lawyers. Without them, the city would not be Atlantis at all. And more humans entered the city every day, bringing their children and setting up homes and businesses in the city's bustling ports. They joined the army, delivered cargo, farmed the arable lands outside the city's borders, and fished its abundant seas.

Dislike was one thing, but why Hypatia could possibly want to get rid of them was beyond anything Shaloris could understand. The poisonous attitude had taken root in Eumelia at a young age. Shaloris had seen her draw back from them in the street, shudder when they passed, sniff as if she couldn't stand the smell. Eumelia's learned mindset was that humans were fragile, they died too quickly and easily, they had no magic. They were good only for serving, making things. They were like horses or cattle.

Shaloris's stomach clenched and her mouth felt dry. She was sickened by what she'd heard and she wondered if she had the right to hide any longer. Not from Eumelia and Hypatia, but from her destiny and her magic. Did she not have a duty to protect the humans of Atlantis if they were in danger? Did a human not deliver her from her mother's womb? Did a human not feed her and care for her and teach her all manner of wonderful things?

Something quaked deep inside Shaloris and now she was afraid. Afraid of what it would mean if Eumelia became King Bozen's heir. But she was also afraid of what it would mean if she stepped up and showed that she wanted it. What would it mean if she claimed her magic? How would she change? Would it give her the courage she lacked?

TWENTY

The day of King Bozen's name day baked under the summer sun, heat bouncing off the white marble at the center of Atlantis.

Atlantis was a sprawling but organized metropolis, with a main port to the ocean and an outer and inner ring of riverways. These passageways for deliveries in and out of Atlantis were wide and deep. With many ports along its waterfront, it was easy to distribute goods and travelers to anywhere in Atlantis. The very center of Atlantis was reserved for wealthy residences, glittering temples, and rich gardens fed with freshwater diverted from the high waterfalls to the north. Fresh spring water both hot, from the thermals, and cold, from deeper underground, was fed through pipelines to every home. Everyone, no matter how young or old, how rich or poor, had access to fresh water. Every family was given a small plot of land for a garden. Sometimes only a few square meters of soil, but it was enough to feed four if well-tended.

At the heart of Atlantis was an exquisite temple with fat

white pillars and a huge dome with an oculus. This way nothing would be hidden from the gods and all activities would be lit with either sunlight or moonlight. Directly beneath the oculus was a pool fed directly from the ocean itself. Saltwater, though a deity for the Mer, was also revered by Atlanteans, for the ocean is what gave the nation its power.

Shaloris stood beside her mother, Valgana, both of them resplendent in white robes. Their long dark hair was half piled on top of their heads and festooned with white flowers. Valgana held a golden goblet inlaid with the stone of Atlantis—aquamarines. At her throat was a fine golden chain from which dangled an aquamarine pendant.

The temple was abuzz with excitement as the most elite citizens and guests from afar partook of the King's feast.

Shaloris was full to bursting after the feast. It had included fish baked in lemon and butter, roast lamb, tender sea vegetables, soft salty cheese from the northern highland goats, fresh cucumbers dressed with sweet vinegar and fresh herbs, and sweet wine made from almonds. Within reach at any moment were trays carrying piles of black and green grapes, bowls of olives soaking in oil, fresh soft figs, and tender roasted chicken on little wooden skewers. The place smelled of many tantalizing foods, as well as salt from the ocean-fed pool in the center of the party.

King Bozen had come down from his seat to drink with his councilors.

Hypatia and Eumelia leaned against a pillar on the far side of the room. Whenever Hypatia's gaze passed over King Bozen, her eyes filled with a longing so obvious that Shaloris flushed and turned away. It was embarrassing. Shaloris tried several times to catch Eumelia's eye, but her sister was pointedly ignoring her. Instead she and her mother were in near constant whispered conversation as Hypatia educated Eumelia on the who's who of Atlantean aristocracy.

Valgana had already introduced Shaloris to each guest in turn, taking her time and moving slowly through the party before the meal began. She'd told Shaloris that people would remember her better if they were not distracted by the food. Shaloris thought this was probably true. So the bulk of their mingling was finished before the incredible platters of food were brought in. Shaloris felt exhausted from all the talking and smiling and wondered when it would be okay to leave the party and go back to the quiet of her home. Maybe even climb the cliffside to the high temples overlooking the ocean and relax in the stillness while most people were occupied with the nighttime celebrations. She knew better than to ask her mother for permission to leave.

Valgana took Shaloris's hand and led her to a place not far from the king's right hand. There they'd have a good view of all the wonderful things the king would be presented with. At the mention of gifts, Shaloris glanced at Hypatia and Eumelia again, and noticed they were maneuvering themselves to the edge of the pool.

Representatives of surrounding nations and beyond jostled themselves into position, waiting to present the gifts they'd taken great pains to bring from as far away as the Pelopponese cities, the sea-states of the Aegean and the Mediterranean. Even the exotic and unimagined places of the south where skin was dark, the languages unique, and the magic mysterious and earthy.

Men and women in colorful costumes and headdresses

gave skins of spotted animals; huge ivory tusks decorated with gold; yards and yards of brightly dyed handmade textiles; barrels of fine spirits, nut oils, and vinegars. Colorful spices filled the air with warming scents. One king from an island with a name Shaloris could not pronounce led a great stallion that looked like he'd been painted with gold. When the sun's rays illuminated the animal, the crowd gave a pleasing gasp, for the truth was revealed. The horse had not been painted, but had a naturally glittering coat, even to the curly long hair over its hooves. King Bozen appeared appropriately awed.

When Shaloris and Valgana took their turn, King Bozen was effusive with his appreciation for the tailored and newly dyed purple robe they'd had made, and the tunic of aquamarine silk. Once Shaloris had returned to her place, she felt she could relax and enjoy the rest of the celebrations with her part out of the way. She took a sip of the wine a servant had placed on the table beside her and made herself comfortable in her seat.

When the king's herald announced the Sovereign of Okeanos, Sisinyxa of the nation of the Mer, Shaloris straightened and strained for a good view. The herald also announced Sisinyxa's husband, Ajax.

They approached King Bozen in a little more silence than the other guests. The Sovereign of Okeanos was a great mystery. Shaloris had heard that no one even knew where Okeanos was, that it was completely hidden beneath the water, that it was a place of great rich mines.

Sisinyxa was a striking woman with a powerful bearing. She was not overly tall, but with her shoulders back and the way the light illuminated her flawless complexion, she was positively regal. She wore a simple dove-gray dress fastened at one shoulder with a clasp made of the precious yellow metal from her own mines. The fabric was not embroidered or dyed, just flowing and clean. It fell to the floor and moved like a ghostly curtain as she walked on unadorned feet. Her hair fell in gleaming waves over her shoulders, and a fine circlet of the yellow metal encircled her forehead.

Every male eye followed the Sovereign of Okeanos the way moths throw themselves against candlelight.

Shaloris tore her hungry gaze from Sisinyxa to drink in Sisinyxa's husband, Ajax. Tall and lean, with the same unblemished skin as his wife, Ajax walked silently across the marble. A dark-blue skirt covered him from waist to knees, but that was all. He moved the way Shaloris had seen cats pick their way across the rooftops. Smooth and liquid. He looked like a statue come to life. In his hands he carried a beautiful, tall box that was strange in its own way. Only the frame of it was solid, while the sides were made of a rough fabric pulled tight and fastened to a frame of yellow metal.

Sisinyxa spoke. It was brief and she did not raise her voice, so all those present strained to hear her. Shaloris thought her voice was like music. Sisinyxa wished the king a happy name day and a prosperous year.

Ajax set the box upright and it was nearly as tall as Ajax himself. With a tug, he unfastened the fabric and it fell away from the box.

A murmur passed through the crowd as their eyes took in the bright yellow armor. Aquamarines lined the neck of the gleaming breastplate. The set included a scabbard, greaves to protect the shins, vambraces for the wrists and forearms, and a perfectly round shield which was so bright in the sunlight one could hardly look at it without squinting.

Aquamarine gemstones had been laid in the shield, outlining the shape of Atlantis—three concentric circles.

As King Bozen thanked and embraced Sisinyxa and Ajax, and could not keep himself from trying on the set of vambraces, Shaloris whispered in her mother's ear.

"It's so yellow, surely it's not gold." Shaloris knew that solid gold made poor armor. Some wealthy Atlanteans plated their armor with it because it was pretty and a sign of wealth, but gold itself was too soft to be good protection in battle.

Valgana whispered back, "It's orichalcum. It's much harder, and more valuable even, than gold."

When Sisinyxa and Ajax had done their part, Shaloris watched them slip to the back of the room and wait there a few moments until the stares dropped away from them to focus on the next gift. Then they quietly slipped away.

The gifting was coming to an end. Remarkable and exotic things piled up on the tables at the outer walls behind the king's seat, and servants had begun to slip in and take them away.

Shaloris fought to keep her eyelids from drooping. She was full and tired. She stirred when her mother's arm slipped around her waist and squeezed her, bidding her to pay attention. One gift was left, and Eumelia and Hypatia had stepped forward. Shaloris came fully awake. Of course Hypatia had waited until the very end; that way Eumelia's gift would be the last one to be given and the one soonest remembered.

"King Bozen, may your years be long and prosperous and your name day full of joy," Hypatia began, launching into a rather drawn-out birthday blessing.

Shaloris stole a glance at her father's expression. King Bozen had retreated to his seat and reclined with one hand resting at the base of his goblet of wine. His other hand was at his jaw, his knuckles curled under but his index finger poised thoughtfully against his lips. His kind gray eyes focused only on Hypatia as she spoke. Shaloris saw with some disappointment that his expression was dripping with love, even if it was tinged with sadness.

She felt her mother stiffen beside her and wondered how painful it was for her to see the king gazing upon her rival with such affection.

Shaloris wanted to ask why the king had set aside Hypatia if he loved her so much. Was it because she was Mer? The rumors of the city said she had magic to hold him, something beyond even the magic sirens had over humans. Perhaps his own councilors were afraid that she had been controlling him.

Both Hypatia and Eumelia had empty hands, and there was no gift box or basket anywhere near them.

"Our daughter, the Princess Eumelia, wishes to bestow upon you a gift of great value, one only she can provide. I beg you wait and watch with some patience, my King." With this, Hypatia gestured dramatically to where her daughter stood at the ocean pool's edge, directly across from King Bozen.

Bozen's eyes moved from Hypatia to where Eumelia stood with her head held high and proud. Shaloris could see her chest rise and fall. The skin of her forehead and cheeks glowed with a thin sheen of perspiration. Eumelia lifted her hands slowly, her fingers moving elegantly, but she did not tear her eyes from her father's face.

The room seemed to hold its breath, waiting for...what? Was she going to dance and sing? Atlanteans loved theatre, and leaned forward eagerly, their eyes on the young woman with the hair like fire and skin like marble.

Shaloris's skin prickled and her pulse quickened as Eumelia's eyes shifted from green to bright blue. A moment later, the room reacted with a sigh of amazement. King Bozen leaned forward in his seat, enthralled.

"Look the water!" someone cried.

The water in the ocean pool was moving in a circle. Little sloshing sounds began to fill the air as the whirlpool picked up speed. A divot formed in the centre as Eumelia's hands moved in the air, manipulating the water...bending it to her will.

Another gasp rose as a thin line of water, no wider than a pinky finger, crept upward from the centre of the whirlpool. It climbed and climbed, defying gravity until it reached eye level. At the top of the staff of water, a bright blue glow appeared like a star. It grew bright but never lost its teal color. It began to fatten and crawl outward in both directions, making an intricate symmetrical pattern. The bright blue thing widened and then curled upward at the edges. A hole appeared in its center, making a ring. Not a ring...

"It's a crown! Oh, wonderful!"

The voice was right. Eumelia was turning the ocean water into a bright blue crown filled with light—aquamarine—Atlanteans' own royal gemstone. ·

"Clever girl," Valgana whispered under her breath, and Shaloris felt her mother's grip tighten around her waist.

Taking her time, Eumelia made a display of crafting the crown with a practiced artfulness. Shaloris wondered how long she'd spent working with this magic in secret. Deep in her heart, a small, cold seed of fear took root.

Was it just a crown? Or was there some other kind of magic infused into this crown? Might it actually make a difference in King Bozen's choice? Was there a way

Hypatia and Eumelia could sway his decision with this spectacular magic? Or was it a trick, simply done to impress and make everyone remember Eumelia? Her name would be on everyone's lips for a long time to come, and she'd forever be the young woman who made King Bozen a crown out of saltwater, turning it into Atlantis's own most-valued gemstone the way alchemists had tried and failed to turn substances into gold. Surely this was a woman touched by the gods. Surely, she would be the next ruler of Atlantis. She would be the first female ruler of the great ocean nation and she'd be accepted by even the men of the council, because she'd been witnessed doing great things.

The crown was soon complete, and it spun on watery fingers as the pool itself passed the crown to its edge where Bozen only had to get up and step forward to take it.

Suddenly, Hypatia was there, fingers reaching out to take the crown from its watery perch. She plucked it like it was a ripe fruit and the water holding it up sank slowly back into the pool. The whirling water slowed and grew still.

Holding the crown aloft, Hypatia walked slowly toward King Bozen, who waited for her solemnly.

King Bozen got up from his seat and then went to his knees so Hypatia could reach his head. The circlet of orichalcum on his head was removed and taken away by a servant. With great drama and ceremony, Hypatia settled the glowing aquamarine crown on King Bozen's bright red curls.

"To your name day, to your long life, to your reign." Hypatia's voice rose and fell like a wind through stringed instruments.

The crowd was galvanized. They got to their feet and the room erupted with applause and shouts of congratulations. People were smiling and laughing and talking to one another about the remarkable magic they'd witnessed. This was not something one saw everyday, from the king's own daughter, did you know?

Eumelia and Hypatia shared a triumphant look.

Shaloris began to wither.

TWENTY-ONE

A fortnight after King Bozen's name day celebration, a servant from the palace whispered to Shaloris, "The king will visit you this evening."

Shaloris felt honored and a little frightened. She'd not been close to her father as she grew up. He'd always been good to her, loving and kind, generous and sweet. But he'd not raised her and the relationship had been one of princess and king more than daughter and father. She'd observed his rule from a distance, and had learned much from him that way. But as a man, he was a mystery to her.

Stealing a glance in one of her mirrors, she was pleased to see the color still high in her cheeks after having spent much of the day outdoors. Her curls were still in place and the wispy robe of greens and blues was tidy. The day had been warm and lovely and she'd begged her tutors to take their lessons outside. They'd agreed and moved to the gardens at the back of the palace. When her lessons were over, Shaloris had gone to one of the larger parks, flanked by two guards and a chaperone, as she always was when she left palace grounds. She could ask them to walk far enough behind her that she could forget they were there, and if she went to the ocean, she could ask them to remain where she could not see them. She'd not always been trailed this way, cossetted like a precious jewel who might at any time get snatched away. The extra security had been added only in the past year. Valgana had told her that the security had been added to Eumelia as well.

Shaloris settled in her sitting area, an airy room with a high ceiling and filled with the warm flickering light of torches. A cluster of lounge chairs sat around a low marble table topped with a gigantic vase filled with sea-lillies. Their sweet, fresh fragrance filled the room, and their pastel blue and green hues soothed the eye.

"King Bozen," announced a lady servant.

Shaloris stood when he entered her sitting area. Then she crossed to him and knelt before him, taking his hand and holding her forehead to the back of it.

She felt his warm hand on the back of her head and smiled at the floor. She had never had time completely alone with her father before. Shaloris stood and invited him to find a place to relax. After waiting until he chose a seat, she gestured to the tray sitting on the low table.

"Would you like some wine?" she asked, and was pleased to find her voice steady.

But King Bozen shook his head. "Thank you, please sit."

Shaloris did. She surveyed her father. His hair looked a dark copper in the firelight, and his skin a burnished bronze. King Bozen was sometimes called 'The Bright King' because he had unusual coloring. His hair was the kind of glinting red that was normally paired with pale, freckly skin. But his skin was tanned and smooth in tone. His gray-green eyes were pale and reflected any light in the room. 'The Bright King' was a name which suited him.

When she looked at her father, she saw Eumelia. The tanned skin and the red curls, only Eumelia's eyes were an otherworldly green. They were the kind of vivid shade Shaloris had only ever seen in Mer people. Atlantis had its share of Mer citizens, and they were easily spotted by their skin and their eyes. It was the Atlanteans and the humans who were impossible to tell apart.

"I thought it was time we had a private talk," King Bozen began, after clearing his throat. He knotted his fingers together.

Shaloris realized with a jolt that he was nervous, and this in turn made her nervous. What was so important that he'd have to say it in private and in person?

"I'm listening, Father King," she replied, hoping the strength of her voice would help him say whatever had to be said.

"It is a strange and wondrous thing," her father went on, "how you and your sister came to be born at the same moment of the same day."

Shaloris knew the story well. As a young king, Bozen could choose whomever he liked to bring to his bedchamber. Unwed and not yet taking the idea of a bride seriously, King Bozen had been drawn by Valgana's beauty and magic. But he'd fallen in love with Hypatia, madly and deeply, or so Shaloris had heard. Shaloris felt the old questions rise in her mind like bubbles exhaled underwater. Why then had he set Hypatia aside?

"I liked your mother very much," Bozen said. His eyes reflected the torchlight, and Shaloris thought they seemed bright with moisture. "Valgana is a wonderful woman of many gifts and it is easy to see who gave you your beauty. I am sure your talents may even one day surpass your mother's, so well you've been raised and cared for."

By talents, Shaloris knew he meant her Atlantean magic. The magic she herself had not yet claimed and was a little afraid of.

"You know that I have a difficult decision to make," King Bozen said.

He's preparing to reject me, Shaloris thought. *He's going to choose Eumelia for the crown. Why else would he be flattering me?*

Her breathing remained steady but she felt suddenly caught in a thicket full of emotional thorns: dismay and hurt at the rejection, relief that she'd not need to bear such a heavy burden, and fear at what Eumelia and Hypatia might one day do with the power which would pass to them.

"Already I have delayed too long, my councilors warn me," King Bozen said with a dry chuckle.

Wanting to ease her father's discomfort, Shaloris spoke. "I think I understand, Father."

"You do?"

"Yes. Hypatia was your true love, therefore Eumelia must be your heir."

He seemed to freeze in place for a moment, then he smiled. "No, little minnow. I'm doing a terrible job, forgive me."

King Bozen moved to a chair closer to Shaloris. He took her hand in both of his big ones.

"I did love Hypatia," King Bozen admitted. "*Do*, for the gods know I love her still, with all my heart."

"But...you set her aside."

"I had to. My councilors convinced me that to remain so close to a siren was not in the best interests of our people."

"We have sirens among our population." Shaloris shifted in her seat to face her father more directly. "They are part of our people, the diversity that gives Atlantis its strength."

"Yes, but there are far less of them than there are of us, and the humans living among us. The Mer are wild, unpredictable, and in possession of some powers that are not fully understood. My government does not wish me to be manipulated by one of them. To remain impartial and in full control of my own faculties and judgment, I separated myself from Hypatia. It is one of the most difficult things I have ever had to do. To be honest, I am not entirely sure why Hypatia has not taken Eumelia and gone to Okeanos. It is their way."

"I can tell you why."

Bozen looked at her for a moment, then dipped his head in appreciation of her honesty. "Yes, you are right. I know as well. But, Shaloris, I cannot give them what they want."

Shaloris's stomach went into a tumble of somersaults. Her heart began to pound almost painfully and her armpits felt suddenly damp.

"Do not look so afraid!" King Bozen looked alarmed. "You will not be required to rule for a very long time, unless something should happen to me."

"Gods, no," she wheezed.

He smiled and touched her cheek for that.

"But, you could yet take a wife," she went on, "and father many other children."

Her words were tripping over themselves in her desperation to convince him to change his mind. Suddenly her concern for what Hypatia and Eumelia would do with the crown evaporated and all she wanted in that moment was to be released from the colossal weight she felt moving into place overhead.

"I can't."

Shaloris blinked in surprise. "Can't?"

"I can't have any more children." King Bozen said this with some sadness but appeared remarkably composed. Like it was old news, news he'd come to terms with a long time ago.

"How do you know? You already fathered two daughters."

"I just can't. I know." His tone was blunt enough that Shaloris understood the subject to be closed. "I will not choose Eumelia because her mother has poisoned her mind. She is not suitable to rule. They do not know that I have ears all over this city, and I know their true feelings toward our people."

The humans, Shaloris thought.

"They would be the destruction of Atlantis as we know it today."

There was a prophetic ring to his words, one that echoed in Shaloris's mind on repeat. The hair on the back of her neck spindled upright. Her forearms, legs, feet, and hands felt chilled.

"I need you to be the queen Atlantis will need once I step down."

Her father, the mighty King Bozen, slid off his seat and went to his knees in front of her. He took her other hand, which was now as cold as ice and trembling. He looked up into her face.

"I can see that you do not want it," he said softly, "but my daughter, you are my chosen. You will not be alone, not ever. And you will have me at your side, teaching you and showing you a way to rule that you can then adapt for yourself when the time comes. Will you do me the honor of stepping into the role of heir to the throne of Atlantis?"

What could Shaloris say? Her own eyes misted up and

though her voice trembled and she was terrified, she said, "You humble me."

King Bozen's face broke into a grin so wide and happy, it was like a whale suddenly breaching the flat calm of the ocean. He pulled her into his arms and held her next to his solid warmth.

She realized in that moment that he'd truly been afraid she'd reject him. And if she had? He'd have had no choice.

Her heart thumped against his and for a moment, they were bonded in what only the two of them in all the world knew.

Shaloris pulled back. "Can we keep it a secret a while longer?"

Her father touched her cheek in that way he had. "For a little while, my minnow. But I will have to make an announcement within the month. The council grows restless, and a restless council is not a good thing. They will not be settled until they know. They are planners, the lot of them."

He stood and brought her to her feet as well.

"I will have you come to meet them in private before I make the announcement. They must know before anyone else in the city learns."

Shaloris nodded, thinking it was the last thing in the world she'd go shouting from the rooftops.

King Bozen kissed his quaking heir goodnight, and left her to her thoughts.

TWENTY-TWO

Shaloris heard her mother Valgana come in calling to her daughter, a smile in her voice. Hearing her mother from where she was taking a breath of night air on the terrace, Shaloris entered her rooms and gave her mother a hug. Shaloris had been keeping the secret even from Valgana. Tonight, Shaloris would tell her mother, for King Bozen had made the announcement to the council that day. Tomorrow she would be presented to the people and it would be a secret no more.

Shaloris dreaded Eumelia and Hypatia's reaction, but it couldn't be helped.

"I'm glad you're here." Shaloris took the heavy basket covered by a blanket from her mother's hands and set it on the floor. Taking Valgana by the wrist, she pulled her to where they could sit facing one another. "There is something I need to tell you."

Valgana's robes rustled as she sat down, a knowing smile on her face. "I'm listening."

Shaloris took a breath and told the story of King Bozen's visit, trying to relay her father's words exactly to her mother.

Valgana listened without reacting.

"I'm to rule Atlantis one day, Mother," Shaloris finished, a tremble in her voice.

Valgana put both of her palms on her daughter's cheeks. "And what a queen you shall make, my love."

Shaloris studied her mother's dark eyes. "You knew?"

Valgana released Shaloris and took her hands. "King Bozen did not visit Eumelia's rooms."

"How do you know that?"

Valgana gave Shaloris a sly look. "There is not much that happens in this palace without my knowing about it, Shaloris. You too can have this power."

"But why should the king not visiting her rooms mean that he would be choosing me? It could easily have meant that he came to me to temper my disappointment ahead of time."

Valgana shook her head. "I know him," she said quietly. "Don't forget we were once lovers. The king does not like to deliver bad news, and often has his states-people do it for him. In this case, I knew that wanting a private moment with you meant that he wanted to see your face when he told you he'd be choosing you as his heir."

Shaloris's mouth quirked up in a smile. "I was not exactly happy about it."

"Do you still feel this way?"

Shaloris lifted a shoulder in a half-shrug. "I have had a month to become accustomed to the idea that I shall have to work to become a good queen. I was afraid because I was imagining the expectations being set upon me would be enormous from the start. But, truly, provided the king does not encounter an untimely death, I will have decades, perhaps even a century or longer, to learn from him. Surely, by then I shall know what I am doing."

"You are already showing the wisdom of a queen, my sweet girl," Valgana replied. "You do have time, and you can ask all manner of questions and take part in every council meeting. You know deep in your heart what an honor you have been given, and how much you can influence the happiness of your people and the strength of your nation."

Something like determination fluttered at the edges of Shaloris's heart as she agreed with her mother.

They sat quietly for a moment, listening to the night insects and the call of the birds of peace.

"The king said he could no longer father children," Shaloris ventured, keeping her voice almost at a whisper.

Valgana's brow pinched and she blinked in surprise. "Really? He told you this?"

Shaloris nodded.

"Did he say why?"

"No, and it didn't feel like I should ask."

Valgana chewed her lip. "This is news to me, I must admit. I cannot think of any reason why he should not be able to have many more children."

"Perhaps when he was ill with a fever, two seasons ago?" Shaloris ventured.

Valgana looked doubtful.

A whine penetrated the darkness.

Shaloris sat up straight in surprise. "What was that?" Her eye fell on the basket. "What have you got in here?"

"Ah, this is the reason for my visit," Valgana replied, releasing her daughter's hands and getting up to fetch the basket. "It is a gift for my daughter, the heir."

Shaloris waited for her mother to sit with the basket on her lap. She scooted forward to the edge of the seat.

"A gift that whines?"

Valgana pulled back the blanket to reveal a puppy. Two

sets of eyes blinked up at Shaloris in the sudden light and one of the heads gave a whine. The puppy put its paws up on the edge of the basket and reached its noses out to sniff.

"Oh!" Shaloris squealed with pleasure and picked up the squirming pup, not much larger than a squirrel. "An Atlantean hound! He must have cost a fortune!"

The two-headed dogs were native only to Atlantis and forbidden to be traded or sold outside the city. Only royalty and aristocrats had the right to own the breed. One of the reasons they were so expensive was because they were reputed to have magic, though only those who owned one were told of this magic by the breeder—Tesya.

"He was not cheap, but Tesya and I have been friends a long time. He wanted you to have the pup as well. He's the smartest of the litter, or so Tesya says." Valgana smiled widely as she watched her daughter kiss and stroke the puppy.

"I shall have to think of a clever name for you," Shaloris told the puppy. "Show me your nature and within a week, I'll have the perfect name. I promise."

"If the myths are to be believed, the Atlantean hound lives as long as the one it bonds to," Valgana said. "He'll protect and love you for your entire life."

Shaloris gasped in amazement. "Is it true?"

"Tesya says yes. King Bozen has had his hound Lia for twenty-three years already and she's still as spry as a pup."

"How marvelous!" Shaloris put her forehead to the foreheads of the puppy and stroked his ears. "What other magics do you have, wee one?"

"They are fierce in battle, as loyal as it is possible to be, and they never get lost. No matter how far apart you may become separated, he will always be able to find you. He will protect you with his life."

"And does he like to swim?" Shaloris asked.

"Naturally." Valgana laughed. "He is Atlantean."

Shaloris put the puppy down and watched him sniff her feet and wander around exploring his new home. She hugged her mother.

"Thank you, he's the most spectacular gift I have ever received. I'll take good care of him."

"I know you will. Every monarch of Atlantis has had an Atlantean hound, and you shall be no different."

"I'm not a monarch yet."

"No, but the King gave me permission to give you the hound early," Valgana answered and her voice glinted with something hard.

Shaloris watched the puppy sit on his haunches and one of the mouths open wide in a yawn. "Are you sure this is not rubbing our victory in Eumelia's face?"

"You should not concern yourself with what Eumelia or Hypatia will think or feel or say," Valgana replied. "Eumelia is nothing more now than the king's bastard daughter, and Hypatia nothing more than a past dalliance."

"They are confident that Eumelia will be queen," Shaloris murmured, "I would not want to be anywhere near them when they find out."

Valgana rose and dropped a kiss on her daughter's head. "You won't be. You'll be standing beside your father the king. Now get some rest. It's a big day tomorrow and you need to look well-rested and beautiful."

———

THE DAY of her designation was hot and the air was still. Not a breeze flicked the leaves on the fig trees or lifted the water to lap along the stone canals of Atlantis. It was still not yet noon. A songbird could be heard outside the window, and calls from the flower sellers in the street below.

"You must wear white today." Valgana bustled happily about Shaloris's rooms, sifting through dresses and hair pieces.

The Atlantean hound sat under the window, both tongues lolling out and both heads panting as he lay on his side in a sliver of shade.

Shaloris sat nervously watching in the mirror while one of her ladies wrestled her long hair into coils of braids on top of her head. Teasing out a few of the curls softened the sharp planes of Shaloris's face. Valgana had directed the maid to leave some long waves hanging down Shaloris's back.

"Why white?"

"White says purity, integrity, virtue..." Valgana's voice dimmed as she disappeared inside the room that held shelves of dresses, wraps, and sashes. She returned, holding up a simple sleeveless white gown of layers of gauze. Even the fine spiderweb fabric barely stirred in the close air. "It will say you are a clean slate, ready to learn and stand at your father's side as he prepares you for your future."

"All that from a color?" Shaloris replied with a smile.

"All that and more," Valgana replied, laying the dress out on the bed. "Never underestimate how powerful an impression your physical person gives to all who lay eyes on you."

Within the hour, Shaloris stood as her mother tied a thick belt of leather discs rimmed with orichalcum at her waist. Shaloris's skin dewed fetchingly with a light layer of sweat, but Shaloris thought that another hour or two and she'd look more like a greasy rat than a glowing young woman.

"Why must they always have these things under the hottest sun of the day?" Shaloris grumbled, brushing a damp curl back from her forehead.

"High noon is a moment full of promise and power," Valgana explained. "And speaking of which, let's not delay." She ushered her daughter from her rooms and down the long halls leading to the palace foyer where a carriage waited to take them to the center of Atlantis.

It was a day for celebration and anticipation. Happy citizens lined the streets to wave as the carriages trundled by. Shaloris and Valgana rode in a carriage pulled by four horses. The prancing beasts had been dusted with crushed marine powders, changing their white hides into glittering blues and greens.

Valgana waved at the crowds, but Shaloris remained in her seat, under the shadow of the carriage-top, too shy still to show her face to the people.

The carriage took them through the long, curved streets, over a bridge toward the innermost circle of Atlantis and the gates of the central temple. Citizens crowded against the yellow gates of orichalcum but were not allowed inside.

A long line of similar carriages moved slowly along the temple front. Beautifully dressed aristocrats and council members were helped down from their coaches and walked slowly between the tall narrow trees. Some of them waved to the cheering citizens, others remained unsmiling with gazes forward, solemn and serious.

When her feet alighted on the stone and she began the long walk beside her mother, Shaloris craned her neck in search of the red hair of her half-sister.

"Do not gawk." Valgana tugged on Shaloris's hand. "A princess of Atlantis does not goggle like a common person."

Shaloris returned her gaze demurely to the head in front

of her and made the long walk in silence and stillness. At the top of the temple steps, Valgana and Shaloris were directed to the far side of the intimate amphitheater where some of Atlantean law was discussed and debates were held. It was the same room where King Bozen's name day had been celebrated.

Servants holding massive feathered fans stood at every pillar, waving continuously and lifting the air in the room to cool the guests. Seats had been erected in semicircular rings not unlike the layout of Atlantis itself. Valgana and Shaloris made their way to the far side of the front row.

It was then that Shaloris spotted the red hair of Eumelia, at the other end of the front row. Her sister looked every bit a queen. Her unruly curls had somehow been humbled and forced slick against her head. Her hair was tied up and back and topped with a circlet of orichalcum glittering with aquamarines. She too had chosen to wear white, but her gown was anything but plain. It caught the light and shimmered and was tight to Eumelia's body even as it twisted around her like a column from chest to knees. Lace dangled from the hem in delicate floating trim and the same lace dangled from the back of her head. The bodice of her gown was encrusted with aquamarines and diamonds, glittering as she turned this way and that. Kohl lined her eyes and colored powders accented her cheekbones and lips.

Eumelia's eyes drifted about the room until she found Shaloris, but they lingered only a moment. Though Shaloris smiled, Eumelia did not.

Hypatia took her seat at her daughter's side, resplendent in a green gown of heavy fabric which must have been baking her body inside it.

King Bozen was the last to enter, and just as everyone

had found their seats, they were required to stand again. He was smiling and nodding at friends as he passed through the crowd, around the pool in the center and up to his seat upon the dais.

This was not only a day for announcing the chosen heir to the Atlantean throne, but also a day for acknowledging the contributions of other citizens to the betterment of the nation.

Shaloris felt herself wilt as two council members whose names she'd already forgotten awarded titles, lands, and gifts to various people in the room. She wanted to whisper to her mother that she wished she'd been warned the ceremony would be so long, but she knew better than to complain. Her mother would have no tolerance for whining, especially today.

King Bozen barely spoke during the first hour of the proceedings. He rose to kiss his citizens on the cheek, to grasp elbows, to hug. Sometimes Shaloris could hear the deep rumble of his voice as he murmured something only the one being recognized could hear.

Shaloris felt herself grow sleepy. She fought to keep her eyelids from drooping and her mind from wandering.

Suddenly, out of a long drone of toneless words, someone had said her name in an authoritative voice. Her mother was pressing urgently on her elbow, almost lifting her from her seat. People were getting to their feet all around her and the sound of applause and some shouts of her name injected her with adrenaline so powerfully that her limbs shook as she got to her feet.

She took the steps up to the dais on quaking legs, to where her father stood with his arms open for her. Stepping into his embrace, she blinked numbly as he kissed her cheeks and murmured words she could hardly comprehend in her ear. Her father laughed and gently turned her to face the room.

Before her, every face was alight, and she felt her heart thrumming in her chest. Her shallow breath made her feel dizzy.

Someone had her by the hand and something cold was being slipped onto the index finger of her right hand. It was her father, slipping the heir's ring on her finger. Bright yellow orichalcum cradling a large flat stone of aquamarine bearing the seal of Atlantis—an upright trident. Only the king had a ring like it. His was slightly larger, and his trident had a crown imposed behind it, blending its forks with the tines of the crown. Shaloris could use this ring to seal letters, give commands. Even before she became queen, she would have a breathtaking power.

Her body grew warm as she looked up into her father's smiling face. He held her beringed hand in his, turned to face the crowd, and lifted the ring to shoulder level, holding it above his own.

The glittering eyes and teeth of the crowd caught her gaze as it flitted around the room. She never expected the previously solemn crowd to come to life, to fill with excitement on her behalf.

It hit her square in the chest then, like a soundwave from the blast of a war-horn. The citizens of Atlantis had wanted this. They had wanted *her*. And they were her people now, as much as they were her father's.

She felt her heart grow full to bursting, and her skin prickled with determination. She would do everything in her power to make King Bozen proud and to do right by her people. She was not only his chosen heir, she would be the first queen. Even when she took a husband, a foreigner chosen to strengthen Atlantis's position in the world, her husband's power would not equal her own.

As these thoughts flew about the edges of her consciousness, Shaloris did notice a few faces in the crowd whose smiles seemed frozen and uncertain. Most were the elder men of the council. They were not ready for a queen. Shaloris made a silent promise that she would be ready for them. She would show them that a queen could and would rule justly.

But there was another face, another set of eyes, and these ones did not make an attempt to disguise their ire for and jealously of the new heir. She had almost forgotten about Eumelia in the blur of celebration. The siren's beautiful face had turned ugly, and there was poison in her eyes. Her own mother's expression could not match Eumelia's face in hatred.

Shaloris swallowed and looked away, her smile faltering. Blinking back tears, she focused anywhere but at her half-sister, but her body felt like she had been struck with ice water, despite the heat of the day.

The hubbub lessened as the crowd settled into their seats again. Servants began to move through the crowd carrying trays of red wine. The real celebration could begin now. A group of musicians stood waiting to set themselves up to play.

But as the citizens took their seats, one redhead remained standing. Eumelia's glare iced first Shaloris and then the king.

The conversation faded further as people noticed the king's other daughter had not sat with the rest of them. Even Hypatia, who had at first taken a seat, glanced up at her daughter unhappily, and then got to her feet to stand beside her.

The room grew quiet, then silent.

Shaloris had been seated beside King Bozen on the dais, and now the king leveled his dark gaze on his other daughter.

"It is a time for celebration," King Bozen said directly to Eumelia, his gaze troubled. "Will you not take a seat and drink with us?"

"The king is in error," Eumelia replied, with a voice like cold iron.

A murmur went through the crowd.

King Bozen's face turned thunderous and he got to his feet. "You will be gracious. You will apologize. You will sit. And you will drink." Each direction was a command. "So soon you disappoint us?"

"Us?" Eumelia spat.

Hypatia put a hand on Eumelia's forearm, her growing alarm apparent. Eumelia shook her mother off.

Eumelia's eyes took on a faint glow and Shaloris felt a prickle of fear at the look she cast. The siren stepped forward into the space in front of the dais, her eyes only for King Bozen and Shaloris.

"You shall rue this day," Eumelia hissed. "Do not make this mistake. I have done and been everything you have asked of me."

King Bozen looked taken aback at this and Shaloris thought she knew why. King Bozen had never asked anything of his girls. Only that they grow up well, behave, and be studious. It was expected of royalty the world over.

"This is not becoming of a princess of Atlantis," someone shouted from behind Eumelia.

It was slight—tiny, really—the twitch in Eumelia's fingers. But Shaloris did not miss the motion.

A loud crack sounded through the room and several people cried out in surprise.

"You dare humiliate me!" Eumelia's voice began to rise. "Do you not know who I am, *what* I am?"

A crack appeared in the floor between Eumelia's planted feet. It shot forward toward the dais and back toward the pool. The water in the pool sloshed in the still air, splashing up onto the floor.

King Bozen's eyes were alight with rage.

"Do not threaten your king!" he bellowed, louder even than Eumelia.

Eumelia bellowed back, and her voice became the sound of trumpets. "You will die for this! You will all die!"

Shaloris cringed into her seat as Eumelia's eyes lit with a white-hot light and she spun, looking at all of those in the room. Her hands had become stiff, her fingers talons.

"Take her away," King Bozen called to the guards.

Atlantean guards materialized to surround and take hold of Eumelia. The crowd drew back, some leapt to get away from the apoplectic siren.

A sound like rolling thunder cracked miles from Atlantis, then barreled across the sea, growing closer and closer.

Eumelia was taken from the room. She did not resist the guards; in fact she looked up at the sky through the oculus, which had grown dark with clouds.

Shaloris shuddered at the look of euphoric rage on her half-sister's face.

TWENTY-THREE

A deep, grievous groan of heavy stones being shifted out of place reverberated through the temple. It was as if the stones that held the city of Atlantis above the ocean were being rearranged.

Valgana bolted from her place in the front row to her daughter's side.

"Move, Shaloris. It's not safe here." Taking her daughter by the elbow, she led her toward the arch through which they'd entered.

"What is it?" Shaloris panted as she was swept along. "I don't understand!"

Startled and confused expressions crossed the faces in the room. People murmured, asking one another to confirm that they were all hearing the same gritty protestations vibrating under their feet. Dirt and mortar spattered against the stones as it fell from supports overhead. Puffs of dust shot from the seams in the floor.

As she reached the arch, Shaloris heard people begin to move. Suddenly, people were running across the wide walkway leading from the temple, pouring over its steps. Though there was no visible threat, panic spread like the shadow of storm clouds sweeping across a prairie.

The groaning grew louder, then a hissing sound expelled from the temple behind them. Shaloris looked over her shoulder as her mother dragged her toward the front gate, calling ahead in a loud voice for them to be opened. A bright white column of water exploded from the temple top, directly through the oculus. It belted toward the sky in a great geyser, catching the sunbeams that had broken through the gathering clouds—beautiful in the strength of it.

Shaloris's jaw dropped and her neck creaked as she followed the water's trajectory, watched it slow. It appeared to stand almost perfectly still before it began its fall back to earth. A loud crack like the sound of cannon fire brought a trembling hand to her mouth as a fissure appeared in the temple roof. Water sprayed from the wound. A column tilted. The entire roof went off-kilter like a tilted hat. Then she lost view of it as the geyser crashed around the temple on all sides, sweeping away Atlanteans as they ran for their lives.

"Just move!" Shaloris heard her mother shriek.

The gate had opened only a few feet, abandoned by the guards who'd begun to push it inward. Valgana and Shaloris squeezed through the space, ripping their clothes as they caught on the locking mechanism. Shaloris left a long strip of fabric hanging from the metal. A moment after Shaloris passed through, the gates slammed shut as the weight of the panicked crowd trying to get out hit the orichalcum-coated iron at full force.

"Father!" Shaloris screamed, pulling against her mother's hands. She'd lost sight of him as she left the temple.

Yanking her hand from her mother's grip, Shaloris

returned to the gate, sloshing through the fast-rising water. Dull thuds against her shins made her look down and she bit off a scream as the bodies of dead fish floated by in the foam.

Water flooded through the legs of the crowd behind the bars, now dirty with mud and leaves picked up as it crossed the parkland surrounding the temple. The din of voices and screams of terror combined with the sound of the rushing water—which had not abated in strength—was near deafening.

"Back, get back!" she screamed to the panicked faces through the gate. "Get back or you'll be trapped!"

Some of the guards remembered who they were and took up the call for the crowd to move back.

King Bozen's face flashed at her once, eyes wide, and then he was out of sight in the crowd once again. He was still inside!

The guards pulled and Shaloris pushed, the water flow increasing. Valgana recovered some of her composure and joined her daughter in pushing the gates open. Those who still had their wits held back those who had lost all sense but fear, keeping the weight off the bars. Slowly the gates opened and bodies poured out into the street along with the water.

A deafening sound brought all eyes to the temple as the roof caved in. The geyser continued to stream up into the heavens, gaining power as the roof tumbled.

Shaloris and Valgana were swept along with the crowd, keeping their hands clasped tight. Shaloris looked around wildly for her father, but could not find him in the fray.

Another hissing explosion brought Shaloris and Valgana to a halt.

A second geyser, shaped more like a wall than a column,

pelted upward into the darkening sky near the innermost harbor. It sounded like a growling beast and seemed to climb forever before arcing and falling.

The crash of its landing filled the skies with mist and Shaloris felt her face grow damp.

"This way!" Valgana pulled her daughter away from the center harbor, heading down the broad street to where a bridge connected the middle ring to the central ring of the city. "We need to head to higher ground!"

Screaming and yelling punctuated the continuous sound of massive amounts of falling water. Water swirled in the streets, carrying dead fish, lost shoes and clothing, and other bits of refuse. The geysers did not abate, the water in the streets was now knee-deep. Someone jumped from an upper window and landed with a splash behind them.

Shaloris' chest burned, her muscles ached and shook from exertion and still they sloshed through the deepening water. Going with the flow of the crowd, they approached the bridge leading to the middle ring of the city. Shaloris was bumped and pushed by Atlanteans panicking to get to the dry parts of the city. The groans of buildings leaning and stones falling could be heard all around them. Shaloris was too afraid to look back. The hiss of the geysers did not abate and it seemed to her ears that the sounds of additional jets of water were joining as every moment passed.

Ahead, two women and one man stood on the rails of the bridge, shedding their clothing. Each stripped down to complete nakedness then leapt into the river. As the last one disappeared, Shaloris caught the flash of a long powerful tail: Mer. They'd get out of the city faster by swimming than by running.

"Mother," Shaloris panted, "let's jump. We can swim out!"

Valgana did not stop pulling her daughter over the bridge, but she'd seen what Shaloris had seen. More Mer joined the three who'd already jumped. They would be out of the city in minutes if they swam fast enough. Unless...

Another explosion of water burst upward behind them making a wall of water between middle Atlantis and its center. The wall grew and grew, crawling sideways and following the riverbanks, before crashing down on either side. Roofs collapsed under its weight, stones fell, voices screamed in terror.

"It's not safe," Valgana yelled, "we have to get there!" She pointed toward the northern cascades. To the west of the cascades were walkways of stone leading straight up to the temples on the cliffs overlooking the ocean. It was the only safe place remaining.

Water slid over half of the bridge, but soon they were running on dry stones again. The geysers were doing the most damage to the eastern side of the city.

The bridge groaned and swayed with the weight of panicked people. It had a seam running through the center, allowing it to open for ships but destabilizing the entire structure.

Shaloris and Valgana led the crowd, doing their very best to stay in front. Adrenaline and terror fueled their bodies. Their now sopping wet hair had fallen from the elegant updos and slapped wetly against their backs and their faces. Their clothing grew heavy, sodden with saltwater.

The water below the bridge rushed and boiled as seawater was sucked up by the geysers, drawn in from the ocean. Anyone swimming would be battling against the pull. Shaloris doubted her own abilities and was thankful her mother hadn't let them jump. There were no stronger swimmers than the

Mer. Atlanteans could stay underwater indefinitely, but Shaloris had often felt herself succumb to the pull of strong tides. If they had jumped, they'd have been sucked up into the geyser to be dashed down upon the stones of the city.

No sooner had their feet struck the solid stone on the other side of the bridge than the rushing waters, or something in it, struck the underside of the bridge hard. The bridge and all those still on it went flying in all directions. Something struck Shaloris in the back of her shoulder and she cried out in pain, falling into the rush of water pouring over the street.

Valgana yanked her daughter to her feet and pulled her away from the bridge. A rectangular stone the size of a carriage crashed down in front of them, nearly crushing Valgana. Her mother gave a shriek unlike any Shaloris had heard before. They altered course.

They staggered through the water toward an alleyway. Shaloris's shoulder throbbed. Somewhere in what remained of her logical mind, she equated all of this destruction with a single siren. Could it really be Eumelia doing all of this? The sheer magnitude of the destruction threatened to overwhelm her. Surely one siren could not be doing this alone. Were the gods involved? So much death and horror for no crime committed? The gods had to be angry with Atlantis; it was the only thing that made sense.

Valgana and Shaloris paused in the alleyway, sucking in air.

Shaloris's vision blurred as hot tears leaked from her eyes. Through the shock and panic, Shaloris wondered what would be left of Atlantis. When would the destruction stop?

And beneath all of the questions and fear—something

Shaloris herself was not yet fully aware of—a simmering rage. It birthed its ugly way into her heart like a thing with leathery batwings and sharp teeth.

A group of screaming, panicked horses running by the mouth of the alley brought Shaloris from her thoughts.

"We can't stay here, it's not safe," she wheezed at Valgana.

"There is a way through. This way." Valgana grabbed her daughter and pulled her farther down the narrow alley of stone.

Water streamed and burbled past their ankles. The walls on either side were close enough to touch both at the same time.

A wall loomed, but Valgana did not slow. They rounded a corner into a connecting, even narrower, alleyway. A head appeared from a window high above, and a pair of wooden shutters slammed shut. Droplets of water and grit fell from the sky. The light was like dusk, though it was early afternoon.

An angry rushing growl behind them drew Shaloris's attention backward.

"Mama!" she squeaked, as the wave hit them in the backs. It shoved her into her mother and sent them both floating through the alleyway on a surge of seawater. Something hard hit Shaloris in the nose and salty blood trickled into her mouth. They were expelled into a small courtyard with a single slender tree in the middle. The wave lost some of its power as it spread across the stones.

Using the tree to stand, Valgana helped her daughter up and they were off and running again, through yet another alleyway. A terrific crash of stones behind them spurred them on.

Her lungs burned and her nose throbbed. Her thighs quivered with exhaustion.

They ran, and ran, and ran.

TWENTY-FOUR

Shaloris woke in the middle of the night, her face wet from her Atlantean pup licking her face. She wept from happiness, astounded that the dog had survived. Valgana had been right.

"I'll call you Epison," whispered Shaloris to the pup as it snuggled into her side. "My little survivor."

Shaloris had made it to high ground, but her mother had not, and neither had King Bozen nor a great number of Atlantean citizens. Standing atop the northern mountain range, where she and the other survivors had taken refuge two days ago, she could not tear her eyes away from the ruin that had been her home.

Before her was a great semi-circular field of mud, jutting stone ruins jumbled with garbage including broken bits of carriages, wooden shutters, clothes, and the bodies of humans and animals. Like a shooting star with a fat tail, to the north and the east, the elegant curve of the city limits could easily be seen. But to the south and west it was nothing but a mudslide with a path that disappeared into the ocean.

Shaloris's feet were bare, her clothing, skin, and hair still crusted with bits of dried mud. She'd rinsed the worst off in the little pools of water that gathered by the top of the waterfalls, but had yet to bathe fully. The mists of the northern falls clung to her like grief. The sound of falling water was a drone of white noise, numbing her in the wake of a disaster of impossible scope.

Soft footsteps behind her made her blink but she did not take her gaze from the ruins below. The pup stirred in her arms and one of the heads yawned and licked her forearm. The other head stirred and gave a whine. She set Epison down where he sat at her feet and began to groom himself.

"My Queen?" It was a voice she did not recognize.

Tearing her gaze from the scene of death and ruin below, she looked upon a man whose face rang a distant bell of recognition. A council member, that much she knew. An Atlantean, much respected among his peers. Nestrin? Nestan? *Nestor*, the name finally came to her. He'd addressed her as his queen. It sounded so odd that she had to make an effort not to let out the laugh of hysteria tightening her throat.

"We await your command," Nestor said, lowering his eyes deferentially before peering up at her between his brows.

Her command?

He must have seen something in her face, for he rushed to make a suggestion.

"The flooding has ceased and the mud has stilled, but it may not yet be safe enough to search for survivors. Though, if that is your wish, we shall do our best."

She blinked at him vacantly. Her world had ended. Both her parents were dead. Only by some miracle had she survived the collapse of the pillars that had trapped her mother. Atlanteans were homeless now, and utterly without power. What should they do? The question seemed as far from an answer as her mother was from life.

"If I may, make a suggestion..." the councilor continued.

Shaloris could do little more than nod. How this elder might suggest they move on from this, or what he thought they should do next was of great curiosity to her. Herself? She could see nothing but killing herself and joining the rest of her people in their fate. What else was there?

"Send a small group to Okeanos to ask the Sovereign for a place among them. I would be happy to lead them."

"Okeanos?" Shaloris's voice sounded little more than a hoarse rasp.

"I'm told they have plenty of room, shelter, and an endless supply of food."

"No one knows where it is, is that not so?" Shaloris felt her focus begin to sharpen. Her mind clung to Nestor's suggestion like it was a lifeline.

"One of my colleagues, Renlaus, he knows where they are. He's been there many times." Nestor put a hand on his stomach and the other overtop of it. Hands still streaked in mud and grime.

"And what of the humans among us? They cannot live in underwater caves. The damp would kill them. And they can't swim there. There are no ships or boats left; they were destroyed in the harbor."

Nestor's face stilled. "There *are* no humans among the survivors."

Shaloris's eyes widened and she looked over Nestor's shoulder to the temple beyond and the group of dazed Atlanteans tending to one another as best they could. They rested, wept, or lay flat out on the ground in prostrate prayer. A few were at the pools near the northern falls, rinsing blood and mud from their clothing and themselves.

"No humans?" Shaloris thought of her maids, of many of the palace guards, the cooks, the market vendors, the children running in the streets.

"No Mer, either," Nestor added. "They've all gone to Okeanos where they'll be safe. And so should we. It is too far for us to journey on foot to Hirion or Antarchus, but we can—all of us—swim to Okeanos. Renlaus tells me we could make the journey in less than a day."

"But we have injured…" Shaloris gestured to where several Atlanteans were having wounds cleaned. Those with broken bones were being made to be as comfortable as possible.

"Which is why I'm suggesting you send me and a few of our strongest only. Sisinyxa cannot turn us away, not after what has happened. They will have felt the waves, even as far away as they are. They will be expecting us, perhaps, or that is my hope." Something like ambition gleamed in Nestor's eyes, but it seemed so in contrast to the near despair Shaloris herself felt that she barely recognized it.

Hope was a small moth fluttering in her chest. It was stay here and die or go to Okeanos where they could rest and recover. Perhaps another plan would come to her. She scanned the survivors. These people were her responsibility now. Dread slipped through her like a cold shadow. They would die up here if something was not done.

She looked at Nestor, waiting for her response. She took his hands. "Go to Okeanos, then, as quickly as you're able. Take whoever you think can make the journey. You have my thanks. We will pray that Sisinyxa will be compassionate and we will await your return tomorrow or the next day. Please be no longer than that."

Nestor bowed his forehead to her hand with thanks, and then turned and strode back to the temple where she watched him have words with a few of the stronger looking Atlanteans among the survivors. Within the hour, Shaloris and several of her people watched as the group picked their way down to the Atlantic and disappeared beneath the waves.

In the time between their departure and their return, Shaloris allowed the hope to grow. Sisinyxa was sure to have pity, was sure to provide them with the shelter and safety they needed. Shaloris found herself beginning to dream of building a new life for her people.

She watched as Nestor and his followers climbed the long winding switchbacks to the clifftop, stroking her hound and speaking his new name softly to him so he'd learn it.

But as Nestor approached, her heart drifted down. The expression on his face and those around him did not speak of hope.

She got to her feet, letting Epison drop to the dry grass and yelp at the group as they crested the last of the climb.

"What say you?" Shaloris was barely able to stop herself from sobbing at the look on Nestor's face. Those with him appeared beaten, exhausted, haggard, and looked even worse than when they'd left.

Nestor shook his head. "I am sorry, my queen. I was wrong. Sisinyxa was not sympathetic to our cause." He expressed confusion and hurt. "She sent us away under threat of death." His brows pinched and anger clouded his features.

Shaloris stepped backward in shock. "Surely not?"

Her mind went back to the vision of the Sovereign as she and her husband Ajax moved through the crowd to present King Bozen his gift. She had thought then that a creature so beautiful could only be just and kind. But Sisinyxa had shown herself to be as treacherous as Eumelia and Hypatia.

"She wishes us to die here on this mountain top?" Shaloris spluttered.

Nestor nodded. "Perhaps it is we who are the fools. I have long felt the Mer were not to be trusted. They love only themselves, and held relation with us only as far as it suited them to do so." He turned haunted eyes on the ruin of Atlantis in the valley behind. "It was Mer who did this to us, and Mer who refuse to help us up."

Shaloris was lost for words. Rage simmered deep under the surface of her calm exterior.

Nestor was right.

Shaloris had only ever thought of Eumelia as an individual, a sister whom she loved once, a sister who had betrayed her. Eumelia had proven more deadly than any Atlantean or any human were capable of being. The Mer had been made welcome among them for centuries and now they'd turned their backs during Atlanteans' deepest moment of need.

Eumelia and Hypatia were doing only as their natures dictated they could do. They were selfish, cruel, heartless, greedy, and murderous.

A vision of Valgana looking up in terror, her hands up as though they could prevent the collapse, filled Shaloris's mind. Her hand flew to cover her mouth and keep in the cry that threatened to spill out as grief ripped her heart in two.

Sirens did this. Eumelia, Hypatia, and now Sisinyxa.

Sirens would pay.

THE MUD HAD DRIED and became compacted sand, encasing the ruins of the city in a dense sarcophagus. The ruins were a tomb for the dead, the only grave most of the population would ever have. They'd been returned to the earth without warning, without preamble, without ceremony. But Shaloris could not bear to leave those nearest the surface exposed to the elements to rot in the sun and be picked at by the vultures and scavengers who'd moved in as soon as the ground was stable.

Taking the strongest of her remaining people, they combed the broad area for bodies. They were not difficult to find, one only had to follow the clusters of gathered birds. The bodies they recovered were excavated and wrapped in fabric. Shaloris designated a place where the earth was deep for the one marked mass grave. Animals were buried alongside humans and Atlanteans, leaving nothing visible for the scavengers to pick.

Shaloris found Valgana's body far from where she had imagined it had come to rest. But Atlantis was no longer recognizable and already her memory of the city's geography was fading.

Valgana was wrapped and buried along with the rest, but Shaloris stood at the grave for a long time after her people returned to their makeshift camp. She wept until she felt she could weep no longer. She apologized to all of them, and to King Bozen, who had never been found. She cried until she could hardly see, until the sun touched the horizon. She cried until the time for crying was over, and then she wiped her eyes.

When her vision cleared, she saw a silhouette among the rocks at the edges of the city ruin. Someone was standing there. Gooseflesh rose on her body. It was not one of her people, she could *feel* the menace baking off the person like heat waves. Sick with grief and unafraid, she walked toward them. The shape was familiar. A slice of setting sunlight lit the curly red hair for a moment.

Eumelia.

Emotions tumbled her—hatred, rage, confusion, disbelief. There was a sliver of hope, too. Hope that she was wrong, that Eumelia was somehow not responsible for this disaster, for killing everyone she loved and burying her home.

Her footsteps on the sand made Eumelia turn and look, and in that moment Shaloris knew. It had not been a mistake. Eumelia looked like an artist pleased with her latest sculpture.

Shaloris hissed as she came to a stop a few feet from her half-sister. "Are you proud of what you have done?"

Eumelia stared calmly at Shaloris, her expression vacant. She looked almost bored.

"The king did this," she replied. "We warned him of what would happen. He did not believe us."

"You...warned him?" Shaloris asked in a tone of disbelief. "This was your plan all along? If you were not given the kingdom, you would destroy it?"

"My mother was right," Eumelia went on, seeming to ignore Shaloris's words. "Those gifted with power have a right to change the course of destiny. Otherwise, we would not have power at all. It is gods-given. We warned him, and he did not heed us."

"He was your father!" Shaloris cried. It dawned on her that she was not dealing with a sane being. And still she tried to find some sense, to make Eumelia understand. "These people were your people. Atlantis was your home!"

"Admittedly, I did take things a little further than we

intended," Eumelia replied in that stony way she had. "I only wanted to prove that I was the rightful heir."

Shaloris was so angry she could not speak. Her fingers curled into stiff fists, the hairs on her body spindled to standing.

"Death is too good for you," Shaloris said. Inside her chest came a blooming, a warm surge of power opening outward like her heart was unfolding like a flower. Her body grew warm. Tingling energy swept up from the soles of her feet and raced along her bones, lighting her up inside.

"Listen to me now." That heat coming from her heart swept up her throat and warmed her tongue and teeth. It poured from her mouth like it was an open oven.

"A curse will fall on you and all of your kind..."

Eumelia's eyes widened and the sunlight cooled, the rays slicing across the horizon dimmed as the sun sank.

"You will never have a home, as you have taken my home from me. You will never have a family, just as you have taken my family from me. Just when you think you are happy, you will be uprooted. Just when you think you have found love, you will lose it. Your daughters will be born under this curse and will pass it on to their daughters. Your sons will be powerless and your heart will be broken with the birth of every son. You will be a slave to the seasons, and to the salt that gives you your power. You will never feel genuine joy again, for you will know that just as happiness comes close it will be snatched away. This curse is my answer to what you have done, and the misery every siren must bear in her long lifetime is thanks to you. Remember it. Bear it. Forever."

The sun dipped fully below the horizon and shadows swept over both of them.

Shaloris was shaking, but she found that the fiery rage

that had risen up in her at the sight of her half-sister had abated. She'd claimed her magic, and it had satisfied her.

Eumelia stared at Shaloris for a long moment and then crossed her arms, her lip lifted in a sneer. "Is that all you've got?"

Shaloris turned her back on her sister and walked away. All she wanted to do was lie down and sleep for days on end.

TWENTY-FIVE

Shaloris and her remaining people went north to the coastal city of Hirion. There, they were given shelter and food. Six years passed, and in that time Shaloris assembled something that looked like a life.

Nestor asked if he could work on assembling a fleet with which he would take Okeanos by force, and she agreed without hesitation. Shaloris had no city over which to rule, but she had some sway as the daughter of the great King Bozen, last ruler of Atlantis. She also had her magic, which grew stronger as the years passed. She became a woman to respect, even to fear. She spent her days and nights drumming up support and making deals on behalf of Nestor. It would take years, but what else did they have but time? They were the last of their kind, the last Atlanteans. Their nation had been destroyed by a siren, they'd been refused aid by a siren; it was only fitting that they take the sirens' home for their own.

Nestor spoke of mines full of orichalcum, and sold shares of those mines as payment for military and naval support from the wealthy citizens of Hirion and beyond.

Every year, Shaloris made a pilgrimage by ship down the coastline, back to the place of her birth. She took Epison with her. She visited her mother's grave and wept with fresh pain. She mourned her father, her people, her city, and in this way kept her ire and grief alive.

No one returned to Atlantis with her aside from Epison and two Atlantean guards. No one seemed to wish to return and Shaloris could not blame them. But she felt some responsibility as the queen to keep the memories of the fallen alive.

On this day she visited the temple and made gifts of flowers and fruit, though she felt the gods were no longer resident in this desolate place. The clifftop temple had begun to age and decay. Weeds and vines sprang up around it, covering it with greenery. Water pooled in the worn places in the stone floor and the fountains grew furry with moss.

With only Epison for company, she made her way down to the graves. It seemed to her that the ruins were sinking deeper every year, and very little vegetation took root in the salty soil. She knelt at the border of the wasteland, sitting in the lush low grasslands which once stretched out beyond Atlantis for miles. Before her was nothing more than a scar on the land, beneath which all the dead lay entombed, the buildings and beautiful architecture of Atlantis broken and crushed under the earth.

She should have died—she told herself—alongside her father and mother. But then she would remember Nestor and the seeds of hope he'd planted in her heart: Atlantis would one day rise again. They would make a new home for their people, on the bones of the ones who'd taken their own away.

Shaloris had hired a scribe to write down her version of

events, and in turn that scribe had taken the story to an artist to render into beautiful mosaics. The work had only just begun, but one day she planned to set that story into the very walls of Okeanos.

"Sister."

The word was so soft it sounded like the wind. Shaloris was shaken from her meditation, her eyes opened but she saw no one. She had imagined it. She closed her eyes again and went back to making plans for Okeanos once it was hers.

"Sister."

Her eyes flew open. In front of her stood Eumelia.

She was barely recognizable.

She was thin and pale, her hair hung well past her hips. It had lost its curly spring and hung from her head in lank strands. Her eyes appeared hollow and haunted. Strife hung from her, so heavy her once straight shoulders seemed to sag under an invisible yoke.

"What are you doing here?" Shaloris snapped, hardening her heart toward the pitiful creature.

"I came to find you." Eumelia's voice was soft and dry, like a weak wind. She sounded like an old woman. "I know that you come here every year."

Shaloris said nothing, not caring to ask how Eumelia had come by this information. She supposed it was no great secret. Mer had the run of the oceans and saw all passing ships.

Eumelia got to her knees and bowed her head. "I came to beg your forgiveness. I have never been more regretful for anything than for what I have done to our father and our people."

"Good." Shaloris bit the word off. "Now go away and let me mourn in peace."

Eumelia lifted those haunted eyes. "I beg of you, remove the curse."

"I seem to recall your response to the curse was something to the effect of, 'Is that all you've got?'" Shaloris sneered.

"You were right to do it. I deserved to be punished. I never thought—" Eumelia swallowed so loudly that her sister had no trouble hearing it. "I would rather have death than this."

Shaloris felt a slow smile creep along her face. She leaned forward. "That was the point."

"You don't understand," Eumelia whined. "Something you could not possibly have intended has happened because of your cursing us."

Shaloris cocked her head like a curious bird.

"We have become...unnatural." Eumelia's voice dimmed to a husky whisper, and shame burned in her cheeks. "The salt—it sends us away to—to mate."

It so pained Eumelia to say these words that Shaloris almost laughed. "Sends you to land, you mean."

Eumelia nodded, looking relieved. "I'm glad to see you understand. Now you must lift the curse, for nature did not intend us to live this way."

Shaloris drew herself up to standing. "All curses go against nature; that's what makes them curses."

Eumelia stared in disbelief. "You cannot have meant it. It's too horrible. It makes us mate with humans. *Humans!*" Disgust filled every word and marred her once beautiful face.

"That's what I would call poetic justice," Shaloris replied, growing bored of the conversation. "What you did was unforgivable. I will not lift the curse. Your kind will pay for all time. Now leave this place. You have no right to set so much as one miserable foot here."

Eumelia's expression transformed slowly into something less hurt and more angry.

"I left a son," Eumelia croaked, her eyes dark with pain and rage. "Because of you. I have urges I cannot control. My memory fades and returns with the salt like a siege-engine to torture me. I gave birth to a child who was not like me, was nothing more than a human boy. Gods help me, I loved him, but I left him. It rent my heart into pieces. This is what you have done."

Shaloris looked down her nose at her sister. "Live with it. At least you have your life. With every season that passes and every child you leave behind, remember that it is your penance."

Eumelia bared her teeth, her fingers curling into tense claws. She stepped forward.

Shaloris put a hand up. "Don't tempt me..."

But she stopped talking when she realized her feet were wet. Looking down, her eyes widened in surprise. Water was seeping up from the ground and swirling around her ankles. Cracks appeared in the sandy soil, spreading outward from where she stood, lifting at the edges like a pie splitting in the oven.

"What are you doing?" She glared at Eumelia. "You can only destroy Atlantis once. You want me to drown? Go ahead. I welcome the chance to join my father and mother."

But she didn't want to die anymore, not really. She backed away from Eumelia. The water was now at knee height and rising fast. It seemed to be crawling up her body unnaturally, against gravity. Horror clawed at her throat and her very flesh crawled. She made to run but at the twitch of Eumelia's fingers, the water hardened and became a bright blue stone.

Epison began to bark shrilly and run back and forth along the edges of the strange water. He seemed to understand he shouldn't touch it. He whined and growled and snapped at the water, seeing it as more dangerous than the woman who was making it come.

"You wanted to rule Atlantis?" Eumelia's voice shook with righteous anger. "You can rule it from your prison. I'll make you a crown unlike any a ruler has had before you. You make me a slave to the salt? I'll make you a slave to your own dead kingdom."

Shaloris screamed then, struggling to free herself. Her panicked mind grasped at understanding as the stone reached her waist, locking her in place. The aquamarine split off and crystalized, shooting this way and that, forming six-sided columns. They spiked into the sky and locked hard around Shaloris's body, growing as rapidly as water could flow. Her screams were muffled as the gemstone closed over her head and still the crystal grew and grew.

The soil cracked and bubbled as saltwater shot through it, clawing its way toward the crystal to transform. The crystal spiked outward and expanded as Eumelia stepped back from her work.

A bubble of space formed around Shaloris as the blue walls thickened and expanded, cracking and groaning. She found she could move again. She railed against the crystalline walls, the sounds of her breathing and her screams coupling with the otherworldly crackling sound the water made as it transformed into stone. The room inside grew and became a huge hollow cavern lit with the blue of the stone. The sun overhead penetrated the gem and sent beams shooting every which way like a prism. And then darkness crept in, as the gem continued to grow and the earth and soil crept up around it.

"I can curse, too, oh Queen of Atlantis," Eumelia said quietly, though Shaloris could hear it clearly, as the earth bubbled and settled over the massive stone coffin she'd made. "If I must live out my life in a prison, then so must you. These walls will hold you for thousands of years."

TWENTY-SIX

I was sitting. That much I was aware of, because I could feel the pieces of broken crystal pressing into my hips.

There was a crack in the darkness, a lightning shaped fissure through which light leaked. I could hear the sound of my own breathing, and that of Shaloris nearby. The fissure turned blue and widened. Slowly the black bled away and my vision returned.

Shaloris's face began as a blur of pale skin and dark hollows for eyes. A mass of darkness surrounded her head. Slowly, her features sharpened, and the planes of her face and the details of her—her little moles, her eyelashes, the flecks of color in her irises—coalesced to make the woman whose memories I had just lived.

I stared at her and she stared at me. Her chest moved in and out as she breathed and I realized we were breathing in time. Her hands held mine gently, her skin exactly the same temperature as mine. I watched as she blinked and felt myself blink in the same moment. We were fused, she and I. I had had her thoughts, her understanding, her memory, blow through me like an ill gale, and it left me speechless.

"Now, you know what you must do." Slowly, she straightened and released my hands. Her gaze didn't leave my face. "You must free me, if you wish to be free yourself."

But for her, *free* meant *kill*.

Kill. Was I capable of it?

Sensing my hesitation, she grabbed my hands again and held them so tightly I winced. Her expression was fierce, her eyes like fire.

"You *must* do it," she said.

A crackle like birthday sparklers sounded over our heads and echoed throughout the big blue room. Dust and small particles landed on the floor around us. High above our heads, the crevices and valleys of the crystal snaked this way and that. Long, sharp stalactites of aquamarine hung down from the ceiling. I half expected to see bats fluttering among the columns of crystal.

Another loud snap echoed and a long, sharp stalactite broke off and plummeted point-first to the floor.

A scream tore from my throat and I turned my face away from the stalactite, throwing my arm up as it struck the floor a few feet away. Shattering into a million tiny shards, it peppered us with tiny blue scimitars. I peeked around my arm at Shaloris. She reached up a hand and pulled a small sharp sliver from where it had penetrated her cheek near her jaw. A thin trickle of blood snaked down to her jawline and dripped. In the blue light of the crystal, her blood appeared a dark green, almost black.

She dropped the bloody sliver and gazed at me expectantly. "Why else did you come here?"

"I'm not a murderer." I lowered the arm that had been protecting my face and shook shards from my hair.

Overhead, a gritty groan echoed through the eaves.

"You'll die here, if you cannot kill me." She got to her

feet and shook out her clothing. She cast about on the ground where shards of all shapes and sizes spread out around us. She bent and picked up a long, nasty looking blade of blue. She turned it in her hand and held out the dull end to me. "Your people will go on suffering unless you can do it."

I got to my feet, my chin trembling. Taking the shard, it was all I could do to look at the sharp edge and picture it slicing into skin, spilling blood, ending a life.

A greater fear than I had ever known before welled up inside of me like the swell of a growing wave. I was afraid of what I had to do, afraid of who I would become if I did it.

Shaloris took a step closer to me. "Think of the suffering, think of the madness, the abandoned children. I did that. Me."

A crack overhead was followed by a long groan and another stalactite broke off and shattered behind Shaloris. A spray of aquamarine spattered across the floor, skidding to a halt at her feet.

Shaloris stepped even closer, so close she could have wrapped her arms around me. She lifted her chin, exposing her throat. With a finger, she lifted the gleaming blade in my hand and directed its tip toward her neck.

My hand tightened on the dull end. My heart sped up. I sucked in air through my nose. My skin felt clammy and my mouth felt dry. I pressed the sharp end into her skin.

She closed her eyes and waited.

The blade trembled and I hesitated. A thin trickle of blood traced its way down her throat and I watched it, my vision blurring as tears welled in my eyes.

Shaloris's eyes snapped open. She moved, her one hand flying up toward mine and her body shifted to move her neck forward into the blade.

"No," I cried, realizing what she intended. I pulled the blade from her throat and threw it to the side, screaming. My head pounded from the force of the scream. "I'm not a murderer!"

The blade struck the walls of the crystal, but there was no shattering crack. Instead there was the sound of a splash, then a trickle and then nothing.

Shaloris's eyes widened and both of us looked to where I'd thrown the blade. There was a splotch of wetness on the wall and several streams glinting wetly toward the floor. A small puddle oozed across the aqua floor.

I stared at it, confused.

There was a thud to our left. A dull sound, not the sound of breaking stone. A dark shape was moving out there, not just one, but two. There were several more thuds. A crack appeared in the wall, stretching from the floor and jaggedly running toward the ceiling. Particles and chunks of stone landed around us. Overhead the pointed ends of stalactites seemed to waver, threatening to fall and impale us.

I bent and picked up a large chunk of aquamarine, staring at it. I looked at the wet spot on the floor and back at the stone in my hand.

"Eumelia made this stone out of saltwater," I murmured. My eyes narrowed. Speaking to the stone, I whispered, "Return to your original state."

The stone burst into water and splattered at our feet.

Shaloris and I stared at one another. She shook her head. "You are running out of time."

Several more thuds against the wall to our left resounded through the space. I heard the very faint calling of my name.

"There will be no murder here today," I said to Shaloris.

"Killing you will not end the curse, or Eumelia would have killed you rather than entomb you. This stone has been keeping you alive, just as it has kept alive the siren's curse. We need to work together to end this, just as you and your sister together were responsible for creating it."

She cocked her head, her brows tightening.

I closed my eyes and saw Eumelia, her face full of rage and her elemental powers coursing through her as she drew saltwater up through the earth and hardened it, making a coffin around her sister. Nike was wrong. I did not need to be stronger than the speaker of the curse; I needed to be stronger than the elemental who had built this crystal cage.

I saw my mother walking into the Baltic, her face a white mask of suffering as she surrendered herself to sea, leaving me broken-hearted on the beach. I saw the faces of beautiful baby boys, small chubby fists clenching on empty air, searching for a mother's comforting touch. I saw Antoni, looking out at a blue ocean stretching before him, thinking that his heart had drowned though his body still lived.

Something moved inside me. Some huge thing, like an earthquake, but it felt good. A face rose unbidden in my mind. It was a face I loved but it was a face whose details had faded, the exactness of my memory telling lies as the years passed by. It had been a long time since I had looked upon this face and I didn't understand why I was seeing it now, but my heart blossomed like a rose in the heat of a summer's day.

The face had a copper beard and laughing hazel eyes. My father, Nathan. I could almost feel his strong arms holding me, almost hear the beautiful tenor tone he used to sing to me with.

A memory surfaced, like his face was only the tip of a very large moving landmass. It was a memory I had locked away, had no access to until this moment. I was too young to have the rights to this memory, even though it was mine.

I was a baby, probably not much over a year old. I could hear my father calling for my mother from my crib. It was night. My mother did not answer. The older Targa knew why she was gone, but the baby Targa knew only the confusion and fear she'd picked up from hearing her father. My father came into my room and picked me up, swaddling me in a blanket. He cradled me against his chest, and his heart pounded and his breath hitched. He left with me, down the front steps and onto the sidewalk in front of the two-story house. The house where I'd been born on the bathroom floor.

My father called my mother, eyes flashing down one side of the street and then the other. He called louder. A voice yelled at him from some upper window but he ignored it.

Then there was my mother's voice, behind us and down the street. He spun around and I felt him sag to the street in relief. Footsteps running on the sidewalk grew loud, but not the sound of shoes, the slapping sounds of bare feet...bare, wet feet.

I felt two warm droplets on my face and didn't know what they were then, but I knew what they were now. I was well acquainted with tears, but they'd always been siren tears—my mother's tears.

These ones were my father's tears.

All this flashed through my mind in an instant, as Shaloris looked expectantly up into my face and the crystal crumbled and groaned around us.

Tears of a man who believed himself abandoned, and tears of a baby too young to understand. The memory of those tears on my face rushed in on me, swept over me, like a wave breaking against the stones.

Never again and no one, my mind whispered.

My father's tears. Tears born of the fear of loss, fear of abandonment, and the sick feeling of helplessness. Tears of saltwater.

I swayed on my feet and nearly came to my knees as another realization struck me like the whump of a strong wind. This was why I had been born and given the powers I'd been given. This was why my father was my father and my mother was my mother and all that was between them resulted in me. I still didn't fully understand, but I felt its truth as surely as fire gives heat.

"Never again and no one," I whispered fiercely, opening my eyes and looking at Shaloris.

Shaloris's brows pinched in confusion, her eyes locked on my face.

Salt held us captive, and salt held the secret to our release.

Thrusting my arms out to the sides, my hands reaching out toward the crystal walls, I cried out, tears now streaming down my face.

My ears filled with the sound of rain as bucketloads of saltwater crashed over my head and poured over my body. My eyes closed tightly in reflex and my hair plastered to my face. My clothes pulled at my frame from the force and weight of the water raining down over us. I forced my eyes open and even through the saltwater running over them, I could see the woman in front of me, her face, and the sudden understanding that crossed it as her gaze clashed with mine.

"I revoke the curse!" she cried out.

I could see *through* her. Her being had turned to smoke

and the rain poured through the memory of her. Her hair and clothes were wet, even though droplets fell right through her. I saw one pass right between her eyes.

The ghost's lips formed a half-phrase...

"Thank—"

The ghost of Shaloris dissolved like a light mist under the heat of a burning sun. Her image blurred, drifted, and was gone.

Soaking wet and covered in gooseflesh, I blinked and looked around.

Several meters away, my mother and Antoni stood completely drenched, frozen in a caricature of postures. Antoni held a mallet in his hands, the same one we'd used to pound the pegs in when we erected our tents for the night. My mother held a pick-axe, the kind used for digging through compacted stone. Her hair was plastered to her head and her clothes were stuck to her body. Antoni wiped the water from his eyes and blinked at me in happy surprise.

Beyond them, Nike was seated on a rock and Petra knelt nearby, holding the lid from a thermos. They both stared at me, also frozen.

Emun stood at the edge of the rubble pile, holding a small, brass-headed hammer. He too was staring in stillness.

"Targa!" My mother was the first to move. She dropped her pick axe and ran forward. She threw her arms around me with a slap of wet clothes. A moment later, Antoni threw his arms around both of us and I was crushed in a soggy bear hug.

"What the hell just happened?" Jozef's voice echoed in the cavern. "One second I'm giving the two-headed pup a drink and the next moment he's gone! Where's the crystal? Why is the floor all wet?"

Antoni and my mom released me, Mom took my face and held my forehead to her own.

"I thought I'd lost you."

"It's over," I replied, holding her by the shoulders.

The moment we released one another, Antoni swooped in for another hug.

The three of us moved to join the dry members of our little search party.

"I don't understand," Petra said, getting to her feet.

She handed Nike the thermos lid and the sorceress took it. She was smiling at me over the lip of the cup but she looked exhausted.

"What happened to you?" I asked the white-haired siren.

"It was tiring, trying to hold back your mother," she replied.

I glanced at my mom, and she had enough grace to look sheepish.

"I heard you scream..." She didn't have to finish. I knew what had happened next. That's what all the thudding and thumping had been.

"The gemstones are gone." Jozef held out the sack that used to hold them. It was dripping.

Nike nodded. "All of them. Mine and Sybellen's, too. They became water at the same time as the crystal did."

"Can you tell us what happened in there?" Petra rested a hand on Nike's shoulder. "Now that your mom seems to have gotten control of herself again."

"Let's get out of this cave," I said, feeling like if I ever went underground again it would be too soon. "I'll tell you everything."

IT TOOK us about an hour to get out of the temple and set up camp. We were glad Petra was along—she was a human GPS and led us out without any wrong turns.

Once we were settled around the fire with food, and Antoni had radioed Ivan to report the mission accomplished and we'd be back the following afternoon, all eyes turned to me.

"So, who was she, Targa?" Nike asked, pouring some water into the lid of her metal water bottle. "Was she a siren?"

I shook my head. "She was Atlantean, actually. You were almost right about the curse, almost. But not quite."

Nike cocked a slender eyebrow over the cup at me as she drank.

The words came easily as the sun drifted down and disappeared below the horizon. I explained how the curse was the responsibility of a pair of half-sisters who had been torn apart by sibling rivalry and greed. I added what details about the Atlantean culture, society, and city I could recall, especially for Petra's sake, but everyone seemed to sit on the edge of their seat, breathless to hear more.

"I don't understand how you can know all that...all that detail," Petra said when I stopped to cool my throat with a drink of water. "She must have been a hell of a storyteller."

I laughed, realizing that I had taken for granted that Shaloris had used magic to show me her memories, just the ones I needed to understand.

"I'm sorry, I didn't explain very well at the beginning. Shaloris was a sorceress. She was able to use her magic to take me into the past, show me her life, her memories, I even picked up her understanding in some places. What she knew, I knew." I looked at Mom, sitting there with Jozef, their fingers entwined and light from the fire dancing over their faces.

"Like the Hall of Anamna," she said.

"Trippy." Petra let herself slide off the rock she'd been sitting on to settle on the sand. "All that knowledge passed in fifteen minutes."

My eyes stretched wide with shock. They felt as big as doorknobs. "That's it?" I gaped at my Mom, then Nike, then Antoni.

"Yeah, but after ten minutes your Mom couldn't wait any longer," Nike added, with a sly smile sent in Mom's direction.

"We didn't know what was going on there. There was no sound, no movement in what felt like forever," Mom explained. "I thought you were dying, or that it was all a big mistake." Her eyes flicked to Nike and I wondered just how fiery their disagreement outside the crystal had gotten.

"So you tried to break me out?"

"As far as I was concerned, we'd tried it your way and it wasn't reaping any rewards..."

"Not yet anyway," Nike injected.

"And you," I looked at Antoni where he was sitting beside me with his chin on his hand and his elbows on his knees. "You had a tool in your hand as well."

Antoni straighted and his eyes darted around the group guiltily. "So did Emun!"

"Hey if you can't beat 'em, join 'em," Emun said lazily and without any of the embarrassment coloring Antoni's cheeks.

Everyone laughed.

"Plus you're my sister, and it didn't feel right. It may have been only fifteen minutes, but it felt like hours you were inside that thing."

The crystal had nearly fallen down around my ears and stalactites could easily have nailed Shaloris or me to the floor, or both of us. But my family didn't know that, all they'd wanted was to get me back, so I let it go. It had all turned out for good in the end.

"So the pup..." Jozef said, speaking for the first time since we'd settled around the campfire for story time.

"Epison," I said, nodding. "That was his name. He was alive because his master was alive. His was an Atlantean breed that obviously went extinct when Atlantis was destroyed. His name meant 'survivor.'"

"Well, survive he did," Jozef murmured. "Poor thing."

"Which makes me wonder," Nike mused, "how do you suppose the original triton managed to get a piece of that crystal with a raging two-headed dog guarding it?"

"Could be that he found a piece that was jutting through the earth above and broke it off the larger chunk. The crystal went straight up into the mud above it, so that's a possibility," Mom suggested.

"Or he doesn't have a problem with tritons," said Emun, "we know he hated sirens but we didn't try to see how he reacted to just me."

There was a murmur of agreement followed by a thoughtful silence.

Then, Nike spoke. "You said that Shaloris told you that she'd tried to revoke the curse once before?"

I nodded. "Why?"

"Just theorizing that maybe that's why the gemstones worked to protect us from the curse. Her attempt to revoke it was somehow infused into the piece the triton found."

Emun nodded but his eyes were half closed as he stared into the fire. "Good theory, makes sense."

There was another murmur of agreement and I fought

the urge to break out laughing. We sounded like a bunch of amateur sleuths ruminating clumsily in the dark, pipes smoking as we muttered things like, 'Oh come now Watson, do you really think...' and, 'Elementary, my dear,' and, 'You have *seen* but you have not *observed*.' I got the giggles but quickly stifled them when Antoni shot me a wary glance, a half smile on his face.

I realized that I was beyond exhausted. I got up and stretched, letting my movements speak for me.

There was another murmur as everyone agreed it was time for bed. There were some popping bones and yawns as we moved about brushing our teeth, putting out the fire, and in general winding down.

"You've got a big job ahead of you, bro," Antoni said quietly as he and Emun stood side by side brushing their teeth, mouths encircled with foam.

Emun made a questioning grunt and his brows shot up as his toothbrush froze.

"Sounds like no one can increase the triton population except for you." Antoni spat out his foam, rinsed his mouth, and tucked his toothbrush into his toiletries kit. He gave Emun a close-mouthed smile full of meaning and whacked him twice congenially on the shoulder.

"Best get to work then, no dawdling."

Emun snorted and then bent over to prevent spilling toothpaste foam all over his chest.

Calls of goodnight echoed in the dark and the desert fell into a relative peace and silence.

ON THE FLIGHT back to Nouakchott, Petra pointed to the ground. "See that dust? Any bets that it's someone heading to the Richat Structure to check out the new topography?"

"You weren't kidding when you said seventy-two hours," said Jozef.

In Nouakchott, Petra and I had a moment to chat as the others transferred bags from the chopper to the plane.

"Thank you doesn't begin to cover—" I began, but Petra waved me to silence.

"Are you kidding? I got to walk through Atlantis! That is an archaeologist's dream come true."

"Still, you put your life on hold to come and help me. If there is ever a time you need my help, I'll be there when you call."

She nodded and pulled me into a hug. "We're elemental sisters," she said quietly beside my ear. "I'll not be shy from now on, and neither should you."

TWENTY-SEVEN

We returned to Gibraltar to rest a few days before the longer journey back to Gdansk. Jozef wanted to pack a proper bag as it had been decided he'd be moving into the Novak manor until he and Mom decided what they were going to do next.

"Do you feel different?" I asked Mom as we carried our bags inside the house and dropped them in the foyer. I had meant to ask her earlier, but between explaining the Shaloris and Eumelia story, getting ourselves sorted to travel, and sleeping on the flight from Mauritania to Gibraltar, as well as the ride back to Jozef's house, there hadn't been a good moment. Turned out the air-sickness was still there, but I felt less drained than I usually felt, so maybe the dissolution of the curse had lessened the extent of it.

Her eyes widened and brows went up. "You don't?"

"Well, I'm not terrified of accidentally touching an aquamarine anymore, but otherwise..." I shrugged. "Not really, no."

But I had never really felt the pull of the siren's curse

the way my mother had. Either it was different for me as an elemental, or my time had not come for its power to work on me. Now I never would, and that was all right by me.

Emun and Jozef came in carrying more bags and paused to listen.

"I feel like dark clouds were hanging over my head and they just moved away," Mom said as we stood in the foyer. "I feel like I didn't even realize that the clouds were there until now. They've been there for so long that I didn't realize the sky could look any different."

Jozef stepped closer to my Mom, his face dreamy as he listened to her talk.

"My thoughts are clear, my memories are intact, and best of all, I have no fear anymore. It's just gone."

I swallowed down a lump in my throat as Nike and Antoni entered the house last, carrying their bags.

"What are we talking about?" Antoni asked, setting his bag down and straightening.

"Whether Mira feels different," Emun replied, taking off his jacket and hooking it on the hatstand beside him. His eyes found Nike. "Do you feel different?"

Nike hesitated. "I do," she said slowly. Her eyes drifted to my mother's and held them.

"But?"

"But I always was a little different from other sirens, and my desire to get underwater for good is as strong as ever. And..." she trailed off, eyes still on Mom.

"We need to go to Okeanos," injected Mom.

I looked at her with surprise, but she and Nike were looking at each other like an understanding had passed between them. Like it was something they'd both felt for a while now.

Finally, Mom's eyes passed to me. "Would you like to come?"

"I think that's a wonderful idea," said Nike, brightening. "It'll give Targa a chance to see where her mother is from."

I loved the idea, and part of me marveled at how I hadn't though of it yet myself. "Absolutely, I do. We might never be as close as we are now." In fact, we had been closer when we'd been in Africa, but it wouldn't have been right to leave the non-Mer hanging out in a strange city for a few days while we went for an aquatic jaunt.

"It won't be the way it was," Mom said, finally. Her expression softened. "But now is the perfect time to go." There was something in her eyes I couldn't put my finger on. A knowing she wouldn't voice. Nike had that same look, like there were shutters behind her eyes giving just a hint of some warm unknown source of light.

I glanced at Antoni. He smiled at me. "It's a great idea. Go. I'll hang out with Emun until you get back."

"Uh, you mean you'll hang out with *Jozef* until we get back," Emun replied, and I realized his eyes were also lit with the fire of curiosity. "I wouldn't miss seeing Okeanos for all the classic cars in America!"

That settled it. After a good meal and a rest, Mom, Nike, Emun, and I slipped into the waters at the Drakief's private boathouse and began the journey toward the Azores. It was a journey that would take most of the night, yet somehow no one bothered to suggest waiting until morning. There was an eagerness connecting us.

It felt wonderful to be in my siren form again. The last of the stress from our desert journey crumbled and broke away as the saltwater soothed my skin and my soul. Though traveled together, the four of us drifted apart. We didn't converse, and weren't always even within yelling distance. Even Emun seemed like a kind of peace had stolen over him. In an adjacent way, the curse had been hanging over him, too.

When our heads broke the surface beyond Mount Califas, the eastern horizon was painted with pale peaches, greens, and indigos.

"That's it," Mom said as she bobbed beside me, her wet hair gleaming and her eyes dark in the early morning light.

Mount Califas was as she had described it. Steep, very tall, and what might have been bare cliffs once were now completely encrusted with vegetation. The base of Califas nearest us was a clutter of black rocks and breaking surf. Nike led us in a large semi-circle to a section of white beach where we found our footing and walked up on the sandy soil of Okeanos.

I was going to ask if this was the same section of beach Claudius had come to before he'd kicked all the sirens off their own land, but I could tell from Nike's grim expression as she looked around that it was. As the light bloomed with the sunrise, my eyes found dark spots in the mountainside that might have been the entrances to caves, but they were so grown over it was difficult to tell for sure.

An explosion of screaming seabirds drew our attention to a crust of flat rock a little less than a quarter of the way up the mountainside.

"Look!" Emun's voice was an excited whisper.

A siren had appeared on the ledge as the last of the birds flew away. She was naked but her curly black hair was dry and little wisps of it blew in the light breeze. Her pretty frame made a sharp silhouette against the rock behind her for this siren was much darker, darker even than Nike.

I heard a sharp intake of breath and glanced at Mom.

She was looking at the siren just above us without surprise, as though she had known someone would be here.

The siren looked down at us. It was too dim and she was too far away to see her expression clearly. A moment later, she disappeared.

Movement at the base of Califas drew my eye, and there was another siren, this one milky white with long auburn hair and wearing a simple shift dress. She emerged from the cave at the base of Califas, picking her way over stones and shrubs. Another siren appeared behind her, and another. A very young siren appeared from another cave entrance farther down the beach. She paused and eyed us, said something to someone invisible behind her, and then came out and walked toward us. She was followed by more sirens. Suddenly there were dozens of them, coming steadily out of the belly of the mountain and joining us on the beach.

As they drew close, I saw some of them were weeping in the siren way, no sound, just an endless flow of tears. Their expressions varied from neutral to happy to awe and even a kind of ecstasy. They closed around us, putting my mother and me at the center. Nike took a few steps back, taking herself out of the little circle forming on the beach.

Emun, standing several feet to the side of Mom and me, was getting his own little encircling crowd. Siren hands found his skin and stroked him, as if making sure he was real. Fingers touched his face and a few voices murmured wonderingly in a language I didn't recognize. Emun glanced over at me and cocked a kind of awkward crooked smile. His eyes said he wasn't quite sure what to think, but that it was okay. These sirens had never seen a triton; to them he'd always been a creature of myth, and now he was standing there naked and dripping. His dark hair hung nearly to his shoulders, his blue eyes as dark as ever as he looked into their faces. He let them touch, and those sirens who had already convinced themselves that he was real, moved aside to make room for others who wanted to put tender and questing hands on him.

Suddenly, *she* was there, the black siren with the long body and huge thick curls. She stood in front of Mira, with eyes only for my mother. It came to me suddenly, that they knew each other and my mother had even told me once about her. She could only be one siren.

"Polarisin?" I said.

Her beautiful dark eyes came away from Mom's face and she smiled at me.

"You look just like your mother," she said, and her voice was a warm cat's tongue to my ear.

The murmur of voices died down as the last of the sirens came to the beach and joined the strange party. Sirens of all ethnicities and—from the sound of it, languages—had come to Okeanos. They'd been pulled by some invisible tether.

Mom stepped close to Polarisin and put her fingers to the tall siren's throat. She kissed Polarisin's cheeks and dipped her head in a respectful bow.

It jarred me, and another realization came rushing in upon me as Mom and Polarisin said the words that many sirens had said before as the mantle of Sovereignty passed from one to the other. All of the Mer around us had felt what was to come, they had felt the changing of the guard, the transition of power from one Sovereign to another. But I had not felt it. Somehow, I was one of them and yet different, the way Nike was.

In my periphery, I found the white-haired sorceress and watched her. It occurred to me that maybe I had been in the presence of another elemental all along, and just not known it. We were the same as our people, but different. We were part of something, and yet separate from it. I wondered at this difference, wondered at it because though salt gave the powers of Sovereignty, I had never felt that my elemental status had come from salt, but rather from somewhere else, somewhere broader, somewhere inclusive of the ocean but also beyond it. Maybe, like Georjie had theorized, my powers had come from that magic imbued by Gaia, nature itself.

This realization shook me as I stood there on the sand, and the sirens began to mill around Polarisin, kissing her cheeks and whispering to her. I was an elemental, and nature had chosen to release me from whatever bond held sirens together. It had chosen to bond me to other beings instead, other elementals. It had to be why I couldn't feel my mother's Sovereignty, and I couldn't feel it passing to Polarisin now, the way the rest of the Mer could.

The moment came when I was the only Mer on the beach who had yet to greet Polarisin as the new Sovereign. Thinking that I had to perform the deferential ritual or risk insulting her, I lifted a hand and reached for her throat.

She looked down at me with those luminous dark eyes, and her hand came up and caught mine in mid-air. I looked at her with surprise as she held my hand. She lowered it, and reached for my other hand so that we were standing hand in hand.

"Not you," she said, and I was jarred again to see tears filling the new Sovereign's eyes. They overspilled her lids and tracked down her cheeks. She released one of my hands and touched my face tenderly, then she bent and kissed first one cheek then the other. She released me and stepped back, wiping the moisture off her face.

"You'll always be one of us," she said and her head tilted

a little before she went on, "but you are also *diachorîso*, set apart." She gestured widely at the crowd of silent Mer around us. "When our gemstones turned to water, all sirens were afraid, until we realized that it came with a...a falling away. A freedom settled over us that we had not felt before in our lives. I came here without fully understanding why. The Salt called us, so we came. We were joined by others along the way, who also felt this call."

"But, you're from the Pacific," I stuttered, "how did you get here so fast?" After all the curse had been broken not yet for a full three days.

"I might be from the Pacific, but a siren can travel the world, no? I was not far away when I felt the Salt invite me." She tilted her head to indicate the others. "These are the sirens who were close by, and thousands more are on their way. They'll arrive over the coming months." She cocked a dark slash of eyebrow. "I would like to be able to tell them what happened, *why* they've come. Even the Salt has not given me its reasons. Perhaps you can help me understand?"

She wanted the story. None of these sirens knew what had happened to their gemstones, why they'd suddenly dissolved. They only knew it was a good thing, and somehow, they knew that it was because of me. Perhaps because they could feel that I was outside of the invisible netting that connected them all.

I looked at my Mom, then Nike, and then Emun. They were listening with interest but also waiting for my reply. I looked at Polarisin again and smiled. "Yes, of course. I'll tell you the story."

Polarisin took my hand and tucked it into my elbow as she steered back toward Mount Califas. "Good," she said. "And perhaps I'll have someone with artistic skill immortalize it inside this mountain. It seems we were once creators of fine mosaics." She smiled and a little dimple appeared in her cheek. "The art has fallen into a little... disrepair, let's say. And I aim to restore it."

"I'm very happy to hear that," I said, smiling back.

EPILOGUE

Mom and I sat on the end of the wooden pier jutting from the public beach that lay between the Novak manor and the Gdansk harbor. The sounds of a busy beach on a warm day hummed on behind us as we faced the Baltic horizon.

"So, what did it say?" my mom asked, bumping me with her shoulder.

"What did what say?" I replied innocently.

"The letter from Lusi, what else." If an eye-roll had a tone, my Mom's voice was infused with it. "No need to be coy."

I reached into the kangaroo pocket in the front of my tanktop and handed her a crumpled envelope. When we'd arrived home in Gdansk, Adalbert had said that Lusi had been by a few days earlier wanting to see me. But rather than waiting for some undetermined amount of time for us to come home, she'd scrawled a letter and asked him to give it to me. It was this letter I handed to my mother now.

Mom unfolded it and read aloud. "Dear Targa, I don't know how you did it, but you have, and one day I want to hear all about it. I'm sad I can't stay and wait to see you in person, but duty calls. Speaking of 'calls,' the next time you ring me I won't be so resistant. I promise. Signed, Lusi." Mom folded the letter up and gave it back to me. "What was so private about that?"

I shrugged. "Nothing, really."

The truth was that I didn't fully understand myself why I found myself treasuring this rather messily hand-written letter from Lusi. Maybe it was because she could be the oldest known siren in the world, maybe it was because I found my mind drifting to her from time to time, wondering if she'd ever tell me *her* story.

I let my mind release Lusi for now. It drifted back to the crystal and to Shaloris and to the mysteries of magic that had brought her into her aquamarine cell. It might look sinister on the face of it, but the same magic that had taken her there had also released her. I mused that the mysteries of magic might not be so different from the mysteries of the heart. Each seemed as enigmatic and full of secrets as the other.

"You want to know something strange?" I asked Mom.

"I bet I can guess," Mom replied, leaning back on her palms and flicking the water out toward the horizon.

I felt surprise steal over my features as I looked at her. "You can?"

"Sure." She turned her face to the side and tilted her cheekbone roughly in the direction of the beach as if to say, *The shenanigans going on behind us.*

Blankly, I looked at the beach. Kids screamed happily and ran as an older sibling chased them. The chatter of conversation and laughter filled the air as families and couples sat on blankets and beach towels or at picnic tables, or just in lumps of ankle-deep sand, enjoying the bright warm day of late spring.

Jozef lay on his back on our picnic blanket, an open book crooked over his face. I supposed he must be dozing. Antoni sat on the second blanket we'd brought, his knees bent, his feet on the sand and his arms wrapped around his shins. His shoulders were sloped and relaxed. Emun was standing in the background, his phone held to his ear, his hand moving in the air as he spoke. My gaze found Antoni again. I couldn't tell where he was looking, thanks to the sunglasses shading his eyes, but after a moment, he lifted one hand in a single, still wave.

I waved back. "I don't get it," I told Mom.

"The beach, the people." Mom lifted one palm and gestured to the scene behind us as a whole. "It's strange, right?"

"You mean because we're so used to abandoned beaches with no one around?"

She nodded.

"Well, yeah, it is a bit strange now that you mention it, but it's a good strange. It's a strange I could get used to." I gave Antoni a smile before facing the Baltic again.

"That doesn't surprise me."

"No, I guess it wouldn't." I was unlike my mother in this way. She could leave the human life behind for many years and never miss it. Thanks to who she'd fallen in love with, that possibility lay open to her without ever having to break her own heart or anyone else's. I knew she would take it, and soon, but at least the decision wasn't coming under duress. With no curse, she could do as she liked.

"But that wasn't what you were talking about, was it?" she asked.

"No." I looked down in my lap as the memory of the memory bobbed to the surface. "Inside the crystal, right before I...broke it, I thought of Dad."

Mom looked at me and was silent for a moment. "Did you?"

"Yeah. In fact, he was all I could think about, and there was something weird about the way he just popped into my mind, like my memory didn't conjure him up consciously. He just...blew through me. You know?"

My mom listened quietly as I told her about the memory from my childhood, the one I shouldn't have. Her bright blue eyes drifted down to the water and glazed over a little, unfocused as her own memory took her back.

"I remember that night," she murmured. "It wasn't often he caught me missing, but it did happen a few times."

I nodded. I knew. When I was finished telling her my memory, we fell silent. The sounds of laughter and waves and seabirds screaming from high above drifted around us.

"I have something strange to tell you, too," Mom said, suddenly. "I wasn't going to say anything about it to you because I thought it was irrelevant. Just a bit of Atlantean trivia, really. But now that I know Nathan visited you inside the crystal, I think I should."

The way she'd put it jarred me for a moment—that my father had visited me inside the gem, like he was a ghost or a being from the past with consciousness. I didn't see it that way, but I supposed these things could be interpreted a million different ways by a million different minds.

"Jozef was telling me back in Gibraltar how his father had died, that Loukas had discovered a little late in the game that Atlanteans who spent too much time on land and not enough time in saltwater got a kind of wasting disease."

"Okay," I replied, patiently. Waiting for the punchline.

But Mom looked at me expectantly, like I should have had something click by now. When I still looked clueless, she said, "It has symptoms that look a lot like MS."

"Multiple sclerosis?" I cocked my head and the question was still clear in my tone.

She let out a long sigh. "I guess you're too young to remember, or you forgot..."

Then it did hit me, straight in the chest like a bag full of cement.

"Grandpa—" I wheezed, and was unable to finish the sentence.

Mom's arm slid around my shoulders and she pulled me into her side. I was grateful for her support. Without it, I might have slid into the water and just stayed down there forever. In shock.

Nathan's father had had MS. It was fairly advanced by the time I'd been born and in every memory of him that I had, he was in a wheelchair. That wheelchair was as much of a part of him in my mind as his hands or his hair.

I found my voice. "You don't think that's a coincidence?"

Mom shrugged. "You tell me."

Nike had said that I would be able to break the curse because there was something that linked the curse-maker and me. It had never been made clear what that link was.

"Born of a siren and an Atlantean," I said, "just like Eumelia."

"And not only that, but born of a Mer mother and an Atlantean father who had genuine love," Mom added. "They made an elemental. So did your father and I."

"Do you think he knew?"

"Nathan?" Mom shook her head. "I don't think so. By now lots of people probably have some Atlantean blood flowing in their veins, even if it's a tiny amount. It doesn't necessarily mean they can make gills, or even that they have a longer lifespan."

"Do you think Grandpa knew?"

"I doubt that, too." She planted a kiss on my forehead and drew one foot out of the water, placing it on the dock as she made to get up. "It's a mystery I can live with without solving, what about you?"

I laughed and knew exactly what she meant. "Yeah, I've had enough of solving mysteries to last me a lifetime. It's enough."

And it really was. For once, my mind wasn't pulling or tugging at a problem. I felt light, happy, and curiously refreshed.

Mom got to her feet and pulled me up by my hand. We walked the dock heading back to the beach and back to our men arm in arm.

It was enough, I thought as my eye panned from my brother, to my mother's long-lost love, to my own Antoni.

They were *more* than enough.

***

THE END

AFTERWORD

Thank you dear reader for making it to the end of The Siren's Curse trilogy! I had such a blast writing Targa and Mira's stories. When I was a little girl I dreamed of having the freedom of a mermaid to explore underwater realms, so the manifestation of these stories is really the manifestation of a childhood dream of mine.

If you loved these stories please take a moment to review them on Amazon. Positive reviews help authors like me and readers like you in more ways than you might realize. Not only do they help to make a book more visible in the Amazon store, they help readers find stories that they'll enjoy the most. Thank you in advance for your reviews!

Thank you to my VIP readers, my editors Nicola Aquino and Theresa Hull, my designers at Damonza, and to my friends and family who support my author career.

I'm gonna go dive into starting book one of the next series now, so maybe I'll see you there. Curious about what that might be? Join my private group on Facebook (AL Knorr's VIP Reader Lounge) or my newsletter at www.alknorrbooks.com to be the first to get fresh news!

Keep reading!
Abby

ALSO BY A.L. KNORR

The Elemental Origins Series

Born of Water

Born of Fire

Born of Earth

Born of Æther

Born of Air

The Elementals

The Returning Series (Mira's Story)

Returning

Falling

Surfacing

The Siren's Curse Trilogy

Salt & Stone

Salt & the Sovereign

Salt & the Sisters

Elemental Novellas

Pyro, A Fire Novella

Heat, A Fire Novella

The Kacy Chronicles

Descendant

Ascendant

Combatant

Transcendent

Register at www.alknorrbooks.com to receive a free copy of
Returning and to be the first to learn about new releases by
AL Knorr.